Y0-BRR-032

The Garden of Two
Vicki-Ann Bush

Cover Art:
Michelle Crocker

http://mlcdesigns4you.weebly.com/

Publisher's Note:

This is a work of fiction. All names, characters, places, and events are the work of the author's imagination.

Any resemblance to real persons, places, or events is coincidental.

Solstice Publishing - www.solsticepublishing.com

To Zoltan,
Love is never,
truly gone!
Vicki-Ann Bush

The Garden of Two

Vicki-Ann Bush

Dedication

This story is dedicated to Ronnie Bush. No matter what the future brings us, no matter where we are.

You always have been, and forever shall be ... my Charlie.

Preface

I write this not for who we are today, but rather for who we were. We were destiny at her best. We would have united despite any adversity. On any path. Any way they crossed.

We believed that sometime long ago, we were separated and fated to wander the earth; searching until the day we would be reunited.

We were the finest wine because of the sweetest grapes. Where there was warmth, there was safety. Where there was passion, there was comfort. And where there was fire, we were at our most intoxicating.

We were quite simply us. There wasn't anyone who could understand or even begin to try.

This is who we were...

Chapter One

Charlie Murphy was running faster than he thought possible. Everywhere he looked there were bodies, and the yelling—they were the wails of the damned. Some men surrounded him, shooting, while others were also trying to avoid the incoming bullets. But most frightening of all were the soldiers who wandered in a blank haze, unaware of the flying bullets or any form of attack. He'd barely finished high school a few months ago—how could life change so much in such a short time? His days of comfort in Long Island, New York had come to an end. He could only hope it wasn't permanent.

Charlie could not stop to help; he searched for life-saving cover and waited to advance on the enemy. He spotted a disabled truck a few yards away. He dodged and dropped, trying to keep low. When he got there he was frightened; his adrenaline was in overdrive and he was short of breath. He lay on the ground, furiously searching through the haze of apocalyptic chaos.

What he didn't notice were the three German soldiers still trapped under the truck, or their buddies, who were running his way to see if they could release them. A patch of land to his left seemed clear. Cautiously he got up and looked around before firing. As he pivoted, he heard a hailstorm of fire and something incredibly hot hit his chest.

He looked down. A pool of red seeped through the hole in his shirt. He had been shot. He grabbed his chest and tried to keep running, but the mud was slippery. Pain seared through his body and consumed him, a branding iron pressed against the gaping hole in his flesh. He fumbled through the pocket in his coat for the compass. His hand clasped it, squeezing it tight and close to his body.

Collapsing, he sank into the mud. His eyes, clear of the muck, looked skyward, where he thought he saw Lillie's face. The very last thing Charlie could remember was the hazy vision of the woman he loved and the compass that would get him home. Then his world went completely black.

***

Fourteen months earlier

Charlie was rushing to get to the grocery store. He had stayed a few extra minutes after school, and now he was worried he might be late for work. This was his last year and graduation couldn't come soon enough.

As he ran down the store lined blocks of downtown, he could feel the sweat dripping from his forehead and running down to his chin. It was an exceptionally hot spring.

Growing up without a dad, he had worked at odd jobs since he was twelve. The money he earned wasn't much, but it helped his mom with groceries. As the various stores whizzed by him, he thought of all the different jobs he had done. Harrison's Feed & Grain, hauling many a fifty-pound bag to the local stables for delivery from there. And Barker's Tools, pushing the cart for the salesman, sometimes nine hours a day in the summer. When he turned fifteen and got the steady job at Johnson's Grocery, it was like a vacation. Steady work, steady pay, and Mr. Johnson was the nicest person. He knew how hard things had been for Charlie and his mom since his dad had passed away. Mr. Johnson even worked around his school schedule and gave him the option to work weekends or not.

Breathing heavily, Charlie spotted Johnson's Grocery just across the street. That seemed to be an incentive, as he took in a deep breath and ran full-on to the front of the store. Now gasping to get more air into his lungs, he pulled out the brass pocket watch. It had belonged to his dad; his mom had given it to him after he had passed away. Charlie popped open the front to reveal the dial—four o'clock on the dot. He was on time. He took a second to admire the watch. It wasn't fancy, but yet was regal somehow. The simple scrolls that swirled around the cover to the face made him think of mountain tops. He tucked it back into his pocket and went inside. Mr. Johnson was busy stocking canned goods on the shelf. When he saw Charlie, he waved him over.

"On time as usual, Charlie." Mr. Johnson gave him a smile.

Charlie looked down the short grocery aisle stocked with canned goods and thought, *Just barely.*

"Yes, sir, Mr. Johnson. Right on time."

"I have a little surprise for you," his boss continued. "I know how hard you work and I'd hate to dickens to lose you—but I've arranged and interview with James Whitman for you on Sunday. You can make more money working for his company. It could be a real future for you."

Charlie's heart beat with the speed of a steam engine. He could feel it pounding in his chest. Whitman Construction was the largest company in town and the biggest construction company in three states. This could start his dream. He would finally be able to work with wood, something he'd always loved. And the money—

"Mr. Johnson, I don't know what to say." He extended his hand out to shake, but instead felt a burly bear hug.

"Nonsense. Just say thank you. You've earned it, Charlie."

***

Lillie Whitman opened her eyes and stretched. The May sun beamed through the window and heated the cotton sheets on the bed. She could hear voices streaming from the backyard and threw them off to go take a look. Her window faced the backyard and the beautiful garden that blanketed it. Her father was conversing with the gardener. She grabbed her robe to go see what the all the commotion was.

Descending the large staircase, she glided her hand

over the banister. The wood felt smooth and cool, a contrast to the heat that had soaked her sheets. Walking through the house, she smelled the tantalizing aroma of bacon. *Cook must be making breakfast.* She didn't realize how hungry she was until the smokey scent filled the room.

Lillie opened the glass-paneled doors that led to the garden and stepped out onto the porch. The wooden boards burned the bottoms of her feet. She hopped down the steps to the soft, moist grass. As she walked through the garden, she smiled. Her mom would have been so proud. She had loved the garden and would often sit on one of the many benches, thinking and sharing in its peace. After she passed away, her dad had made a promise to keep it as beautiful as her last memory of it...

He had kept his promise.

As Lillie got closer, she realized her dad was overseeing the planting of new foliage. "Dad, why are you out here so early in the morning?"

"Early? Daughter, you had better get a good look at the clock. It's ten a.m. It's almost early afternoon." Her father, James, peeked out from under his oversized straw hat. This was his favorite hat to wear while working in the garden. Her mother had bought it for him, and although it had seen better days, he wouldn't dare think of wearing another. Lillie had stayed up late reading and didn't realize the morning had all but escaped her; lately she just couldn't seem to fall asleep without first delving in to a good book. Last night it had been *Emma* by Jane Austin.

She edged toward her father, who was holding a shrub she had never seen before. The gardener had placed one of each at the opposite end of the property. "Dad, what are you planting? They're covered in thorns."

"In the late fall, these vines will be covered with deep red berries. The thorns will protect them from the birds. See, we are planting two of them, so that each year they will grow until meeting in the middle. Joining, they'll become one." James gazed out at the two plants. "Fire thorns is what they're called."

"That's beautiful. Mom would have loved them." Lillie gave her dad a hug and a kiss on the cheek and went in to have breakfast. As she walked back through the garden, her mind wandered to her parents. They had loved each other so much. Would she ever know a love like that?

If she were lucky, one day.

Chapter Two

Charlie had gotten up early that Sunday, he was so nervous. While at church with his mom, all he could think about was the possibility of a new job. They had passed the Whitman house many times when he was younger, and he remembered how he had mowed the lawn for their neighbors. The Whitmans had full-time gardeners, so he had never been any closer than their sidewalk. He often wondered what it might be like inside. It must be grand; it was by far the nicest house in the neighborhood.

"Mom, I'm going to walk you home, but then I need to hurry out. I don't want to be late for my interview." Charlie bent his right arm and offered it to his mom. She grabbed it and squeezed.

"I am so proud of you, son. And don't you worry, you are going to do fine." She flashed him that "mom" smile, a grin wider than the Grand Canyon. The one that always made him feel like everything would always be okay.

"I really want this job."

"I know you do. I also know that since your dad died, you've felt responsible for me. But you're not. I appreciate all the help, but you have to follow your dream for you—not me. I'm the parent; it's my job to take care of you. And I think I've done a pretty good one." She winked and patted her back.

Charlie couldn't help but laugh. She was right, he had tried to be the man all these years, but truthfully, she was the one who took care of everything.

They continued walking until they reached the front porch of their home. Charlie noticed the sky looked exceptionally blue and the grass had that newly cut smell. Things were looking up, but he couldn't help feeling a weight on his back. Mr. Johnson had stuck his neck out by lining up the interview, so he had to do well—for the both of them. He kissed his mom on the cheek and headed to the Whitman house.

The closer he came to the house, the more nervous he felt. *Is my suit too tattered?* he thought. He wished his shoes were in better condition. They'd been shined with a kit Mr. Johnson had given to him last Christmas, but they were old. *Nonsense,* he thought. *Mr. Whitman isn't going to hire me for my suit. It will be for my ability. And I know I can do a good job.*

Charlie knocked on the door, making sure his tie was adjusted just so. It wouldn't do to have a crooked tie.

A gentleman opened the door and led him into the study. A huge wooden desk with a luxurious Tiffany lamp and a silver letter adorned the far corner of the room. A plush velvet chair with carved legs completed the set. Bookcases stretched from floor to ceiling. The windows had heavy, dark drapes patterned in a gold and brown paisley print, and framed with a beautifully hand carved wood. It was so rich and posh. Charlie held back on running his hands over the wood. Instead he stayed seated. His excitement built with each passing second. He rubbed his stomach; nausea was settling in. After several minutes, Mr. Whitman strolled in with the confidence of a true gentleman.

"Charlie. Mr. Johnson tells me wonderful things about you and your work ethic. He tells me I'd be crazy not to hire you."

"Mr. Whitman, I love working with wood and construction. I will do the best job you've ever seen." He pulled a small wooden box from his pocket, fumbling, he almost dropped it. He had carved the lid with a design of roses. "I wanted to show you the type of work I am capable of doing."

James took the box and examined it. Running his fingers over the intricate carving, he held it closer for a better view."This is very skilled work. Well, we can't have my friend thinking I'm crazy. How about you start six a.m. sharp on Monday?" James extended his hand and they solidified the new job. Charlie thanked him several times and gathered himself to leave. He couldn't wait to get home and tell his mother.

As he headed toward the front door, he heard someone call him.

"Mr. Murphy!"

Charlie turned and saw a girl running down the hall towards him. As she came closer, he realized it was Lillie Whitman. Charlie had been attending school with Lillie since they were both in first grade, but he could never get the courage up to actually speak to her. And now here she was, coming towards him and shouting his name.

Just answer her, he told himself. *She's going to think you're goopy or something. You don't want to look like a jerk in front of Lillie.*

"Yes, Miss Whitman? Did you need something?" he squeaked. *She is so beautiful,* Charlie thought as Lillie came closer. *And the prettiest girl in class.*

"Mr. Murphy, my father forgot to tell you to make sure you see the foreman, Tommy Monahan. He'll be able to get you started on Monday."

There she stood: Lillie Whitman. She smelled so good. He could barely muster the courage to answer her. "Okay, I will. Thank you."

"So, you're going to be working for my father? He's a good man. I think you'll like working with the other guys, too. They're a swell bunch."

Charlie wanted so badly to speak, he could hear the words rolling around his brain, but every time he looked into her warm hazel eyes, he would get lost and nothing would come out.

"Mr. Murphy. Mr. Murphy. Charlie, are you all right?" Lillie was tugging at his arm.

"Uh, yes. Yes I am. Thank you again. Good day."

Charlie grabbed the front door and exited to the porch. *That was the dumbest thing you've ever done, Charlie Murphy. Lillie Whitman talks to you and you can't even answer her. Now she thinks you're goopy for sure.*

***

Lillie went to the study, where her dad was having tea. He was such a bull of a man and it made her giggle a little inside to see him with a dainty tea cup. "I was able to catch Charlie. He was a bit silly. I was talking to him, but he didn't answer me. He sort of looked right through me." Lillie handed him the morning paper.

"He was just overwhelmed with all the beauty that was in the room." James winked.

"Oh, Dad. Now you're being silly. He wasn't any such thing. I'll be at Claire's house. We're going to review our plans for graduation. I'll be home around four-thirty, in time for supper." Lillie kissed her father and gathered the swatches to show Claire. The graduation ceremony was fast approaching, and she needed to start working on her dress.

***

Lillie arrived at Claire's house and the two girls ran up to the bedroom, laughing and whispering all the way.

"Hey, do you remember that boy in our class, Charlie Murphy?" Lillie grabbed a swatch of material and laid it out on Claire's bed.

"Vaguely. Why?"

"No reason. He came by our house today. He's going to be working for my dad starting Monday. He's good-looking, but sort of odd." Lillie grabbed another swatch.

"They're all odd. Boys, I mean. If you ask me, you never know what they're up to." Claire was a little rough around the edges. She had always been a naturally pretty girl who rarely wore makeup and was not comfortable in anything frilly or overly feminine. But Lillie loved that about her. She always spoke her mind.

From her desk, Claire picked up an article she had clipped from the newspaper. "Have you seen this advertisement for women's undergarments? It's downright criminal. It must have been written by a man. No self-respecting woman would think up an idea like this." Claire hurled the paper on the floor.

"Honestly, Claire, sometimes you get so worked up. It's just an advertisement. Now come over here and help me pick out material for my graduation dress." Lillie also loved her best friend's political views—even if they were a bit too passionate at times.

Chapter Three

Charlie rushed the whole way home. Bursting with excitement, he couldn't wait to tell his mother about starting the new job on Monday.

"Mom!" he shouted. "Mom, where are you?"

When Charlie reached the front door, he nearly took it off its hinges. When she didn't answer, he went from room to room looking for her. As he reached her bedroom, he saw she was sitting quietly in a chair, gazing out the window.

"Mom, didn't you hear me calling you?" He walked over to his mother and knelt beside her. "Mom, are you all right?" She looked up at him. She was very pale. Charlie grabbed her hand; it felt oddly cold and clammy. "Mom! Please, what's wrong?"

He lunged for her just as she collapsed in his arms. He leaned her back on the chair and phoned the doctor.

After what felt like an eternity, the doctor arrived. Doc Clarkson was an older man. He had been practicing for more than forty years and had delivered nearly every baby in town, Charlie included.

It seemed as if hours passed while Charlie waited for Doc Clarkson to examine his mother. When he finally emerged from the bedroom, he was gazing at the floor.

"Well, Doc, what's wrong with my mom? Is she gonna be okay?"

"I'm sorry, Charlie. It seems your mother has suffered a stroke. She is paralyzed on her right side. Her left side is in a weakened state, and her speech has been greatly affected. She will need constant care. I will refer you to a nurse who can come and care for her during the day."

Charlie walked him to the front door; he couldn't wait for him to leave. After the door closed, he collapsed on the sofa and cried. Minutes passed, but it felt like hours. He wiped his face with the back of his shirt sleeve. His eyes were stinging like someone had just poured salt into them, so he went into the kitchen, threw water on them, and then stiffened himself up and went to his mother. She was sleeping so peacefully. A stroke.

Looking at her, Charlie couldn't believe that she had gone through something as severe as this. Her face was smooth and unstressed—her body lying flat and relaxed. Charlie knelt down beside her bed and laid his head next to hers. He took her hand and whispered, "Don't worry, Mom. I'll take care of everything. Everything will be fine."

He stayed with her throughout most of the night.

***

In the morning, a knock at the door brought the nurse that Doc Clarkson had promised to send.

"Good morning sir. My name is Finola O'Grady."

She spoke with an Irish accent that had mixed in with some Long Island. *She's probably been in the States for a while,* Charlie thought. She had a soft smile and a twinkle in her green eyes that gave Charlie a bit of reassurance.

"I'll be home by dark, and I've left a list of things you might need to know. It's in the kitchen." He kissed his mom on the cheek—she felt warm—and then he headed out.

Charlie admired all the different shades of green in the trees and the bright flowers that came with the birth of a new spring. The color, the smells—on any other day he would have been completely happy. But today, it was bittersweet. *Yesterday, this would have been the best day I've ever had.* Now all he could think about was his mother.

The morning thankfully went by quickly, and the crew were a swell bunch of fellows. The work kept his brain occupied and focused. To see a project start from a mere pile of wood and turn into someone's house was mesmerizing, but he couldn't help but worry about his mom. He knew it was impossible to stay home with her, but that didn't make reasoning with it any easier.

Finally it was quitting time. Charlie gathered his belongings and went straight home. When he arrived, he was disappointed to see there had been little change in his mom.

"Finola, have you worked with many stroke patients?" Charlie was looking for something positive.

"I have. I must be up front with you, Charlie. One never knows when it comes to a stroke. It all depends on the person's will."

He thanked her for her services that day. After he closed the front door, he stood in the empty living room and thought about how hard he had worked this year. He would have to study even harder to graduate early and start working full time. He wanted desperately to make life a little easier for his mother and himself. But now everything had changed and he didn't know how to fix it.

The phone rang. It was Doc Clarkson calling to see how his mom was doing. He wanted to perform very important tests at the hospital. "Charlie, would you be available to take her on Thursday?"

"I'll speak to Mr. Whitman and call you back tomorrow. I'm pretty sure he'll understand. He seems to be a reasonable man."

After hanging up with the doctor, he went next door to his neighbor, Mrs. Russo.

"Mrs. Russo, would you mind sitting with my mom? I need to go and speak with Mr. Whitman."

"*Mio caro*, Charlie. Of course I will." Mrs. Russo was a small, chubby Italian woman whose husband was the local butcher. They were kind, and Charlie knew his mom would be well taken care of.

***

Wiping his sweaty palms on the side of his trousers, Charlie was anxious on the walk over, not looking forward to speaking with Mr. Whitman. He had just started his new job today and now he would have to ask for Thursday off. *What will he say?*

Well, it didn't matter. He had to take his mother for the tests and that was that. He felt a moment of courage for however brief it was, but as soon as he reached the Whitmans' front door; his fear greeted him all over again.

Charlie waited in the same room he had been in yesterday. So much had changed in just a day. Shortly thereafter, Mr. Whitman approached Charlie, who was sitting in one of the leather side chairs. Charlie's throat went dry. He waited before speaking. He needed the words to be clear and strong.

"Mr. Whitman, I am extremely sorry, but I must ask you for the day off on Thursday. It's urgent."

"What happened, son?"

"It's my mom. She's had a stroke. They need to run some tests and I have to take her to the hospital. Doc Clarkson will be reviewing the results to see where we stand."

"Doc Clarkson is a good man and an excellent doctor. I am so sorry to hear this news about your mom. Of course you may have the day off. And if there is anything you need, Charlie, just say the word. Family is everything." Mr. Whitman extended his hand and when Charlie went to grab it, Mr. Whitman embraced his arm in a warm gesture of support.

"Thank you, sir." Charlie tipped his head out of respect and left.

"Wait. I'd like to show you something before you go." James motioned for him to follow him out to the back porch. There Charlie saw the most unique garden he had ever laid his eyes on. It was not in season, yet the placement of bushes, ferns and flowers made it appear as if everything in the garden was reaching out to the visitor to be touched, to be hugged. It was magical.

"This garden was for my wife, Elizabeth." James Whitman looked out towards the vast greenery, which seemed to go on forever. "This is a peaceful place, a place to sort out whatever weighs heavily on your mind or heart. When your mother is feeling better, perhaps you would like to bring her here. It might assist her with recovery. It feels like spring even in the coldest months of winter. I know it's helped me over the years." He took a seat on a wooden bench.

Charlie heard a door close and someone calling, "Dad? There you are. I searched the whole house looking for you. Oh, I'm sorry. I didn't see you had company."

Lillie came over. Charlie looked at her as if seeing her for the first time. She had a beauty that went straight to his heart. He stuttered briefly and then regained his words.

"Hello, Lillie. Nice to see you again." Charlie nervously put his hand out. Lillie gently squeezed it with a small shake.

"Yes. Lovely to see you again, too. What brings you out to our beautiful garden this evening?" James explained to Lillie about Charlie's mother. "Oh. Charlie, I am so sorry. Is there anything we can do to help?" She sat down beside her father.

"No," said Charlie, "but thank you both for your concern and generosity. It is really a matter for the doctors now."

James stood up and started back toward the house. "Charlie, why don't you sit here for awhile, gather your thoughts and enjoy the garden? I think you would do well with some peace right now. Lillie, why don't you keep Charlie company for a few minutes? I will call you when supper is ready."

"Of course, Dad. I'll see you in a bit." Lillie smiled at Charlie.

Charlie felt anything but relaxed at this moment. He was sitting alone with Lillie Whitman, and he hadn't a clue what to say. He could feel the heat rising in his cheeks and hoped Lillie didn't notice the sweat forming on his upper lip.

"I really am sorry about your mother. But Doc Clarkson is the best doctor in town. He'll make her well again." Lillie placed her hand on Charlie's.

"I hope so. It just seems so unfair. I finally could do something for her, and now she can't even appreciate it."

"She will. She'll know. It will just take some time."

The more they spoke, the more Charlie began to feel at ease. He couldn't remember why he had been awkward with her all these years. Then it started to get dark, and James called Lillie in for supper. On the way home, Charlie could not stop thinking about Lillie. He wondered when he would get the chance to sit and talk with her again.

***

Later that evening, Claire stopped over to Lillie's with a bag in tow.

"I found the perfect thing to wear for your party. I was walking down town and right in the window of Sherman's our graduation department store, and there it was. It seemed to just find me: the most darling black suit I had ever seen. It's a few sizes too large, but Mr. Sherman said he could take it in just in time for the party. Here, look. I had to bring it by for you to see. I'll bring it back to him in the morning." Claire laid the suit out on the bed. "Isn't it delicious? Just feel that gorgeous silk!"

Lillie ran her hand over the fabric. "It's beautiful, Claire, just like you. You're going to look so elegant."

Lillie gave Claire a hug. She knew her friend had always moved to a different beat and she admired her for her strength and honesty. As she gazed over at the suit, she thought, *Maybe I should invite Charlie.*

***

Over the next few days, Charlie's mind was divided

between his mother's health and the time he had spent with Lillie. It was odd; even though their talk in the garden had been brief, it was enough to keep a smile on his face.

On Thursday morning, Finola arrived to help Charlie prepare his mother for her doctor's appointment. He rang for a taxi, and Finola thought it best she accompany them.

When they arrived, a husky gentleman dressed in hospital clothing came out with a wheelchair and led them to the waiting area. Charlie filled out medical papers while they wheeled his mother away for testing. The nurse told him it would be a few hours before she would be finished and advised that he get a cup of coffee and a sandwich. Finola would wait in the hospital cafeteria. Charlie was too nervous to eat and decided to go for a walk instead. The shops downtown were just a few minutes away. *Maybe buying flowers for Mom will be a good idea.*

Charlie grew thirsty in the unseasonably humid air. After his purchase, he went to his favorite diner. A large, noisy crowd greeted him. During the week it was always busy at lunchtime, with many coming in from the nearby offices. The rush would begin at eleven-thirty and it wouldn't quiet down until about two o'clock. He glanced around; looking for a free space at the counter to order a soda, but every stool was taken. As he was about to leave, he heard someone calling his name: "Charlie...Charlie."

He turned to see Lillie sitting at a booth with Claire, whom he had seen in school but never really spoken to. Lillie motioned for him to come over. His heart was beating so fast he could feel it pushing through his chest, and his hands sprouted a dampness that not even rubbing them on the sides of his pants could dry.

"Charlie, this is my friend, Claire. Why don't you sit down and join us?"

"Thanks. I was just leaving, though. It's so crowded in here and I just came in for a soda."

"I know. It seems as if the entire town came in for lunch," said Lillie. "What brings you here today? Oh, that's right. Today is the day your mom is getting her tests done. How is she? Any news?"

"No, no news yet. She's still at the hospital. They said it could take a few hours, so I thought I'd just walk around for a while, fill some time, and here I am, almost lost in this crowd."

***

Lillie's stomach was positively doing flips, her hands were damp, and her heart felt as if it had forgotten how to beat regularly, but in a strange way this all felt good. *He's so adorable and sweet. I just have to ask him to my party.*

Suddenly, Lillie was at a loss for words. She could feel herself wanting to say them but couldn't seem to pull them from her mouth! *What's going on here?* she thought. *There isn't one boy alive who makes Lillie Whitman nervous. Get a hold of yourself.*

But she couldn't. Every time she looked into his emerald eyes, she became lost. Lillie could hear Claire asking Charlie about his mom. *Perfect. It'll give me time to take a breath and then ask him.*

"Charlie, about graduation...Do want to come to my house? I mean, I'm having a graduation party on Saturday. I'd like it if you could attend."

"Yes, I'd like very much to come, but I have to wait and see how my mom is doing. She can't be alone right now."

All the air escaped from Lillie's body, but she knew Charlie had to put his mom first. "I understand. You are welcome if you can make it."

"Thank you. I'd better get back."

Claire laughed a little as Charlie left the diner. "What's going on with you? I think you really like this boy."

"Oh, don't be silly. I'll admit, he is kind of cute. His eyes are very green. Did you take a gander? How could you not notice! But no, I was just being polite." Lillie peered out the window. She didn't dare look Claire in the eye. Claire was her best friend, and if anyone knew she was trying to avoid something, it would be her.

"You were being polite? You are so full of air—you like him! Admit it, Lillie, you have a crush on Charlie Murphy." Claire pressed up against Lillie, pushing her into the window.

"Fine, then. I do like him, I'll admit it. But don't call it a crush. It makes it sound childish."

***

Charlie listened to the doctors' explanation of his mother's condition, but the more he listened the less he heard. They spoke in an incomprehensible language. Finally he interrupted. "What is it the both of you are trying to tell me? Please, keep it simple."

The doctor apologized. "Your mom has suffered extreme damage to her brain. She will never be the person she was before, and it is more than likely she will need constant care for the remainder of her life." Charlie's ears buzzed and his head swam. This couldn't be possible. She had been so full of life—so capable.

"I'm going to recommend a good nursing home for her. I feel this is your best course for treatment. She will need the kind of care that you just can't give at home."

"No. I would never put her in a rest home. I have the nurse, and I can care for her when I'm not at work—she'll be going home with me."

The doctor kept trying to reason with him to change his mind, but Charlie proceeded to place his mom in the wheelchair. He was not having any part of it.

***

Charlie's thoughts wandered on the ride home. Everything he had wanted to do for his mother had shattered in a matter of days. When they arrived, he settled her in bed and then prepared supper. It was quiet in the house, and his mind went to Lillie and the time they had spent together today.

He wondered what it would be like to hold her hand for more than a second or to kiss her soft lips. He had more than a feeling about Lillie: it was a yearning. His body surged with heat, and his hands become sweaty again. His heart pumped wildly, as if his entire body would explode. He missed her already and the more he thought of her, the more he longed to be with her all the time.

The teakettle had begun to whistle and it startled him. He felt guilty for getting lost in his own selfish thoughts. His mother needed him. Lillie would have to wait.

Chapter Four

Lillie put the finishing touches on her graduation dress, and she ordered the food and flowers for the party. Not satisfied with the centerpieces on the tables, though, she and Claire went to Wilson's Flowers. Claire convinced her that daisies would make a more lively addition than roses.

"Roses are so formal and stuffy," she said.

Lillie looked at her friend and smiled. *I'd be lost without her,* she thought. Choosing flowers for her party was such a simple task, but one a girl wanted her mother there to help her with. After deciding on the flowers, the two girls went to the bakery to confirm the cake order. This was the first party at her house since her mom had passed away, and Lillie wanted to make it as easy as possible on her dad.

Later that evening, she called Claire to discuss their plans for the next day. When Claire answered the phone, it was clear by her voice something was wrong.

"You sound blue. What's up?"

"Oh, you know, Lils, same old stuff as before."

Claire's home was very different than the one Lillie shared with her father. Although Claire had both of her parents, from what Lillie understood, she might as well have lived alone. They made little effort to understand her, and it seemed as if they didn't want to, either. Her mother and father, who both came from a long line of wealth, enjoyed maintaining a certain level of class in society. Her mother was ashamed of Claire's insistence on wearing pants and rallying for women's rights, because it did not fit their perception of right society.

Any self-respecting lady, according to Claire's mother, would not bother with such issues. After all, that was something for the men to worry about. It was this way of thinking that embodied everything Claire despised—a wedge driven between her parents and herself for most of her adult life. Lillie could not understand why it was such an issue for a woman to have her voice heard or to wear what she wanted, whenever she wanted.

"Is it your mom or Gwen this time?"

"Sort of both."

"Gwen visiting again?" Lillie heard the sigh on the other end.

"Yes. She's perfect as usual. Or at least that's what my mother thinks. I don't understand how anyone could be so superficial. And now, there are two of them running around the house together. They cackle like witches. Only these are the kind that are really scary, because you don't realize it until it's too late and they pounce you. They look normal so you can't tell, but doom and gloom are right around the corner."

Lillie's heart sank for her friend. There was a lot of hurt for Claire where Gwen was concerned. Apparently, Gwen was the daughter that Mrs. Dumont wished she had. Instinctively, she had to get her friend out of there or she would continue to be miserable.

"Tell your mom I need you. Tell her something has gone wrong with the decorations and you simply must come and spend the night to help me. She'll understand something like that."

"I'm not sure, Lillie. She really wants me to spend time with Gwen. She thinks Gwen might have a positive influence on me. Can you imagine? That woman hasn't a clue who I am. I choose who has an influence on me. I like who I am. I don't want to be some fluffy-headed little girl who needs a man to take care of her. I can take care of myself!"

"I know," said Lillie. "I'll go talk to my dad. He'll ring up your mom. She won't say no to him."

"Do you think he'll do it?" Claire seemed hopeful.

"He loves you like a daughter, Claire. He'd do

anything for you."

"Lils. I feel as if I'm a second class citizen in my parents' house. Sometimes I think it would easier to be what they want, but I can only be me. Honestly, Gwen should have been their daughter."

"Don't worry, I'll get you out of there for a while. Hang up and wait for my dad to call."

When Claire arrived, Lillie was waiting on the porch for her. They spent time in the garden until a chill made it impossible for them to stay any longer. This spring had been excessively warm in the day but beyond chilly at night. Lillie raced with Claire up to her bedroom. Falling over from laughter, they made themselves comfortable in a pair of overstuffed chairs, talking all through the night. They shared what was serious, lighthearted, and everything in between.

The girls spent most of the next morning just sitting around being lazy. They knew the day after would be busy and wanted some time to just enjoy doing as little as possible. For the first time in what seemed weeks, the temperature had cooled a bit and a garden picnic was perfect.

"You think your dad will ever stop planting back here?" Claire gazed out at the massive garden.

"I'm not sure. It almost seems that he needs to keep planting. You know, to keep her alive. He misses my mom so much. And even after all these years, he still won't let her go. I don't know if he ever will." Lillie lay down on her stomach and rested her chin on her hands. "I hope I find a love like that someday."

The time passed quickly and before they realized it, their lazy day was gone and Claire had to go home. Lillie watched as she got into the car and drove away. *Just look at her. She is one of the only girls I know who drives.*

Lillie spent the rest of the evening concentrating on last-minute preparations for the party. She wanted everything to be in the bag, altogether beautiful.

***

The next few days flew by, and before Lillie knew it, it was Saturday morning, the day of the graduation party. The Whitman house was bustling with staff and delivery people coming and going. Gardeners were taking special care to set up everything as exactly as planned. Lanterns hung along the back of the property line and from various trees in the yard. Green vines snaked along the trellises and white linen clothes draped over the round tables. The housekeeper set out the most elegant silverware, and as a surprise for Lillie, James had her mother's finest china unpacked from storage. The grounds looked spectacular.

Inside the kitchen, the most tantalizing smells filled the air as the cooks prepared a meal that would have dazzled royalty. Flowers were delivered and placed throughout the house on both the front and back porches. Inside, ribbon and vines of tiny flowers draped the central staircase. The centerpieces were arranged with the daisies Lillie and Claire had chosen at the florist's and set on delicate lace doilies.

Upstairs, Lillie was sitting in her room, thinking about her mother. She missed her so much. *How much different would this day be if she were here?*

There was a knock at her door, and Claire came charging in before Lillie had a chance to answer. Instantly she felt better. As Claire hopped on the bed and rolled on her back, Lillie thought, *She's so beautiful!*

Claire wasn't one of those "glamor girlies," the type that wouldn't do a thing that could possibly ruin her hair. She was strong and intelligent and darn proud of it. Claire never worried what other people thought or what was the popular fad at the moment. She made her own way and most definitely had her own style. She was beautiful both inside and out.

"What's the word? Why are you still in your

pajamas?" Claire said, pulling some of Lillie's clothes out of the closet. "Come on, lazybones. We have to go downtown. You made that appointment at the beauty parlor, and I have to pick up my suit from alterations at Sherman's."

"I was just thinking about my mom. But I'm okay now. My sister's here."

Claire's cheeks turned a little red and she waved her hand in the air. "Yeah, yeah, I'm great—I know it." Then she looked away.

Lillie put her lips together and raised her mouth on one side in a smirky smile. "Oh yes, you're great all right." Then she jumped off her bed, got dressed and off they went.

***

Charlie had a few errands to run, and since it was Saturday, he asked Mrs. Russo again if she would sit with his mother. He went to the butcher's for their meat, mailed a letter to his aunt in New Jersey, and picked up his mother's prescription from the drug store. Once he was home and putting the meat away in the icebox, Mrs. Russo came in from his mother's room.

"She's sleeping. I made her a bowl of soup and then she drifted off."

"Thank you so much for staying with my mom."

"You're welcome, Charlie. Did you hear about the big party at the Whitmans' house tonight? I think all the young people in town will be there."

"I'm going to stay home. Anyway, the only suit I own is so old, the black is now gray. All the other guys will be wearing suits that would put mine to shame."

"Nonsense, Charlie Murphy. A nice young lady invites you personally to her party and you're not going? Now isn't that rude! Yes, you will go, and I will stay with your mother tonight. As for a suit, Mr. Russo has some beautiful ones he can't fit into any more. You know he loves his pasta a little too much. I'll go get a few for you to try on."

As she started to leave, Charlie called to her, "Mrs. Russo, thank you. I can't think of what I can do to repay you."

"Just have a good time, Charlie boy."

Charlie crept into his mother's bedroom and sat down on the edge of the bed next to her. She was sleeping so peacefully you couldn't tell something as serious as a stroke had happened to her. He was so excited about going to the party, but he couldn't let go of his nagging sense of guilt. How could he have fun when she was just lying in bed, unable to go anywhere? He pulled the blanket up, carefully tucking it under her chin, and kissed her on the cheek.

Then he heard Mrs. Russo come back into the house, calling to him. Charlie silently made his way downstairs.

"Mrs. Russo, I can't go. I can't leave her here and go to a party and pretend everything is fine when it's not." Charlie sat down on the couch, and Mrs. Russo went and sat down beside him.

"Charlie, you're such a good boy, and what a son—No one is better than you. You take care of your mother, but she also wants you to be happy. If she knew that you had stopped living because of her, oh, Momma would be so sad. You know, Charlie, part of taking care of her is taking care of you, too. So you go to the party, and I don't want to hear anything about staying home, you understand?"

Mrs. Russo handed Charlie the suits. He couldn't help but smile as she shooed him into the other room to try them on.

***

Lillie walked among her guests, making sure she hadn't missed anyone who had arrived. The lanterns were lit with tiny lights that glowed in the trees, and the large branches built a canopy that magically twinkled overhead. Lillie smiled and laughed as everyone congratulated her on her graduation, but inside she was nervous and waiting for one special guest. An hour had passed and she was giving up any hope that Charlie was coming. She walked over to where Claire was engaged in conversation and took a seat.

She listened as Claire captivated the boys at the table with her political savvy. Lillie was still searching the crowd when she scooted around in her chair and looked behind her. There was Charlie standing on the porch, peering through the crowd of guests; he hadn't spotted her.

He's here! Her heart fluttered and her head spun. She wanted to jump up and run to him, but instead she held her breath for a moment and walked over with grace.

"Charlie, I'm so glad you could come. How is your mom?" She wanted in the worst way to feel his arms around her, but instead she maintained her calm.

"She's about the same, thank you for asking. Our neighbor is staying with her tonight just so that I could be here."

Then Lillie asked him to join her on a walk around the garden. She wrapped her arm through his, squeezing gently. They got to spend so little time just the two of them. She wanted to soak in the moment and enjoy just being close to him.

They came to a bench and sat down. Charlie broke the silence first. "It sure is a beautiful night. You look lovely in that dress."A wave of butterflies zipped through her stomach. He was so good-looking, even better close up. "Thank you. You look very handsome yourself."

"Are you blushing, Charlie Murphy?"

"Uh, no. I just felt a bit warm. Is it warm to you? I think the heat is coming back."

Lillie wanted to laugh, but managed to hold it to a giggle. "No, nope." She shook her head in denial. "I think it's rather a bit chilly."

She couldn't help but take a little joy in watching him squirm. "So how is it going at my dad's company? You getting along all right?"

"Oh yes. It's great! I love my job. I see a real future for me there."

"That's so nice. I'm glad things are going well."

"I was worried about my mom, but the new job pays so much better. I can help meet the medical bills."

"That must ease you a bit. You can concentrate more on her recovery."

"Yeah, it's a relief. Would you like to take a walk?"

"Sure. That would be nice." Lillie quickly fluffed her hair when his head was turned and grabbed his arm when he extended it out to her. They walked in silence. Being close was enough.

***

The evening raced by at the speed of a bullet and before they knew it, guests were beginning to thin out and go home. Charlie didn't want to leave, but he needed to. There was no way he wanted to take advantage of Mrs. Russo's kind offer.

His heart ached at the thought of leaving Lillie. Oh, how lovely she looked! He wished he could take her in his arms and never let go.

"Lillie, I had a wonderful time tonight, and you really do look beautiful in your dress." He gently placed his hand on the small of her back as they walked to the front porch. "Maybe we can get together again sometime soon?"

He kept taking his hands in and out of his pants pockets and moving back and forth on his feet.

"Yes, I would like that very much," said Lillie.

He looked into her eyes for a moment longer. He was sinking fast, his heart beating with such speed he could feel it pound against his chest. Heat rose from the pit of his stomach and spread an uncontrollable burning throughout his body. He was trying to be the perfect gentleman, but all he wanted to do was kiss her. He could feel the heat in his face surging to every part of his body. It was getting harder to resist scooping her up into his arms and enveloping her with his body. A minute longer and he wouldn't be able to stop himself from kissing her. But he knew Lillie was above all else a lady. There was only one thing left to do: he would thank her again and take his leave.

***

Lillie stayed with her lingering guests until the very last one had left. She was thoroughly exhausted. While the staff was still busy cleaning up, she kissed her father on the forehead and went up to bed.

Alone and in blessed privacy, she buried herself deep under her covers and cuddled up to her downy pillows. She closed her eyes and gave in to the thoughts of the most perfect of nights: the twinkling lights, the delicious food, and the garden as witness to the beginning of her and Charlie.

She imagined them together with a family and just so happy. Could it ever happen? How she wished it would come true. Charlie would be a fine husband and would someday make an excellent father. One look at how he cared for his mother, and Lillie knew he had all the tenderness and warmth she would ever need or want.

Chapter Five

Lillie couldn't believe school was over. Life would be different now. How often would she be able to see her friends, and which ones would she never see again? It felt strange to think about not spending time with the same people she'd grown up with. Very strange indeed.

Lillie plucked up her courage and knew she was ready. The girls decided to go downtown and have lunch to celebrate what was to come. Would they decide to stay at home or embark on new adventures?

Only time would tell.

On the way, they passed by the new housing development her dad's company was working on.

"Claire, do you mind if we go in? I want to see if Charlie is here."

Claire smiled at her as they headed over to the construction site. They saw Charlie hammering on the second story of one of the houses and when he spotted them, he quickly climbed down.

"Hi, Charlie, how is your mom today?" Lillie once again wanted to kiss him, but remained composed. It was getting more difficult each time they were together.

"She's about the same. Thank you for asking, though." At that, Claire started to giggle.

"What's so funny?" Lillie snapped.

"My, the two of you. Stop dancing around each other. Charlie, just ask her on a date already, will you!"

Charlie gave a little nervous laugh; Lillie was mortified.

"Claire, how could you?"

"No, she's right." Charlie turned to Lillie. "Lillie, would you care to join me for lunch this Saturday? I will meet you at your house at one o'clock."

Lillie was so excited she didn't think she could stay calm for another second.

"One o'clock would be perfect."

***

"U.S. CAUTIOUSLY WATCHES WAR IN EUROPE"

This was the headline Lillie saw on the newspaper being passed around the diner. When the girls arrived, they were unprepared for what they saw. The patrons, usually chatting about the weather or the diner's delicious apple pie, were in turmoil. The men were in a heated conversation about the fate of their country if it joined the war. The reports were saying how this was the worst war the world had ever seen, and that if the United States did become involved...

Lillie and Claire sat down at a booth and ordered lunch. The discussions grew more disturbing with each passing moment. After quietly eating their lunch, they left with dread.

***

The week dragged on endlessly. *Will Saturday ever come?* Lillie tried to keep busy by getting ready for her trip to Princeton. She wouldn't be leaving for several weeks, but it at least gave her something to do.

Finally, Saturday arrived, and Lillie woke up early to dress. She chose a pale blue sundress with a cream and blue flowered hat.

Charlie met with Lillie at her house. They both looked forward to their picnic lunch at Greyson Park. There was so more they wanted to talk about. Lillie went into greater depth about her mother, and Charlie discussed how hard his mother worked to support them after his father had died. Afterward, Lillie invited him back to sit in the garden. There the conversation continued well into early evening, neither one of them wanting their time together to end.

"This is truly the most beautiful garden I've ever seen. Your father must have loved her very much." Charlie fidgeted with the buttons on his jacket and then he cupped her chin. Slowly, gently, he pulled her face towards his.

And then it happened....their first kiss. He felt her lips, they were as warm and sweet as summer honey. He dipped down for one more taste of her while brushing the hair away from her face.

"Charlie, hold me close." Her whole body trembled, and her head floated towards the late afternoon clouds of deep peach and pink.

As they sat together in a comfortable silence, Mr. Whitman had come out to say it was getting late and perhaps Charlie should be heading home. Lillie slowly walked him to the front porch, where Charlie kissed her ever so sweetly again.

That night in a dream, Lillie replayed how glorious the day had been and smiled.

***

That summer was a haze of days and nights falling more deeply in love. Lillie and Charlie spent as much time as they could together despite Charlie's busy work schedule and duties caring for his mom. Their favorite spot was in the garden. They would sit on its scattered benches, breathing in its heavy fragrance and holding on to each other in complete contentment.

Outside the gates of their garden, the war was growing worse in Europe. The feeling of impending doom weighed on the town. Charlie watched as his closest friend Pete and some of the other boys from school signed on to serve their country. They wanted to be ready for the looming threat of war for the United States and the current conflict with Mexico. It pained him not to join them, but he knew he could not leave his mom; she needed him, and right now that was more important.

It was a warm Friday night, and Mrs. Russo agreed to stay with Charlie's mom so he could enjoy the evening with Lillie. How could he have managed his life without Mrs. Russo? She had helped him tremendously over the past few months, and he would have been lost without her.

Charlie and Lillie dined with the Whitman family happily, but only as a prelude to the garden. That was their sanctuary, the place away from the impending war, his mom's illness and the outside world. Here it was only Lillie and Charlie for whatever time fate had graced them with.

Charlie held Lillie's hand in his. He had never seen a hand so small and delicate, yet each time she held his work-hardened hands in hers, it gave him a stronger belief in himself. And how could he stop himself from just looking at her? It was impossible. Her skin glistened in the light of the moon, and her hair looked so silky and soft. He loved Lillie, he knew this, but he could not tell her. Not yet. There were so many things that he still could not provide for her. She was used to the best in life, and all he had to offer was himself. That was not enough, not for someone as special as Lillie. But someday, with hard work and devotion, he knew he'd be able to give her the life she deserved.

"Lillie. I know I don't have much, but—" Lillie put her finger to her lips and made a soft *shh.* Charlie stopped. He felt in his heart that there was more to her than just money and things; he shouldn't have said anything.

"Charlie, aren't the trees beautiful in the moonlight? It's almost as if their branches are covered in fairy dust. Look at how they twinkle. Do they have a secret only the willow knows and they're giggling at the rest of the world for being left out?" Lillie smiled and rubbed her hands up and down her arms.

"The temperature sure dropped. Are you cold?" Charlie put his arm around Lillie. There was a light chill in the air; a sure sign summer was coming to a close.

"Just a bit of a chill, but I feel warmer now that you're closer to me."

Charlie wanted to feel her body next to his. He'd dreamed of running his hands through her long hair and kissing the nape of her neck. And now it was happening.

Gently caressing her shoulders brought the scent of lilac and roses to the surface of her skin. Lillie always smelled so good, like the garden: sweet, warm, and safe.

***

To Lillie, Charlie felt strong, capable, and smart, as if he could accomplish anything.

"Charlie, what do you think will happen after the summer's over? I will be going off to college and you will be here. Do you think we will be able to see each other?"

"What do you mean? Of course we will. It won't be easy, but I will come up to visit and you'll be able to come home, too. I already spoke with Mrs. Russo, and she agreed to help out when I need her. So don't worry. We'll make it work. You're not getting away from me that easily, Lillie Whitman. Not at all."

Charlie pulled Lillie closer and she rested her head on his chest. Still, she felt sick with anguish at the thought of losing Charlie; she was falling in love with him and she didn't know what to do.

"Charlie, I want to tell you something, but you must take it very seriously. Please don't laugh." Lillie was practically holding her breath; she couldn't believe the words that were coming out of her mouth. After all, she had never been this lost with a boy before. She was Lillie Whitman, the one in control. She was not the kind of girl to feel this helpless. *What is Charlie doing to me?* "I...love you and I do worry about when I go away. What if you find someone else?"

Charlie put his hands up to Lillie's face and murmured, "That is impossible. There is no other girl for me, and for you, Lillie Whitman, I would wait an eternity." He leaned in and kissed her on the cheek. A chill ran through Lillie's body. "I love you. I love so much my heart aches."

They kissed, melting their bodies into one. In that moment, they knew no other would come between them, ever.

The two lovers sat in the garden for most of the evening, surrounded by the wonder and beauty that Lillie's father had so painstakingly nurtured. They seemed to become part of all the living plants trees, flowers, and vines in this garden, the garden of two..

Chapter Six

The air was crisp the morning Lillie left for Princeton. Charlie arrived and drove her to the train station. She had said her goodbyes to her father and Claire at the house; she needed the last few minutes before she left to be alone with Charlie. This memory of him had to last for a while.

As the train whistled for everyone to board, Lillie didn't want to let go of Charlie.

"I don't want to leave, Charlie." Tears streamed down her cheeks.

Charlie placed the back of his hand to her face and with a touch like a butterfly's wings on her cheek, he wiped the tears away. "Don't cry, my beautiful girl. You'll be home before you know it. Go and have the adventure you've always dreamed of. I'll be waiting. I'm not going anywhere."

Lillie rested her head on his shoulder and took his scent in one more time before climbing aboard the train. All the years of imagining her future, she had never planned for this. She was going to miss him so much.

***

She arrived at Princeton late that afternoon. Her dad had arranged for a car to take her from the train station to the campus. At registration, there was a small but very round woman who looked as if she were part of the original staff at Princeton. Her gray and white hair was neatly tucked back in a bun, and the creases in her forehead reminded Lillie of the parchment paper that Cook used for baking—after it had been wadded up. Her pudgy cheeks were flushed, probably because every student in the surrounding eastern states seemed to be in her line.

Lillie waited patiently for what seemed to be hours. When she reached the heirloom of Princeton, she was surprised to find that despite having to deal with crowds of wannabe adults, the woman was quite pleasant.

"Can I help you, dear?" Her voice sounded like a grandmother offering you hot chocolate chip cookies.

"Yes, please. Lillie Whitman. I need my dorm room number and class schedule." She watched her chubby fingers search through the roster.

"Ah, yes. Miss Whitman. Here you are. That will be dorm room number eighty-four. And your class schedule is right here. Your roommate has not yet arrived. If you get lost, just ask one of the other students. They will be happy to show you the way."

"Thank you. Have a lovely day." Lillie smiled and headed for her room.

When she opened the door, she was pleased to see how quaint it was. The sun shone through the south facing window and warmed the room nicely. Two beds with simple wooden headboards glowed in the streaks of beaming light and the matching three-drawer dresser was perfect for all her sweaters and undergarments

Lillie plopped down on the bare mattress. Her new pale green sheets would look lovely with the dark wood. And the checkered green curtains on the window would match. She couldn't wait to decorate. The space under the bed appeared perfect for her trunk and shoes. She scooted off the bed and checked out the small closet on the right side of the room. Just enough space for her dresses and coats.

After she settled in, Lillie grabbed her coat and decided to go for a walk around campus before dark. The buildings were beautiful, their architecture complex and detailed. Each building had a regal bearing as if they knew how truly magnificent they were. The library was her favorite, though. Its huge columns felt so powerful; she couldn't wait to study there. The lovely greenery and trees that filled the grounds reminded her of the garden. *Dad would be impressed,* she thought.

As she walked through the halls and pathways of the campus, she appreciated how lucky she truly was. To be able to experience this, with its opportunities, humbled her. She thought of Charlie and many others like him who had grown up in hardship but managed to overcome it through hard work and faith. She yearned to talk with him and tell him how much she missed him already.

The next morning, Lillie's roommate arrived. She was a tall girl, blond with blue eyes and a slender frame. Carrying two very stuffed suitcases, she barely made it through the doorway.

"Hi y'all. I'm Caroline, Caroline Llewellyn. My family is from Virginia. Daddy's company is in publishing. Boy, it's already getting a little chilly here. Not like home. Honestly, you could literally fry an egg on the steps of my porch. And humid—well, let's just say my hair has a hard time keeping itself in order."

Lillie quickly realized Caroline was the type to ramble on when nervous. "Well, I am pleased to meet you, Caroline. I'm Lillie Whitman from Long Island, New York. And yes, it is getting rather chilly early this year." Lillie grinned with delight. She liked this girl. She seemed energetic and very sweet.

The girls were getting hungry, so they waltzed over to the kitchen, where a tired cook told them it was closed.

"Oh well," said Lillie, "Why don't we skidoo to that diner instead? I spotted it on the way in."

***

"Isn't this walk stimulating? There's so much excitement in the air." Lillie flipped up the collar of her coat, the air was cool.

"Yes. You can feel it. Everyone's buzzing around, looking for their dorm rooms and classes. It's positively exhilarating. This town reminds of those pictures, you know, the ones in the paper." Caroline shook her head. "I can't remember."

"You mean *The Saturday Evening Post*?"

"Yes!"

"Oh, Norman Rockwell. That's the artist. I love his drawings."

When they arrived at the diner it was crowded, so they sat at the counter. After a breakfast of pancakes and sliced spiced apples, the girls returned to campus to navigate their way around. They wanted to be ready for their classes, which started tomorrow.

After a few times around the grounds they circled back to the campus library, the largest Lillie had ever seen. How could there be so many books in one place? They had a fairly current library back home, but nothing like this!

Overwhelmed, Lillie just sat a few minutes at one of the tables and took it all in. She loved the smell of the books. It was as if time had been captured and placed on these pages. After a few minutes, she got up to wander the aisles, choosing three books and bringing them to the librarian. Caroline wanted to stay awhile and listen to one of the local authors, who was there having a reading, so Lillie agreed to meet her back at their dorm room later.

Back in her room, Lillie examined the books she had checked out. The first was *Pride and Prejudice* by Jane Austen, an author with whom she had grown up to love. The second was *The Importance of Being Ernest* by Oscar Wilde, and the last book was different from anything Lillie had read. It was an eerie book by an author she hadn't heard of, Mary Shelley, and the book was *Frankenstein*. It sounded positively frightening, but she had been so drawn in by it she just had to read it.

She snuggled on her bed with a few pillows and began her journey reading about the monster that was created from parts of dead people and brought to life with the help of Doctor Frankenstein. She was so engrossed in her story that she didn't hear Caroline open the door. She nearly fell off her bed in fright.

"Are you all right?"

"Yes, I'm fine." Lillie laughed. "I'm reading this frightening story, and you scared the life right out of me when I saw you standing there. I didn't even hear you come in." She showed Caroline the book.

"Oh yes, Mary Shelly's *Frankenstein*. I've heard of it, but I haven't read it. I'm reading *The Emerald City of Oz*. It's fascinating. How is yours? Do you like it?"

"Absolutely. It's gripping, maybe a little too much!"

Both girls broke out in laughter. After reading for nearly an hour, the girls were getting tired and decided to turn in. Classes started in the morning.

"Hey, Lillie?" Caroline sat up in her bed.

"Yes?" Lillie rolled over.

"I'm glad we're roommates."

"Me too."

Chapter Seven

Time flew by between getting to know new people and figuring out all her classes. Lillie could hardly believe it was almost Thanksgiving. School was challenging, and she loved everything about her experience, but she couldn't wait to get home—home to Charlie. And she missed Claire terribly too. She found herself tapping a pencil on her desk, anything to ease her excitement. There was so much to catch up on. Lillie finished her last class of the day and went back to her dorm room to pack for her trip home.

Caroline was already in the room, closing the last of her suitcases, when Lillie came rushing through the door.

"That's it. I'm finished. Where have you been, Lillie? It's nearly time for the car to get here."

"Actually, he's already here. I passed him on the way up." Lillie was out of breath and throwing the last few articles of clothing in her suitcase. "It's okay. I had packed most of my things yesterday when you were at class. Just a few more and—done."

The two girls hugged each other, and with a quick goodbye and a kiss on the cheek, they ran out the door in separate directions. Lillie hurried to the waiting driver and on to the train station.

The entire ride home, all she could think of was seeing Charlie, kissing him, and being in his arms. She daydreamed about him constantly. She wished the train would travel faster; the trip seemed twice as long going home as it did arriving in Princeton. She wrote to him at least three times a week, and for all the letters he wrote back, it just wasn't enough.

Lillie arrived home to a bustling household. The staff was rushing about making sure the house was ready for the holiday. Exhausted, she went up to her room to freshen up and wait for her dad to get home. He had gone with his foreman, Tommy Monahan, to give out turkeys to the less fortunate in town.

Every year, Lillie's father filled up a truck with turkeys, and the day before Thanksgiving and Christmas, he made the rounds to families who were having difficult times. If not for her father, most of the families he visited would not have a holiday dinner. But he was thankful for what he had been able to achieve in his life and never forgot those struggling around him. Lillie was very proud of her father: he was the best kind of man, a man with a conscience. She knew Charlie would do the very same thing.

Maybe that was why she loved him so much.

Her dad came home an hour later and Lillie ran down to meet him. "So, Dad, have you seen Charlie? How is he doing? How does he look? Is his mom doing any better?"

"There now, Lils. Take a breath. I haven't seen him lately, but Tommy Monahan tells me he's doing a great job. I think his mom is the same, though. That's why he's not coming for dinner tomorrow, am I right?"

"Yes, but I thought that perhaps since my last letter she might have improved."

"Did you ring him when you came home to ask?"

"No. I know he's trying to prepare Thanksgiving dinner tomorrow. I thought he might be busy." Lillie was playing with the food on her plate.

"Honey, I doubt he's too busy to talk with you. Tommy told me Charlie was all nerves at work today. He couldn't keep his mind on the job, knowing you were getting home."

"Really? I'll ring him after we eat." Lillie broke out into a huge smile as she tried to eat as quickly as she could.

***

Charlie longed to hold Lillie in his arms and keep her close. He missed her, but he didn't want her to know just how much. Lillie had always dreamed of going to college and had worked hard to get there; he didn't want anything to interfere with her plans.

He kept busy with long days at work and caring for his mom in the evening and on weekends. Little had changed in his mom's condition. She still hadn't spoken a word, and her mobility was only slightly better. She had been able to keep some movement in her left hand, but her left leg had grown weaker with lack of use. Lillie was coming home today, and Charlie could hardly contain his excitement. Work, something he normally looked forward to, dragged on endlessly. He was hoping to bring his mother to dinner at the Whitman home for Thanksgiving, but given her present condition, that would not be possible. Instead, he was going to steal away a little time with Lillie on Friday, while the nurse attended to his mom for a few hours in the morning.

Charlie was going to attempt to cook his first Thanksgiving dinner; he wanted his mom to have some sense of familiarity. Thanksgiving had always been one of her favorite holidays despite their financial struggle. She would purchase a small turkey and make all the delicious side dishes. Her yams topped with marshmallows were a sweet treat, and the dressing cooked in the bird was always moist and flavorful. She also made the best homemade rolls in town, golden brown and smothered in melted butter. For dessert there was always pumpkin pie from scratch and whipped cream.

While he was busy double-checking the ingredients he would need, doubt crept into his brain and squeezed it tight.

"Mom." He spoke to her often, even if she couldn't answer. "I know you're eagerly waiting for dinner tomorrow night. I'm doing my best, but I'm not making any promises." He peeked in from around the kitchen door. Her eyes caught his and he swore they twinkled. "Yes sirree, we are having a feast." Somehow reassuring his mom quieted his anxiety as well.

Once again his memory brought him back. Dad would take him outside every Thanksgiving to play ball so they wouldn't get in Mom's way in the kitchen. They would smell the food cooking from outside. Every year they tried to sneak in to steal a morsel when she wasn't looking, but she always caught them and chased them back outside.

Such fun and loving memories he had, but now it was time for Charlie to make this a special day for his mom.

After they were finished, he washed the dishes and sat with his mom in the living room until darkness blanketed the sky outside. He could see she was nodding off to sleep, so he put her in the wheelchair and brought her into the bedroom.

Just as he finished putting his mom in bed, the phone rang. It was Lillie. Charlie's heart raced at hearing her voice. She sounded even softer and warmer than he remembered.

They talked for hours, catching up on everything that had happened over the past few months. Even though they had been writing, there was so much more to share.

"Mom's still the same. Not much improvement at all. But dinner was a success. Well, except for the rolls. I cooked those a little too long." Charlie chuckled. "I've missed you so much, my sweet Lillie. I haven't been able to bring myself to go to the garden. It just reminds me that you're not here."

Charlie had tried so hard to hold his feelings in check when she'd left. He hadn't wanted her to change her mind about going away to school. Now that he'd heard her voice again, he couldn't stop himself from expressing his heart's desire: her.

***

His words were intoxicating to Lillie. Everything she had been feeling, he had felt as well! When she left she had felt a nagging sense of regret and worry. What if he had found someone else while she was away? Charlie reassured her with every breath he took and every word he spoke: she was the one for her him. Nothing would come between them, not even distance.

It was getting late, and her father came in to remind Lillie they had an early day tomorrow. Every holiday they visited Elizabeth's grave and brought flowers, a tradition close to their hearts.

They spoke for a few minutes longer, and then Charlie let go. "I love you, Lillie.""I'll see you Friday morning in the garden. Have a happy Thanksgiving." Lillie closed her eyes and placed her hand over her heart. It was beating so fast she thought it might just give out. "And Charlie...I love you, too."

***

Charlie got up early to start preparing the turkey and the other dishes he was cooking today. It wasn't long before the smell of a roasting turkey filled their house. He thought he saw the beginnings of a smile on his mother's face. She had managed to lift the corner of her lips on the right side, and her eyes twinkled with the warmth and love for "her Charlie," as she always referred to him. He wheeled her into the living room and placed her in front of the window so she could look at the children playing ball in the street.

"Remember, Mom, how Dad and I used to go out every year?" Charlie kissed his mom on the forehead and went back into the kitchen to make the yams and marshmallows.

Mrs. Russo came over in the early afternoon to see how Charlie was doing with his meal. They shared a hot cup of tea while Mrs. Russo checked on all of the dishes Charlie had prepared, making sure everything had been cooked properly. "Well, Charlie boy, dinner looks delicious. Your mom will be proud of you."

"Thank you, Mrs. Russo. I just wish she could enjoy it."

"Oh, Charlie, she will. She knows what's going on: I can tell. Just look into her eyes. They will tell you everything. Now I have to get back home. I can't trust Mr. Russo alone with the turkey; half of it will be gone by the time I get there!" They both laughed and Charlie walked Mrs. Russo to the door. Before leaving, she bent down over Ellen and whispered in her ear, "I know you understand what's going on, so don't worry. Charlie is doing fine."

Ellen closed her eyes and squeezed Mrs. Russo's hand.

***

Lillie was lying on her bed when Claire came barreling through the door, as usual.

"Claire!"

Lillie leaped from the bed and gave her friend a huge hug.

"Okay, okay. For a little person you're awfully strong. You're squishing me, Lils."

"You're such a dope. I called you when I got home, but your mom said you had gone out."

"My cousin Gwen's in town again. I had to get out of there." Claire plopped down on the bed and Lillie sat beside her.

"I'm sorry. I know how you dislike her."

"Let's forget about her. Have you seen Charlie yet?"

Lillie sighed. "No. He's spending Thanksgiving with his mom. We're going to meet in the garden tomorrow morning."

"Are you and your dad going to the cemetery?"

"I have to get dressed. He'll be waiting for me. What time is it?"

"Eight-thirty. You'd better get a move on."

Lillie could hear her dad calling for her downstairs. "I'll be down in ten minutes, Dad!" she called back. To Claire, she said, "Are you coming back for Thanksgiving dinner?"

"What, are you kidding me? Of course I'll be back. I certainly don't want to spend Thanksgiving at my house. Besides, I don't think my mom will mind. After, all she has Gwen!"

"I'll see you a little later, then. Wish your folks a happy Thanksgiving from me, will you? And don't forget Gwen." Lillie chuckled. She was trying to get a smile out her friend but knew this was a sore subject.

"Sure, I'll tell her you wished she could have come by. Too bad." Claire smirked.

"I bet you will! Try to be nice, Claire. It's only for a few days."

Lillie hugged her friend again and raced to get dressed.

It was bitterly cold outside and all the autumn leaves had fallen, leaving the branches bare and dreary. Lillie and James sat quietly in the car on the way over to the cemetery. She had bought a pair of charcoal-gray cashmere gloves trimmed with black fur. They complemented her fashion sense but were rather impractical because they were not very warm.

There was hardly anyone at the cemetery that day, and Lillie felt lonely as she stood next to James and her mother's grave. They had visited every year at holiday time since Elizabeth had passed away. Lillie thought that through the years it would get easier, but it hadn't.

As she looked around at the rolling hills and barren grave sites, she noticed how some were so ornate and large, while others were barely visible. Was this a reflection of the person and who they once were? Did the larger stones belong to someone who, in life, had to always make a statement? Or perhaps they loved the luxuries in life and wanted the same in death. Were the smaller ones for those who had led a simple life, or did they just enjoy simpler things?

Then her eyes fell on her mom's stone. It was average in height, and the top had a delicate cross etched into the marble. It read: *Elizabeth Whitman, loving wife and mother. I'll wait for you in the garden, love James.* It was simple but elegant, just like her mom had been. Tears swelled in the corners of Lillie's eyes, and she buried her head in her father's shoulder. James drew Lillie closer, hugging her tight and stroking her hair.

"Let's go, honey. It's getting colder. It looks like snow might be coming." He took her hand as they walked back to the car.

***

Claire went home to find her mom and Gwen sitting at the kitchen table, gazing at fashion magazines. *Ugh. I know I was born in the wrong house.*

Her mother waved her over to the table. "Claire, come over here and spend some time with Gwen and me. We're looking for the perfect wedding dress. It seems your cousin is engaged!"

Great, she thought, *now I'll have to hear endless hints about when are you going to meet a nice boy?* She forced a smile and took a seat.

"Claire, would you be my maid of honor in the wedding?"asked Gwen. Claire's mom beamed with delight. The thought of getting her daughter in a dress must have been pure heaven.

"Me? Why? Don't you have a best friend or something?" Claire was horrified by the thought.

"Claire!" said her mom.

"I didn't mean anything by it, but usually isn't it your closest friend? I was just surprised that you asked me, Gwen."

"I've always thought of you as my best friend. And

we're family. What better person than a family member to stand up for you at your wedding? I think it will be perfectly divine! We'll have to hurry finding a dress for you, though. The wedding is only ten months away. We'll probably have a few fittings, and we have to find the perfect accessories, too. This could take months!"

Claire suddenly felt sick to her stomach. Several months with Gwen would be torture. But she knew how much this meant to her mother, and although Claire didn't always get along with her, she was still her mother. "Sure, Gwen. I'd be honored to be in the wedding and stand up for you."

Her mother shrieked so loudly that Claire swore her hearing was permanently damaged, and then she excused herself to go get ready for the Whitmans' dinner.

In her room, Claire laid out the clothes she was going to wear to Lillie's. A cream-colored satin blouse with pearl buttons and a Peter Pan collar edged with black piping—perfect. Black slacks and sensible black shoes. Style with comfort was what Claire's fashion was all about. She could never really understand why is was so important for a woman to wear dresses in their modern society. The world was changing and women with it.

No mind, she was completely happy with her ensemble. She started the bath and went to read for a few minutes while waiting for the tub to fill.

Claire was interested in the politics of Washington and read the paper every day to stay informed. There was an article on Jeannette Rankin and her latest endeavors in the House of Representatives. As she read, she imagined her life someday and how she would live in Washington and really make a change for women in the political world. She respected Jeannette and used the woman's career as groundwork for her own path. As she stepped in the warm bath water, she felt relaxed for the first time that day. She had settled things with Gwen and made her mother happy—life might be a bit easier at home.

***

Lillie and her father arrived home to the smell of turkey and pies baking in the oven. Lillie ran upstairs to dress in time for the guests to arrive for afternoon festivities and dinner. Since they didn't have any family in town, her father had invited a group of close friends to come and celebrate with them. They were like family to Lillie and her Dad, and it was nice to share the holiday together.

Lillie had picked out a soft lavender floral dress that tied in the back with a green sash. She would wear her mom's pearl earrings and pull her hair up in a soft sweep.

When she went downstairs, the first of their guests had already arrived. The evening was memorable with delicious food and loving company. Claire and Lillie sat and listened to stories that her father and his friends told of earlier days and some of the troubles they had gotten into as youngsters.

Lillie laughed so hard her sides hurt, and she had to wait a moment to catch her breath. But through all the good times and laughter, she couldn't get the thought of Charlie off her mind. She would see him tomorrow in the garden, where they could be together, and for a while time could stand still.

The evening finally came to an end as she said goodnight to each guest.

"That was a lovely evening, Dad. Everything was delicious. I think I might have eaten a bit too much though. My stomach feels like it's five feet in front of me." Lillie chuckled as she kissed her dad and went up to bed. Tomorrow would be Charlie's day. She could hardly wait for sleep to take her.

The next morning, Lillie woke up to a loud noise coming from the backyard. As she hurried to put on her robe and go downstairs, the commotion grew louder. From the back porch, she could see her father and a large truck with several men from his construction crew. The truck contained two enormous pine trees, and the men were digging large holes in the garden.

Panic and nausea took over. "Dad, what's going on? What are you doing?"

"Aren't they something? I had them brought down from upstate. It occurred to me the other day we had no pine trees back here. What do you think?"

Lillie tried to remain composed. Charlie would be coming soon and nothing was going to ruin this day. She wouldn't have one moment wasted. She took a deep breath. "Dad, today Charlie's visiting. You know I haven't seen him in two months. We were supposed to have a lovely time in the garden, minus the added commotion of your construction crew."

Her father motioned for the men to stop.

"Thanks, Dad. Today means so much to Charlie and me. I feel like we haven't seen each other in years."

"I'm sorry, Lillie. You know how I feel about your mother's garden. Sometimes I get an idea and I have to do it right then and there, although in my defense I ordered the trees over a week ago. They've already had their first big snow fall upstate, so it was slow getting them moved down here. It's yours and Charlie's day today. I can wait until tomorrow to plant the trees."

***

The nurse arrived a few minutes early at the Murphys'. Charlie was still in the process of dressing his mother. He took her brush and stroked her hair. He couldn't quite do it the way she had fixed it, but he tried. He scooped her up to lift her into the wheelchair, she felt so frail to to him.

"Go ahead, Charlie. Go see your girl. I'll finish her up." Finola had turned into a friend as well as a nurse for his mother. She would stay late and arrive early and never ask for any extra pay. She took excellent care of Ellen, and

Charlie had grown to feel secure when Finola was with her.

"Are you sure? I can finish. I'm almost done."

"I've got it. Ellen and I are going to have a fine day. I've brought some new magazines for us to look through. One of them has an article on the affluent homes of Long Island. The Whitman house is in there. I thought she would enjoy seeing where Lillie lives and where you're off to."

"Thanks, Finola. I'll be home around five o'clock."

Charlie kissed his mom on the cheek and ran out the door. He wanted to stop and pick up flowers for Lillie on the way. It might be silly, bringing flowers to the girl who had the most beautiful garden in the state, but he just couldn't resist.

Chapter Eight

Lillie knew it would be cold out, and she needed to wear her prettiest coat for Charlie. It was a gift from her father last year, and she had waited for a special occasion to wear it. James had taken a trip to Paris, looking for a particular flower for the garden, and while he was there he had done some shopping for Lillie. The coat he had brought back was made from the finest wool, a soft ivory with black velvet trim. It had a large, cape-like collar, and the buttons were handcrafted in clear and black crystal. Lillie had borrowed one of her mother's handmade pearl combs and used it to pull back the front of her hair.

She was brought back to one of her last memories of her mother sitting in the garden. She was on a bench snuggled with a blanket and asked Lillie to sit beside her. They didn't say much, just sat together. A tear caressed her cheek and she quickly wiped it away. No time for sadness: Charlie was on his way.

***

Charlie arrived at the Whitman house and went to the side entrance of the garden. Lillie was sitting on one of the many benches placed throughout the garden, her expression miles away.

He stopped to admire her. She was beautiful, even more beautiful than he remembered. Her wavy hair cascaded over her shoulders, flowing down to the middle of her back. The burning anticipation in his chest made every step leaden. He approached her from behind and stroked her lovely hair.

Lillie turned to look up at him with the sweetest of smiles. And then, with a leap of excitement, she was in his arms and they were kissing passionately and without care. They were the only two people on the planet, and all of the world's beauty belonged to them. Charlie's arms tightened around her waist; every sweet caress of her lips made him yearn for more.

They sat down on the bench, and he held her for a while in silence, just admiring the garden and enjoying being close. After several minutes, Charlie pulled away to look at Lillie's face. "What were you thinking when I first arrived? You looked so deep in thought."

"No, my thoughts were here. I was looking at the two fire thorns. See, they're reaching toward each other. I tried to imagine what it would be like when they finally touched. Intertwined, their beauty will spread the whole width of the garden. How lovely they will be together, so much stronger and brighter. These tiny berries, here on the vine, will grow and cluster, filling the garden with such color. They've grown quite a bit since the summer."

Charlie cupped Lillie's face, drawing her closer and then gently kissing her. This was forever. No one could ever make him feel the way she did. He would never tire of looking into her beautiful eyes, or noticing the way her hair caressed her shoulders and flowed to the small of her back. She was kind and loving with a beauty that radiated from within and a gentleness that blanketed everything she touched. The world was a richer place with Lillie Whitman in it, and lucky were the ones she loved. He couldn't understand why she loved him, but she did, and for her love he would give everything. It was going to be hard when she left.

"Charlie, I was thinking...What if I stayed here and went to school? I could be near and help out with your mom. We could be together. I know my dad wouldn't mind. In fact, I think he'd be happy. He really misses me. It just might be a little too quiet here for him." Lillie giggled, but Charlie became annoyed.

"No, you're not going to give up your dream only to become a nurse to me and my mother. We are getting along just fine. As I've told you before, I will not be the one responsible for taking that dream away from you! Lillie, I love you more than you could ever know. Being with you...It's the reason I breathe. Every day. I want you, all of you. I won't deny your search to experience life beyond this town and your garden. I will wait for you until you return. Please, don't make me your sacrifice. I don't want you that way; I don't want us that way!"

The building frustration choked him as he tried to explain to Lillie without hurting her feelings. He wanted desperately for her to understand what he was trying to say, and at the same time he wanted to shout, "Yes, stay with me! Be with me!" But he couldn't: it was Lillie's time to explore, and he knew she would eventually regret it if she stayed home now.

"Charlie Murphy, I don't deserve you. You are far too good to be waiting for me, but I will be forever grateful if you do."

Charlie laughed and kissed the tears that had gathered on her cheeks. "Silly girl. I'm the one who's grateful you've chosen me."

***

On Saturday, Lillie spent the day with Claire. There was so much to catch up on: Claire's recent and most unwilling role as matron of honor in her cousin's wedding, her job with the local congressman, and her burning desire to be involved with the politics of today and the future of women rights.

"I don't know, Lils. There's so much we haven't accomplished yet and so much we still have to do. I wish everyone would see how important this is. Women need to stand up and be heard. We've settled for so long. We should be able to vote, to work if it interests us and to raise a family, if that's what we want. We don't have to choose—men don't have to choose—and besides, we're smarter and more cunning than they'll ever be. The sooner they realize that, the better we all will be!"

"Oh my. I wish I were more like you, Claire. You

know what you want and who you want to be. There's no doubt in your in mind. I know I want Charlie and beyond that, well, it's somewhat muddled."

"Who are you fooling? You know exactly what you desire! You want the man, the house, the children and, yes, the adventure! You, my dear, want it all. You're just afraid to admit it. Charlie is the center of your world, and all you have to do is just to build around it. It will come together for you. Just wait and see."

Lillie hugged her friend and then sat down on her bed. "You are my closest and dearest friend, and you know me better than anyone. I would be lost without you."

"Enough of this mush. How about we stir up something to eat. I'm nearly starving!" Claire grabbed Lillie's hand and they ran downstairs to the kitchen.

***

That morning, Charlie bundled his mother up and took her for a walk in her wheelchair. It had been so long since she had been outside, and he thought the air would revive her. It was a glorious morning with the sun bright and the air clear and crisp.

Why, it almost felt normal.

It had been terribly long since he had enjoyed a conversation with her. Somehow, just being outside this morning gave him a sense of hope, even if it was only him doing all the talking. Afterward Charlie headed for home to make them both hot soup and sandwiches.

His mom grew tired after lunch and he helped her into bed to take a nap. He sat on the couch gazing out the window for a few minutes before picking up the newspaper to catch up on the latest reports about the war. Many of his friends from school had already enlisted and had been sent for training. He couldn't help but feel obligated to join them.

As he read on, the reports became horrific. The enemy had no compassion. Many men were being wounded and killed with a terrible substance called mustard gas. It was a cruel weapon that tortured its victims with incomprehensible pain before death. Others were coming home completely changed, displaying tremors, facial tics, and signs of complete mental instability. This war was the worst that anyone had ever seen, and there was no immediate end in sight. Europe was in turmoil.

He put the paper down and closed his eyes. He thought of Lillie's sweet face and the horror he had just read about. Charlie was desperately confused. He wanted to stay home for his mother and to start a life with Lillie, but at the same time he was drawn to join the other men who had already enlisted. If the United States entered the war, he knew Lillie would wait for him, but his mom was an entirely different situation. He couldn't leave her in her present state. Holding a spoon with his help was just not enough progress.

No, I will have to stay home for now. Maybe with some hope the war will end soon, although that's unlikely.

***

Sunday came on swiftly and sadly. Lillie boarded the train back to school, and although she was excited to get back to her classes and see Caroline again, she missed Charlie and Claire already. Passing through the different towns, however, she felt a sense of the adventure.

Lillie was never one to just let things go by. On any given day, she wondered about the people she saw just walking down the street. What were their lives about? Whom did they love? Were they happy or merely content? She wondered when she saw an older gentleman or lady, what did they look like when they were younger? How did they act as a child? Did they have loving parents? Did they do well in school. Did they even go to school? How had they become who they were today?

These were the questions that burned inside her. She did have a thirst for knowledge and was truly interested in the people and world around her, but her interest also extended to the things around her. She loved antique pieces that she could hold in her hand and wonder what their stories were.

Charlie was right: she did have more exploring to do, and that thought exhilarated her.

When she arrived in her room, Caroline was already unpacking her belongings. "Lillie, I missed you. How was your trip? Did you have a nice Thanksgiving? What about Charlie? Was he wonderful?"

Lillie giggled. "Yes, to all of it! I missed you too. Did you have a good holiday as well?"

"It was so much fun. My cousins came in from South Carolina, and my grandparents from Georgia. We had so much family and food; I think my mom was cooking for three days. It was the best! I brought leftover pie for us to snack on later. She makes the best sweet potato pie!" Caroline closed her trunk and placed it in the closet.

"That sounds delicious. I'm a touch hungry from the train ride, and pie sounds scrumptious." Lillie began unpacking. When she was done, the girls sat down and ate some of the pie while comparing their holiday stories.

"Lillie, do you think you and Charlie will get married? I know he hasn't officially proposed, but it certainly sounds as if he intends to."

Lillie's face flushed with the question. She wanted to marry Charlie, and Caroline was spot on: he had said they were to be married someday, but he hadn't asked. She wondered for a moment, could not asking her to marry him mean that he was scared to? He didn't seem scared at all, but was he unsure? No, Charlie had made it perfectly clear he was forever in love with her.

Then why hasn't he proposed? Why hasn't he asked me yet? What could his reason be?

But in an instant, she knew the answer to her own question: it was her. He was waiting for her. She needed her adventure and he would wait until she had her full of it before asking.

She smiled. "Yes. Someday when we're both ready, I know he will ask me in the most romantic way." Caroline waved her hand for more and Lillie drifted in thought for a moment. She grabbed her friend's arm. "In the garden of two."

It was the most romantic and beautiful place in the world, and that's where Charlie would propose. She was sure of it. She would wear an elegant ivory dress; white would be too stark, just too bright. She wanted something subtle and timeless. Maybe an antique dress. Maybe her mother's. She would have to ask her dad about that when she went home for Christmas.

The thought of marrying Charlie enthralled her. How wonderful to be Mrs. Charles Murphy!

"Now, wait a minute. Don't you think you should wait until he asks you first before you have the wedding completely planned?"

Lillie smiled wider. "I think you're right. I should try and wait." The girls giggled as they continued talking throughout the night.

Chapter Nine

Although Thanksgiving had just passed, Charlie was already looking forward to Christmas. Lillie would be coming back home, and he had begun work on her Christmas present: a chair from cherry wood to go in her bedroom. It would be her special chair to sit in by the fire and read. Lillie enjoyed reading at night, and her old chair was just fine, but Charlie wanted to give her one that was made just for her, something he had made from his own hands. Every night after work, he would come home and cook dinner for his mom and himself. Then he'd get her settled for bed and spend the rest of the evening working on Lillie's chair. It was bitterly cold in the garage at night, but Charlie didn't mind. He was doing something he loved for someone he loved; for him it couldn't be more right.

It was late on Friday night, and Charlie was busy cleaning up the garage from an evening of sanding wood when one of his former classmates, John McDougal, came up the drive. As Charlie walked over to greet him, he noticed John was also quite drunk, probably on his way home from Duffy's, the only bar in town. It was the usual hangout on Friday and Saturday night for all the local boys. Mr. Duffy had left Ireland when he was sixteen to come to New York with his parents. He joined the police force and after twenty years of service, retired with a full pension and opened Duffy's. His son, William, helped to run the establishment and gave it an at-home feel.

"John, what are you doing out so late? Don't you have work tomorrow?" Charlie grabbed him as he stumbled over. John worked at his father's garage on the outskirts of town. After graduation, he started working there, learning the trade and hoping to take it over one day. But why was he drinking so much? Usually a couple of beers was the limit for him.

"You haven't heard, have you?" John sat down on the cold cement of the driveway. He was swaying, and Charlie leaned in to keep him from falling back on the ground. "I didn't want to be the one to tell you. I only came by to see how you were doing, you know, with the news. What am I saying? Of course you don't know. No one's told you yet!"

"John, quiet. You'll wake the dead. It's very late and you're soused. Told me what? What are you talking about?"

"I'm so sorry, it's Pete. He was killed in Mexico last week, caught in the middle of gunfire from both sides. His mom received the letter today, and we all just had to go down to Duffy's to toast to his memory."

John put his head down on his knees. He started swaying again and Charlie grabbed his arm to keep him steady. "I would have come and gotten you, but I know with your mom it's difficult for you to leave. I thought Mr. Russo might have come by to tell you. He was delivering a meat order to Pete's house when his mom got the news. He must have figured he'd tell you in the morning. I'm so sorry, Charlie. I didn't mean for you to find out like this. I'm sorry, so sorry. I know you two were pals."

Charlie couldn't move. His heart felt frozen.

Sure, he'd heard the stories about all the soldiers who were dying, and it saddened him deeply, but losing one of his friends was a punch to his gut. Not Pete—he was a stand-up guy, his sidekick, the best. When times were tough, Pete was always there for him. When his dad died, Charlie had it especially hard, with his mom working long hours and Charlie being on his own and alone. Pete would bring Charlie home for dinners. Along with his mom, Pete was family. When Pete had signed up for the service, Charlie wanted to do the honorable thing: join him. He desperately wanted to, but with his mom's condition that was impossible.

Charlie collapsed next to John on the driveway, and

the two boys just sat in silence. The cold ransacked their bodies, setting even their souls to shiver. Charlie helped John up as they shuffled towards his house. Back in his living room, he contemplated a drink. He pulled out the bottle of whiskey that had been in the cabinet since his dad had passed away. He poured himself a couple of glasses, numbed every thought and emotion he had, and fell asleep.

***

The next day, with a very heavy heart, Charlie went to visit with Pete's mom, Mrs. O'Leary. He needed to be in their home and with his family. It somehow made him feel as if Pete were close by. Deidre, Pete's sister, had come out to the Island from the city. She was working as a seamstress in Macy's and lived in Manhattan.

"I don't understand. We're not even at war yet! This cannot be happening."

Deidre walked over to her mother and sat down, clasping her hand. "Charlie, I know your reasons for not signing up, and I have to say, this is going to sound strange, but I'm glad. I'm glad this town will have one less boy to mourn. I mean, everyone is talking. We all know it's just a matter of time before we're in the war as well. What am I saying, we're already in a war, even if the President calls it a 'punitive expedition'; I think Pete would agree with me!" Deidre began sobbing uncontrollably. Mrs. O'Leary put her arms around her and held Deidre tight until she calmed down from sheer exhaustion.

Charlie stayed with the O' Learys for most of the day. Gradually, friends from town came over to offer their condolences and bring food for the family. Why did so many people come with food?

Maybe food can be a comfort, he thought. In any case, there was enough food brought to the O'Leary family to feed the entire town for a week. Pete would have loved it: that boy could eat like a horse! He would have begun with Mrs. Russo's lasagna and worked his way through every dish and dessert on the table. Then he would complain he was too full, only to start the entire process over again in an hour. Charlie chuckled. It felt good to have a warm memory of Pete.

Then it was five o'clock and Charlie knew he should be getting home. Mrs. O'Leary wrapped up food for him to take home to his mother. On the way out, Charlie kissed her on the cheek and she hugged him. It made her feel somehow closer to Pete, she said. He promised to stop by later in the week and left to go home to care for his mother.

Sunday morning, Charlie thought he'd try bundling up his mom to bring her to church. It had been quite a while since they'd been. Before she became ill, she had gone faithfully every Sunday. Ellen was an old-fashioned Irish Catholic and Charlie knew how much it bothered her to miss Mass. He had spoken to Father Sullivan earlier and expressed his wish. Father Sullivan suggested that Charlie bring her up to the front of the church, where they would be sure she was comfortable.

It was freezing, so Mr. Russo offered to drive them over with his wife and himself for the ten a.m. Mass. Charlie could see a light in his mother's eyes as they approached the church, and he wheeled her up to the first pew.

Later, when they were at home, Charlie sat for a while in the living room. His mom had gone to bed for the evening, and his mind kept wandering. He couldn't help but think how different life would be right now if his mom didn't have the stroke, how his plans for the immediate future might have been very different, and how he could have changed his mother's life for the better. He was thankful that Lillie understood and was truly supportive of everything he needed to do right now. He knew she loved him, but he missed her so much when she went to school. If his situation were different, he could have gone to visit her more often. Sadly, he hadn't been able to, not even once since she had left. He wanted to see the campus and her dorm room. He would have liked to meet her roommate; Lillie said she was a great girl.

Charlie's head was swimming and he was having a hard time quieting it down before bed. He decided to sit out front for a while, hoping the cool air would tire him and he could go to sleep. He had been outside for a few minutes when Mr. Russo came out to sit as well. Charlie waved to him from the stoop, and Mr. Russo motioned for him to come and join him. As Charlie walked over, Mr. Russo lit up a cigar and began puffing. It filled the air with a sweet, pungent smell that Charlie could detect before he even reached the Russo's property.

"Charlie boy, what are you doing out so late? It's mighty cold." Mr. Russo took another long puff of his cigar.

"Couldn't sleep. My head won't shut off. There's too much going on inside there." Charlie sat back and closed his eyes. "What are you doing out here. Does Mrs. Russo know you're smoking that cigar?"

Mr. Russo gave Charlie a little smirk. "Mrs. Russo has gone to bed, and what she doesn't know is no concern of hers, right?"

Charlie laughed again. "Don't worry. Your secret is safe with me."

"Listen, Charlie. Sometimes we just have to know that everything will work out, and thinking so hard about something will not solve it but obstruct the solution. If you let your head get too cloudy, you can't see past the clutter in your brain. Let it all go. Just close your eyes and think of nothing but space. Soon you'll fall asleep and in the morning you'll feel better. Try it. I guarantee it will work."

"Thanks, Mr. Russo, I will. I'm going to go in now. See you tomorrow." Charlie got up and started walking down the steps of the porch.

"Goodnight, Charlie, and have a good sleep." Charlie waved back at Mr. Russo before going in the front door.

As he lay in bed, he took Mr. Russo's advice, and in his mind he pictured space. It was dark and vast with just the hint of stars in the distance. The more he thought about the wide open space, the more he felt like he was floating, drifting off, and before he realized what was happening, he fell asleep.

***

Ellen watched as her son finished getting ready for work and opened the door for Finola when she arrived. She heard him explain that he had fed her breakfast and she had been sitting in front of the living room window for about an hour. Finola gave Ellen her morning pills and got her ready for a bath. Charlie finished up, and after making his lunch for the day, he kissed his mom and left for work.

Although Ellen couldn't voice it, she had not been feeling well lately. The strength in her left hand had weakened and there was a strange tingling in her fingers. Her body was more limp than usual, and she drifted in and out frequently.

Charlie continued to take her to church every Sunday. She had been a devout Catholic all her life. She believed God would take care of her frustration about her condition in his own way. She would have to be patient.

Chapter Ten

Lillie found that getting back to school was easier the second time around. She had already become familiar with her surroundings and classes. She had her friends and continued to make new ones.

Her favorite class was history and she adored her professor, Mr. Gibson, who was about sixty years old with pure white hair and steel blue eyes that shimmered when he smiled. He had as many lines and wrinkles on his face as the years that he had lived. He spoke about history as if it were the most interesting subject one could ever hope to learn. In his lifetime, he had visited just about every major city in the world. When he was a young man, he had taken ten years after college and decided to see everywhere he could before settling down and teaching. He thought that by doing this it would give him a better perspective on his teachings. He had such passion and enthusiasm that it excited Lillie every time she had his class.

It was early on Wednesday morning, and Lillie was rushing to get to Mr. Gibson's class before the bell. She had overslept because Caroline had been up studying all night for a political science test. Lillie had helped by testing her periodically all night. She just made it into her seat when the bell rang as she scrambled to get organized. She was so engrossed in her actions she didn't notice the new boy sitting right next to her.

"Hello."

Lillie looked up to see who was speaking to her.

"Hello, I'm sorry, did I startle you?"

"No, I'm just distracted; I was trying to get situated before Mr. Gibson started class. I'm Lillie." Lillie put her hand out to greet his.

"Sebastian. My name is Sebastian Penfield, but my friends call me Bastian. Nice to meet you, Lillie. I'm new to Princeton. Just started today. I'm from Long Island."

Bastian shook Lillie's hand and then opened his notebook. "How's this professor? Do you like his class? Does he give much homework? I'm sorry; I ramble when I'm nervous, new school and all."

Lillie covered her mouth. She couldn't help but giggle at this new boy.

"No," she said, "it's fine. He's a great professor. My favorite, in fact. He makes every class so interesting and he's been all around the world! Wait, you'll see how great he is. You'll love this class."

Mr. Gibson walked in and Lillie quickly opened her book to the last page they had left off at. She then leaned over and opened Bastian's book to the correct page.

"Thanks." Bastian smiled at Lillie. She smiled back and whispered, "You're welcome," under her breath.

After class, Lillie invited Bastian to have lunch with her and Caroline, and they agreed to meet in the front of the cafeteria at noon. Caroline was in Lillie's next class, and Lillie told her all about Bastian and that she had asked him to lunch.

"Is he a looker?" Caroline began to blush.

"Hmm, I don't know. He seemed like he could use a friend." Lillie chuckled.

"Yeah, but was he good-looking?" Caroline nudged Lillie on the shoulder. "Well?"

"Well, he wasn't ugly, if that's what you need to know."

"Then he is handsome."

"I guess. As boys go, he was better than most, but I really didn't take notice."

"Lillie, you're impossible!"

"My heart belongs to Charlie. I don't look at other boys in that way. He seemed sweet enough, and he definitely looked like he could use some help getting used to being here. Is that enough for you?"

"I guess I'll wait until lunch to see for myself."

Caroline rolled her eyes and took her math book out for class. “Ugh. I hate math.”

Math had never interested Lillie much, either, but today it seemed especially slow. Every tick of the clock dragged on, and Lillie found her mind wandering back to Charlie. Christmas was only a few weeks away, and she wasn’t sure what she was going to get him for a present. She didn’t want to get him just anything; this was their first Christmas together and she wanted to find something special, something he’d remember always.

On Saturday she would ask Caroline to go with her to the village to visit a few of the charming little shops she had noticed the last time they had gone for a walk. Maybe there would be something there especially for Charlie. She hoped for an antique tool since he loved working with his hands. If not, she could visit the stores back home on her next visit. It seemed silly, coming back to school for only three weeks, but she just had to see Caroline before Christmas. She had picked her up the most darling sweater when she had been home for Thanksgiving, and she couldn’t wait to give it to her.

Lillie spent the rest of class daydreaming about Charlie. She imagined a special house that Charlie built for them, maybe on the Island or in Connecticut. She could have a garden like her mom’s, maybe not so grand, but one she could call her own. Charlie could design and build houses, and she could be the perfect mom to their three beautiful children. And they could travel, see the world, and be together. They would be a happy family, one full of love.

The bell rang and Lillie reluctantly returned to reality.

The girls walked to the cafeteria to meet with Bastian for lunch and satisfy Caroline’s burning curiosity. When they arrived, he was already there waiting for them. Lillie casually introduced him to a blushing Caroline. After they got their food and sat down, there was an awkward silence, and Lillie scrambled to start a conversation.

"So, Bastian, how do you like your classes so far?"

"They're all interesting, but my favorite is Mr. Gibson's class. You were right on the mark. He's funny and his stories are amazing."

Bastian nudged Caroline's arm. "So, do you have Mr. Gibson's class?"

"No, but I hear he's really quite the professor. Lillie speaks very highly of him. I have Mrs. Reed. She's not so terrible, but she doesn't have a sense of humor and she's so conservative; she teaches strictly by the book."

The three finished lunch and agreed to meet later for pie and tea at the local cafe and to explore Main Street. Bastian hadn't had any time to become familiar with the town, and the girls thought it would be wonderful to be his guides.

After he left, Lillie turned to Caroline. "My dear, how do you feel about meeting Bastian?" Caroline looked surprised, so she added, "I noticed your hands were shaky and you seemed, well, nervous."

"You noticed that? Darn. I thought I'd covered it up so well. Oh no, do you think Bastian saw?"

"I don't think so. Besides, he doesn't know you. He wouldn't notice a change like I would. What's wrong?"

"Nothing. Don't worry, it's just nerves. Every time I find a boy cute, I just fall apart. I start to babble and shake, and my palms sweat. I become a complete mess. It's awful when you want to start a conversation with someone but all you can do is mumble a few words. It's horrifying." Lillie chuckled. "Don't laugh. It's not funny. I'm not like you, Lillie. I can't just talk to anyone." Caroline was genuinely upset and Lillie felt bad.

"I am so sorry, Caroline. I wasn't laughing at you. I was just relieved there wasn't anything physically wrong with you. I can help you with this. We'll practice."

"Practice? What do mean?"

"Every time we're with Bastian, try hard to keep up your end of the conversation. Just act as if you're talking with me. After a few times it will get easier, you'll see."

"I don't know, Lillie. What if it doesn't work? What if I sound foolish? You know how I despise sounding foolish." Caroline looked worried, but Lillie wasn't about to give up on this.

"Nonsense. This will work and I will be there to ease any awkward moments, I promise. He'll never know." Lillie hugged her friend before going into class. They agreed to talk more about the subject later, back in their room.

After school, the three met as planned and took a walk to the cafe for pie and tea. They had a great time showing Bastian the town. Lillie was able to glance into a few of the shops, trying to find Charlie's Christmas present. She saw a few things that interested her, but she didn't want it be a distraction from their original plans. Caroline seemed enamored of Bastian, but to Lillie it seemed he might not be as interested. She didn't want to see her friend get hurt. She knew she had to approach this delicately with Caroline later on when they were alone.

It was getting late and the three headed back to school. Bastian walked the girls to their room before returning to his dorm. The two girls put their pajamas on and became comfortable on their beds. Caroline was the first one to break the silence.

"He's so handsome. I wonder if he has a girlfriend back home. He didn't mention one. Did you notice his eyes? They just sparkle. And that smile...I thought I'd faint!" Caroline waited for Lillie to answer, but Lillie was struggling with the idea of telling her friend what she thought. "Lillie, did you hear a word I said? Isn't he just delicious?"

"I did, and yes, he is very good-looking. But after all, you've just met. Why don't you give it time to get to know him better? As you said yourself, we don't even know if he has a girlfriend already." Lillie hoped this would appease Caroline for the moment and she would have more time to sort it out. Was Bastian interested in her? Perhaps she wouldn't have to say a word; perhaps it would all work itself out.

"I get so excited when I'm interested in a new boy," gushed Caroline. "I'd learn to be calm if we could spend more time together. I know I won't sound like a silly goose if I just listen and relax before I say anything. I can do this."

Lillie breathed a sigh of relief. "That's the spirit. You'll be dazzling this boy with your spectacular conversation before you know it!"

The girls chatted for another hour and finished their homework before turning off the lights and drifting off to sleep.

***

The next morning, Caroline had an early class, and she had been gone only for a few minutes when Lillie awoke to a surprising knock at the door. She sprang out of bed and, rushing to put her robe on, ran to open the door.

"Surprise!"

Lillie was speechless for a moment and then screamed. "Claire, what, how? What are you doing here?"

"Well, happy to see you too, Lils." Claire stood in the doorway with a look of sarcasm.

"How did you get here?"

"Congressman Meyer had business in Atlantic City and asked me to assist him. We finished late yesterday, and I thought I'd come and surprise you." Claire walked to the center of the room, looking around. "This is very nice. It's bigger than I thought it would be. Any chance you could spend some time with me this morning? I know I didn't give you any notice, but I really didn't have much myself."

Lillie smiled at her friend. She was so happy to see

her, notice or not.

"Of course I can, but I want to let my friends know. They would wonder what happened if they didn't see me in class. I'll get dressed and then we'll be on our way."

Claire sat down and waited on Lillie's bed while she got ready. When she was done, the two girls headed out the door to look for Caroline and Bastian.

"So, Claire, how did you get here?"

"Congressman Meyer has family close by. He wanted to visit them and didn't mind dropping me off. He's picking me up five o'clock."

"He seems to be such a gentleman. Do you enjoy working for him?"

"I just love it. He's terribly open-minded and believes that women should have the right to vote. He never belittles me and that's rare, working for a man. I am learning that one day, with time and effort, I'll be in Congress and women will vote."

Lillie was suddenly reminded how much she missed seeing her every day. "I miss you. I miss hearing about your causes and the passion you have for what you believe in. You will be whatever you choose, I know it."

The girls went to Caroline's class first. The bell had just rung, and they caught her walking out of the classroom.

"Lillie, what are you doing here? Is there anything wrong?"

"Don't worry, I'm fine. This is my friend Claire from back home."

"I remember. You're the friend in politics. Well, it's finally nice to meet you.

"It's a pleasure to meet you, too." Claire backed away from Caroline and stared out towards the campus.

"Caroline, since Claire's here, I'm going take the day off. Would you mind taking notes in math for me?"

"Sure. What about Bastian? We said we'd meet for lunch."

"I was on my way to ask him if he'd mind if we canceled today." Then Lillie saw the tension in Caroline's face. "Perhaps it might be better if we could all just meet for lunch. That would give Claire and I some time to walk around town. Would you mind, Claire?"

"That's fine. We can all have lunch together and won't it be fun?"

But Lillie knew her friend all too well and gave her a stern look.

"I'll see you both later," said Caroline. "Have fun in town, and don't worry, I'll take your notes."

Lillie waved to Caroline as she disappeared around a bend.

"Claire, that was definitely sarcasm in your voice. Caroline's a good girl. She doesn't deserve to be treated like that. She's been a true friend. You don't know how difficult it was for me coming here, how I felt leaving all of you behind. She's made it more than bearable for me. Sure, she is a little excitable, but that doesn't mean you should be so mean-spirited."

"Excitable is an understatement. Lillie, that girl is perfectly giddy, but I promise to act more, shall we say, *pleasant* toward her." Claire put her arm on Lillie's shoulder. "I'm sorry. I will treat her with more respect. I do mean that."

"You will or I'll call your mother and tell her you thought pink and yellow dresses would be perfect for the wedding."

"You wouldn't!"

"Just try me." Lillie looked at her friend with a devious grin.

Claire scowled. "I promise nothing but sweetness from me."

Lillie shook her head in acknowledgment. "Well, that's settled. Let's go to town."

***

The girls had to hurry back to meet with Caroline and Bastian for lunch. As they reached the cafeteria, they saw Caroline holding a table for them. They were just sitting down when Bastian approached. When he saw Claire, he couldn't take his eyes off of her, although she barely noticed him standing there when Lillie introduced them. Bastian fumbled a hello and quickly left to go get his lunch at the counter.

Lillie was flabbergasted. What was he doing? She turned to her friend. "I'm sorry, Claire. He's never done that before. I don't know what's gotten into him."

"I do." Caroline looked devastated. "I have to go. I almost forgot, there's something I must do right now." Caroline got up and left the cafeteria. Lillie was speechless. She had no idea what had just happened. Claire hadn't said anything out of the way, and Bastian hadn't been there long enough to say anything, either. But as Bastian came walking back, it became clear to her exactly what was going on: he was smitten with Claire.

Oh no, Lillie thought. *He likes Claire. Poor Caroline. No wonder she was acting so odd.* She sat in silence for a moment, trying to think this out. How could she make Caroline feel better?

Not that I'm upset that he likes Claire. She's a wonderful, smart, funny girl and very beautiful. How could he not like her? But he doesn't even know her. Lillie started pushing her food around the plate with her fork. She looked up at Bastian, he was paying at the register and staring back at Claire.

At times she can be stubborn, sarcastic and definitely vocal of her opinions. Wait a minute, she's leaving! Problem solved. They won't have time to get to know each other. After today, everything will go back to normal, and Caroline can take her time letting Bastian get to know her so he can know how truly wonderful she is.

When Bastian came back to the table, he was

focused only on Claire. After a few minutes, Lillie realized that they had actually a lot in common, most importantly politics. Their discussion was both heated and passionate. The longer they spoke, the more they seemed unaware of the world around them.

Lillie listened, overjoyed for Claire but saddened for Caroline. *Things will never go back to the way they were,* she thought. Even with Claire leaving later today, she had a feeling Bastian wasn't giving up. That would go well for Claire, but as for Caroline...She already seemed very far from Bastian's mind. Lillie knew she'd have to have a talk with Caroline later.

After lunch, Claire and Lillie decided to go back to her room to spend more time together before five o'clock. Bastian walked with them to the dorm and lingered out front, talking with Claire before promising to call on her. Once they were back in the room, Lillie grabbed Claire's arm and pulled her over to the bed.

"Claire, what was that all about? I've never seen you react that way to a boy, ever. You agreed to see him again so quickly. You must really like him." Lillie sat on the bed, waiting for an answer.

"I don't know. He seems different." Claire looked out the window at the students walking about campus and then smiled at Lillie. "He's charming and has a great sense of humor, but it's his beliefs I'm truly impressed with. He has this genuine interest in our country and what needs to be changed. We've only just met, but I can't wait to get to know him better."

"This is more interest than you've ever shown in anyone else. I think it's great. Odd for you, but great! My only concern is Caroline. I think she really likes him, so please, if she gets home before you leave, not a word to her about the subject."

"Don't worry. I won't upset 'little miss powder puff.' After all, you have to live with her, and I wouldn't do that to you."

"Gee, your concern for me is overwhelming."

"Fine, I apologize. I guess I'm just being a sourpuss. I miss you already, Lils, and she is allowed to spend every day with you. Since you've left, Gwen's practically moved in with me. My mom is helping her plan the wedding and she doesn't even notice I live at the same house, although they tend to leave me alone, which suits me just fine." Claire ran her hand over the bedspread. It was nice, but not her style. It definitely suited Lillie though.

"I miss my best friend, Lillie. I see Charlie occasionally, but I never know what to say to him. He is so lost without you...Actually, we both are. I have my job, which I am grateful for, but I can't share it with you the way I'd like to. If something wonderful happens in my day, I can't just run over to your house and tell you. It's just not the same since you've left. No, I'm definitely not asking you to come home. I'm just saying it can be very lonely."

Lillie gave Claire a big hug. "I miss you too. Sometimes I ask myself what am I doing here. But I know what Charlie said was true: if I don't do this, I will have regrets. At least I'll be home in two weeks for Christmas, and you'll both see so much of me you'll practically beg me to go, but for now, give Caroline a chance. She makes it easier for me here. She's not you. No one could ever be you.

"Claire, you've been my best friend for most of my life and will be for the rest of it. One day, we'll be the two little old ladies sitting on the porch, reminiscing and comparing notes on our grandchildren. We'll take care of each other and knit sweaters for anyone who will have them. I'm here for you, Claire. Even if we're a distance apart, we are friends forever."

For the first time in her life, Lillie saw tears in her friend's eyes, and she knew how much it pained her to be alone. "I'm glad you and Bastian got along so well. Maybe you could ask him to come and visit over the Christmas holiday and we could all be together. Dad's opening the house on Christmas Eve for the first time in years. You could take him for a stroll in the garden and take that time to learn about each other."

The tears glistened in Claire's eyes as she gave Lillie a half smile.

"That sounds like exactly what I need. I'll ask him when he calls. And sure, I'll be nicer to Caroline, I promise. It truly is a comfort, knowing you have someone watching out for you here. I will remember to thank her as well." The two girls proceeded to lie on the bed and talk for the next few hours before Caroline bolted through the door.

"Oh, you're still here. How was your day?" Then she rushed about the room, attempting to choose an outfit.

"We had a splendid time catching up. What are you doing?" Lillie looked puzzled.

"After I left you at lunch I went to the library to study before class. I was sitting at a table, paying mind to no one, when this boy sat down and began talking to me. As usual, I became nervous and started to babble. I don't need to go into my entire sad routine—you know what happens to me—but this time it was different. He didn't look at me strangely and leave. In fact, he told me he thought I was charming. Imagine that, charming! This is the first time that's happened to me.

"Well, we just started to talk and talk some more, and before you know it he asked me to join him for dinner. I've got to hurry and change this horrible outfit. Just look at this skirt and blouse. They look like I've slept in them. I only have fifteen minutes to meet with him downstairs in the lobby." As she was rushing about, she turned to Claire. "Aren't you leaving soon, too?"

"Yes, in a few minutes, but I wanted to say something before you leave. About earlier, I'm sorry if I..."

"Please don't feel the need to apologize. I could tell

Bastian was interested in you. It's me who should apologize for acting so silly. It was nice to finally meet you, Claire. Have a safe trip home." Caroline gave a quick wave before heading out.

"I wish you didn't have to leave so quickly." Lillie put her arms around Claire. "I really do miss you something awful. Caroline's great, but she'll never be you."

"Of course not." Claire smiled sheepishly. "No one is quite like me. You'll be home in two weeks, and then we can spend as much time together as we can stand." She winked. "I miss you so, Lillie."

Lillie knew how hard it was for her friend to express her feelings to anyone. "And don't forget to ask Bastian, I want to see you all gussied up and on his arm at the Christmas Eve party!"

"You're not going to let that go, are you?"

"Never. After years of hearing you taunt me every time I liked a boy? You'd better be prepared, because I'm going to enjoy this as much as I can!" Lillie laughed and Claire just sighed in agony.

The two girls talked for a few minutes before Claire had to leave, and as Lillie drove away, tears welled in her eyes. She couldn't wait for Christmas and Charlie.

Chapter Eleven

Charlie was anxious. It was his last day at work before the holiday, and Thursday was Christmas Eve, which meant a long weekend. Lillie was finally coming home, and he had finished her chair a few days ago. He couldn't wait to see the look on her face when he gave it to her.

His mom also seemed to be improving. All the time spent exercising her legs and arms was building her strength. He had gotten up a few minutes early that morning and had time to sit with Ellen before the nurse arrived. He told her about his surprise for Lillie and brought it in the house to show her. Charlie didn't expect any reaction from his mom, but to his surprise, she smiled.

He was stunned.

"Mom, you're smiling." She nodded ever so slightly, but enough for Charlie to leap up with excitement. "Mom!" He raced to her side. "You moved your head. Do you think you can do it again?"

Ellen tilted her head again, but this time it was more pronounced. Charlie's whole body shook with happiness. She was getting better, no doubt about it. Ellen looked into his eyes and slowly began moving her mouth. She struggled and looked frustrated, but Charlie could tell she was trying to speak to him.

"Mom, you can do it. Just take your time. I'm right here, and I'll wait as long as it takes. Don't give up. What is it? What are you trying to say?"

Ellen formed her mouth and a noise came out. "Mmewwy Cwismaas."

His eyes brimmed with tears. Holding his mother close to him, he whispered in her ear, "Merry Christmas to you too, Mom."

Charlie breezed through the day, more excited than he had been in weeks. Everything seemed right with the world today and he was going to hold on to every minute. After work, he stopped to pick up flowers for his mom and a chocolate cake from the bakery so they could celebrate. As he came closer to his house, he could see someone waiting on the porch. The closer he got, the more his heart began to pound. It was Lillie. She had arrived home.

Charlie felt his feet try to race faster, but he still couldn't seem to get to her quickly enough. At one point, Lillie leaped off the porch and ran to him. And even with his arms full with flowers and cake, he managed to take her close into his chest and press his warm lips on hers. The passion he had been holding in over the past few months exploded inside him, and he felt as if his heart would burst. The flowers began to fall from Charlie's arms, and they had to break away from their kiss. In peals of laughter, they walked arm-in-arm towards the house.

"Mom, I want you to meet Lillie Whitman." Charlie turned to Lillie. "Lillie, this is my mom, Ellen."

Lillie embraced Ellen. "I've heard so much about you. Charlie speaks about you all the time, and it's lovely to finally meet you."

After a few moments, Ellen was able to speak. "Mmee too."

Lillie's eyes widened and she hugged her again.

***

After Finola gathered her belongings, she wished them all a Merry Christmas and left for home to celebrate with her own family. Charlie and Lillie hastily put dinner together. They wanted as much time together as possible to chat and catch up on what they had missed. The meal was delicious and Ellen was able to sit at the table with them.

Afterward, while Charlie was helping Ellen to bed, Lillie went to the living room, stopping to glance at old photographs of him and his dad. He resembled his father so much, and for a moment it made her think of her mother. She realized just how much they both had lost when they were younger, but then Charlie entered the room and her pain seemed to slip away.

"I've missed you terribly. School is everything I thought it would be, but not being able to see you, hold your hand, or touch your face is sometimes unbearable. I think I've made the right decision being at school, but there are times it just doesn't feel right. Like something is about to happen, something awful. I don't know. I just can't seem to figure it out. If something would happen to you, I couldn't bear it."

"Hey, where is all this coming from?" Charlie pulled Lillie over to him and put his arms around her shoulders, holding her close to his chest. "Nothing is going to happen to me. I'm not going anywhere."

"What about the impending war? You might have to go overseas, you never know."

"No, I don't, but if that happens, there's nothing in this world that would keep me from coming back to you, nothing. I would walk to the ends of the earth to get to you, my Lillie. We're here now. Let's enjoy every second. Not another worry, okay?" Charlie kissed her gently on the lips and pushed a strand of hair away from her face. "Tonight is about you and me, and there's no room for anything else. We're safe and you are in my arms. You will never lose me."

Lillie nestled her head into his chest. She held him as tightly as she could, never wanting to let go. "I'm fine, really. I think my emotions are running high, with it being Christmas and with being home with you again. I always miss my mom more around the holidays."

***

Charlie knew what she meant; he also missed his dad more at Christmastime. But holding her in his arms, he knew they would build a family together some day and he would tell his children about their grandfather and how fine a man he was. They needed to know how much he had been loved.

It was getting very late, and Charlie needed to walk Lillie home. They were anxious for the next day, Christmas Eve, and neither one of them would sleep very well that night. Charlie couldn't wait to give Lillie the chair. He was bursting with excitement to see the look on her face. And as for his mom...Tomorrow would the first time he was taking her to dinner at the Whitmans'. Mr. Whitman had actually arranged for a car to pick them up, and he was generously providing a nurse for his mom so that she would be cared for properly.

Charlie's bed was the enemy of sleep. He tossed and turned for hours before finally going to sit out on the front porch in the cool night air. Whenever he felt his head becoming too busy, he'd sit outside and gaze up at the stars. It was so cold he could see his breath.

As he stared upward, he imagined his life with Lillie. They were married with a quaint house out on the Island. There would just have to be a porch and a swing. He would go to work and come home at the end of the day to his wife and his children. Maybe three. They would have a Lillie-perfect dinner, and afterward he would play with his children in the tree-lined backyard. He could see Lillie's face, golden in the early evening sun, peeking out the kitchen window. Her laughter could be heard over the children's shrieks of fun and adventure. Then together they would carry their children, all drowsy and dirty, upstairs for their baths and then off to bed. Lillie would read them a favorite story, or even two if they were particularly lucky that night, and send them into their sweet dreams with a kiss placed lovingly in the center of their foreheads.

And holidays would be so grand. Christmas would be spectacular with as many presents under the tree as it could hold. And the wrappings...crumbled high as a tower in the center of the living room. If the stars were to favor him, it would be this life, full of love and laughter. If there was such a place as bliss, it was here, tonight in his heart and tomorrow in their future.

***

Lillie awoke early to a commotion coming from the kitchen downstairs. She lay in bed for a while. It was cold, and the blankets were warm and cozy. She was thinking about Princeton, Charlie, and her father. She didn't want to tell Charlie because he had gotten so upset the last time she had brought it up, but she had made up her mind not to return. Her dad would accept any decision she had made, but Charlie was a different story. He would feel guilty, thinking it was his fault. What he didn't understand was that it was her decision to make, not his.

She had wanted to go to a university, but now her mind had changed. It was useless to go and be so unhappy. She would definitely miss Caroline and Bastian, although she had a feeling she'd be seeing a lot more of Bastian if Claire had her way. But missing Charlie was like losing a part of herself; it made her heart ache and her stomach sick, and she wasn't about to do that any longer.

I'll tell him after Christmas. I don't want to ruin the holiday. He will no doubt be furious. Eventually he will understand. It will just take him some time to realize that I'm right and that we can be together sooner.

After breakfast, Lillie went to speak to her dad in his study. He was sitting behind his desk with his feet propped up and the morning paper in his lap; he had fallen asleep. He was snoring, and Lillie chuckled when she saw him. She walked over and gently shook him. "Dad, wake up. I'd like to talk to you before the party tonight."

Her father jumped a little. "What...Was I sleeping?"

"No, Dad, you were sawing wood and very loudly, I might add." Lillie chuckled again.

"Okay, my funny daughter, what was so urgent that you had to interrupt me when I was so obviously hard at work?" Her father laughed and gave Lillie a little nudge.

Lillie held her breath for a moment and then blurted out, "I don't want to go back to school. It's been amazing, but I miss you, and it really isn't what I want any longer. And I know I said I did, but that was then and this is now and now, well, now I don't want to be there. I want to be here! Dad, I know what you're thinking. You're thinking that I haven't given it enough time. No, I haven't been there very long, only three months, but I know what I want and this isn't it. My feelings have changed. I see my future very differently now, and going to college just does not fit the new plan." Lillie stopped, took a breath and waited for her father to answer.

He smiled at Lillie and patted her hand, which was resting on his desk. "Whatever you feel is right for you, sweetheart, is right for the both of us. I would never push you into doing something that you weren't absolutely sure you wanted. If things have changed for you, then you must take the direction that feels right for you, not for me or anyone else. I love you, my darling little girl. Your happiness is my happiness."

Lillie's eyes overflowed with tears. She knew he would understand; he always did, and he never disappointed her. "Dad, I love you. Thanks for understanding and being so patient with me. But I have a favor. Please don't say anything to Charlie. I don't want to tell him until after Christmas. He'll feel guilty. I'll tell him on Saturday while we're having dinner in the garden. Perhaps if we're in the garden, Mom can work her magic and help me out, help him to understand."

Her father nodded yes and got up to hug her. "If anyone can work magic, it's your mom. Wherever she may be, I know she's still watching over us. It's so good to have you back. Welcome home, daughter."

"Good to be back, Dad. Merry Christmas." Lillie kissed her father on the cheek and went in the kitchen to phone Claire.

She spoke with Claire for a while and explained everything that was going through her mind. Claire was excited to hear that she was staying home and promised not to say anything to Charlie or Bastian. Lillie wanted to go back to Princeton after the holidays and pack her things and say goodbye to Caroline. After all, they were friends, and Lillie owed her that. Claire volunteered to go and help her and said she would tell her boss she needed a few days off; she didn't think he would mind.

Following their conversation, Lillie went upstairs to lay out her clothes for dinner and relax in a bath. Afterward she planned to wrap the presents she had gotten for Charlie and his mom. She had bought Mrs. Murphy a luxurious silk scarf that was handmade in France. It was designed with bright red and purple flowers and gold threading spun throughout. For Charlie, she had found an old compass and a pocketknife at the antique store in town. She wasn't sure why she had picked those particular gifts, but she knew as soon as she had them in her hands that she had to get them for him. She was over the moon waiting for dinner tonight; everyone would be together for the first time. To have Charlie and his mom, Claire with Bastian and, of course, her dad constituted the perfect evening.

She took a long hot bath and washed her hair in lavender-scented soap. It smelled heavenly, and she hoped Charlie would get close enough to tell her so. Getting out of the tub was torture. The air was so cold that Lillie nearly put her heavy flannel robe on in the tub. She dressed in her favorite old pajamas so she wouldn't wrinkle her gown for the evening and ran downstairs for red velvet ribbon and some decorative boxes she had purchased. Carefully she wrapped the scarf in tissue paper and placed it in the box, putting the velvet ribbon around it to make a large, beautiful bow. She then went outside and cut some twigs off the pine tree and placed them in the center of the bow. It looked so festive and smelled just like Christmas should.

Lillie was so pleased she wrapped Charlie's the same way.

Sitting in the room, admiring the tree and decorations, she thought about her mom. The house reflected her in every room. She remembered her mom picking out the crystal candle holders that adorned the side tables. They were heavily cut with little red and amber beads hanging from the rims. What fun they'd had shopping that day. Her mom had been determined to purchase new decorations for their Christmas Eve party and couldn't quite find what she was searching for until the very end of the day. They had just about given up, both exhausted and close to suppertime when there it was, beckoning, the one little store they had missed. It had been hidden in a corner at the end of the block and was closing, but her mom convinced the gentleman to let them in for just a minute. Immediately when they went in, she saw the candle holders. Lillie remembered how her mom's face lit up as bright as the red and amber beads. It was exactly what she wanted. And there were two of them, one for each table. Her mom couldn't wait to get home that evening to show Lillie's dad over supper. He had laughed that they had been gone all day and come home with only two candle holders.

But that was Mom, and that's why Dad loved her so much. Something as simple as candle holders could add joy to her holiday.

Lillie checked on the arrangements her father had made for Mrs. Murphy that evening. The nurse would be at the house for five-thirty p.m., and the car would pick them up fifteen minutes later. Lillie wanted to make sure the nurse would be there when Ellen and Charlie arrived. Even though she was doing better, she didn't want to take any chances with her care that evening. There should be no cause for worry tonight. It was the first time Mrs. Murphy was coming for dinner, and Lillie felt better knowing the nurse would be there.

She realized she needed more pine branches to finish with decorating, so it was back out to the garden to cut more. Even in the winter, the garden seemed so alive. She wrapped the pine branches with red-and-green plaid ribbon and placed them throughout the house. The pine not only looked festive but also filled each room with a cheerful holiday scent.

***

At the Dumont home, Claire was helping her cousin with some of the wedding decisions, a task she hated but performed with a forced smile and a promise to herself that this would all be over soon.

"I was thinking about white and pink baby roses for the flowers throughout the church. What do you think, Claire?" Gwen tapped her foot impatiently.

"I don't know, Gwen. Whatever you would like, but don't you think that roses would be too common? Doesn't every girl have roses at her wedding? What about sunflowers? They'll be so sunny and bright, and no one chooses sunflowers."

"Yes, and there's a reason no one chooses sunflowers. They're completely common, and as far as being sunny, I think they're just a dreadful color."

Claire glared at her cousin and very quietly to herself counted to five, and then answered, "It's your wedding, Gwen. Choose whatever you want."

"That's right, it is my wedding, and you are my maid of honor. Honestly, Claire, you haven't helped with a thing."

Claire closed her eyes for a second and tried counting to five again. *One, two, three...*"Forget it, I've had enough. I agreed to be your maid of honor because you're my cousin, but I've never given you the idea I was happy about it. You know I despise all this fussy stuff, so no, I don't care. Whatever you choose—roses, sunflowers, daffodils—I don't care. Just pick something."

Claire stopped. Gwen had tears in her eyes; her mom was going to run her over the coals for this one. "Listen, Gwen. I'm sorry, but I really don't know anything about planning a wedding. Please stop crying and we'll figure it out." Claire handed Gwen a handkerchief. "Now, roses are nice. I was just trying to help by giving you my opinion, but if it's roses you want, then roses it will be. Dainty pink and white ones placed all around the church, just as you wish, and it will be beautiful."

Gwen gave Claire a half smile. "I suppose I did ask for your opinion. I'm sorry for sounding snippy. I think I'm a little overwhelmed."

"I'm sure you are. I'll make us tea and then we can finish up for today, okay?" Claire gave Gwen a smile and a pat on her shoulder. She put the kettle on the stove, and while she waited for it to boil, she thought, *Why do I snap at Gwen like that? It's not her fault. She is who she is and after all, we're family.* Claire promised herself that she would try to be more interested in Gwen's wedding plans. It was the most important thing in Gwen's life, and her cousin didn't need any more stress than she already had.

The two girls sat and drank tea for a while, surprisingly getting along and having a pleasant time. The sun was already beginning to set when Claire realized the time.

"Darn, I have to go get ready. Bastian will be here in an hour, and I still have to take a bath." Claire got up and cleared away her cup.

"That's right, tonight's Lillie's Christmas Eve dinner. How did you get that by your mother? I mean, it is Christmas Eve. Why didn't she insist you spend it with the family?"

"Mom never interferes when it's the Whitmans. She knows how difficult it's been for Mr. Whitman and Lillie since her mom died. This is their first Christmas Eve dinner with friends since she passed away. It's a real event, so she’s allowing me to attend without an objection.”

“Have fun and tell Lillie I send my best.”

Chapter Twelve

The Whitman house was beautiful. The smell of fresh pine and the many dishes cooking in the kitchen were deliciously inviting. The Christmas tree in the formal living room glittered across from the stone fireplace. The decorations hanging from the tree twinkled from the light of the fire and the whole room glowed. It looked as if elves had come and perfectly arranged the room.

Claire and Bastian arrived. When Lillie spotted Claire, she could not believe what she was seeing. Claire was wearing a dress! The hunter green satin flowed to her ankles while the fitted top displayed her figure quite nicely. And as Claire turned, Lillie noticed her hair was lovely, swept back with an ornate silver comb. Bastian, not in the least outdone, had on a black pinstripe suit with a crisp white shirt and shiny black shoes.

Lillie ran to her friend and whispered in her ear, "You look so elegant, and you're wearing a dress!" She hugged Claire and Bastian and took their coats. Claire smiled that don't-say-a-word-out-loud kind of smile.

Lillie understood and nudged her with her elbow. "I'll talk to you later. Come on in and have a cup of hot cocoa."

The three spoke for a while before the Murphys arrived. The nurse was there as planned, wheeling Ellen into the living room so she could warm herself by the fire and enjoy the lush beauty of the tree. Charlie had placed a heavy wool blanket over the back of her wheelchair in case she had a chill and one over her legs for added warmth. Lillie brought her a cup of tea with cinnamon sticks and a dash of spice. It was going to be a charming evening.

***

Charlie watched as Lillie spoke with his mom. She was so gentle with her. Everything he wanted was here in this room. His mom was doing better, he was doing well at his job, and he had Lillie. For a moment, a fear twinged in him. Everything was so perfect. How could it last? How did he deserve this wonderful life. Something had to change, didn't it? As Charlie lost himself in doubt, Lillie sat down beside him.

"Charlie, what's wrong? You look miles away?" Just the sound of her voice was enough to dispense his fear and bring back his happiness.

"No, I'm fine. I'm just watching you and my mom. She's doing so much better, don't you think?"

"I can't believe she's even here. Honestly, a few weeks ago I thought this would never happen. I'm so happy, Charlie. I have you, and everyone is here, just as it was when my mother was alive. I haven't felt this way about Christmas in such a long time. I just want this evening to last forever." Lillie nestled her head on Charlie's shoulder and scooted closer.

"Lillie, your hair. It smells wonderful. I can't quite place the scent," said Charlie.

"It's lavender. I had hoped you would like it." She hesitated and then said, "And I'm about to burst if I can't give you your present right this instant!" Lillie reached for his present from under the tree and handed it to Charlie. "I know we should wait until later, but I can't, so open it."

She squirmed as he unwrapped it. Inside was a brown velvet pouch. He opened it up and saw a pocketknife and compass. He took them out carefully. They were very old, he could tell by the details, but they were both in mint condition. Charlie rubbed his thumb across the back of the pocket knife. He could feel the etching of the design. A stallion, strong and running at full speed. It was graceful and bold. Magnificent.

"They're two very different pieces, but I knew they were meant for you when I saw them. I know how you love to work with wood, so I thought maybe the pocket knife would come in handy. As for the compass, well, that is so no matter where you are, you will always find your way back to me."

Charlie was overwhelmed. What thoughtful gifts! He just had to lean in and kiss her on the cheek. He couldn't say anything for a moment; he just held them in his hands. "I love them. They're so special. My gift for you is simpler. These must have cost dearly. I just don't want you to be disappointed. I'm sorry, Lillie. I didn't have much money. With Mom's treatment and the constant care of having the nurse, I can't give you the same things that you can afford. But I do love them, and my heart will always lead me to you."

Lillie let out a frustrating huff. "Look, Charlie, understand that I do not care how much money you have or don't have. I love you and I want you, no matter where we live or what we have. Life means nothing to me if you're not with me. When I saw these things in the shop, I wasn't thinking about how much money you would spend on my gift; I thought that they would be something special to you and they would have meaning in your hands, just as I have meaning when I'm in your arms.

"You give me direction," she continued. "Everything changed when you came into my life. I was always looking for something, searching, discovering. I thought I had to leave home to find what it was I was missing, but it turns out it was in my own town; I just needed to open my eyes. So please, don't do this to me. Don't make me sound so superficial that I would compare our Christmas gifts. I know you love me more than that. Just accept I love you that much as well."

Charlie was stunned. He hadn't realized what he was doing to Lillie. He was making her seem frivolous and shallow, and there was nothing frivolous or shallow about Lillie Whitman. She loved him; she had told him so many times. How could he doubt the depth of her feelings for him? She was his and he would be hers for the rest of their lives. Nothing else mattered. He was acting like a fool.

"I'm sorry; I just want to give you the world. I love you so much. My darling Lillie, please forgive me and let me get your gift. I'd really like to give it to you now."

Lillie leaned into him and gave him a soft kiss on his lips. Charlie pulled back and looked into her eyes. They were filled with love and longing, but being alone would have to wait.

When he walked back into the room, carrying the rocking chair, Lillie was sitting by the fire. The light from the flames reflected off of her eyes, making them sparkle as they widened. She walked across the room and ran her hands over the back of the chair, where he had tied a large green velvet bow. He watched as her fingers traced the intricate carvings in the wood, which looked like bouquets of flowers held together by flourishes of ribbons. Charlie could tell that he had given her what she had already given to him, a piece of himself.

"Charlie this is the most beautiful chair I've ever seen. Thank you." As Lillie went to hug him, Mr. Whitman came in and spotted the chair.

"Charlie, did you make this?"

"Yes, I did, sir. It's Lillie's Christmas present." Charlie squirmed a little.

"This is one of the finest pieces of work I've ever seen. Why didn't you tell me you were such a fine craftsman, son? You're wasting your talents framing houses. You should be building furniture." Then Mr. Whitman sat down in it and began rocking.

"Thank you, sir, but I'm afraid making rocking chairs doesn't pay the bills, and I really need my construction job."

Mr. Whitman stood up. "On Monday I would like you to come to my office. You and I need to talk business. Perhaps we can start out small, a few chairs while you're working, and see how that goes. If they do well, and I think they will, we can talk about expanding. What do you think?"

Charlie was speechless: this was his dream."Yes, sir, that sounds great. Thank you."

Mr. Whitman patted Charlie on the back and went to greet some guests that were arriving.

"Lillie, did you hear what your father said? I can't believe it! He sounded serious. Do you think he meant it? Of course he meant it, or why would he have said it?"

Lillie started laughing, "Silly boy, of course he meant it. My father would never say anything he didn't mean. That is wonderful, Charlie. You're getting a chance to do something you love. Everyone will want furniture made by Charlie Murphy once they see the beautiful work you create."

Charlie put his arms around Lillie and smiled at his mom across the room. "Tonight is perfect. You're perfect." He kissed her as they walked over to sit with his mom for a while before dinner.

***

After dinner, Lillie suggested they take Ellen for a stroll in her wheelchair around the garden. After a few minutes they sat on a bench in front of the fire thorns.

"Mrs. Murphy, see the different plants? They were brought in from all over the world. Dad had the cobblestone carved out to separate pathways, and wooden benches placed throughout so my mom could sit and watch the birds from anywhere in her garden. As a gesture for his deep love for her, Dad had everything planted in pairs: two of every tree, flower and plant placed side-by-side, growing together. He said they were two lives brought together for eternity. He just planted the two fire thorns along the back wall this past year. We're waiting for the day they'll reach each other and be together forever. Isn't that a lovely thought?"

With her left hand, Ellen she gently squeezed Lillie's fingers. "Thank you."

Lillie gave Ellen a hug, and the three of them sat for awhile before a chill filled the air and they brought Ellen back inside by the fire. After getting Ellen some tea, they walked back to the far garden wall and sat down. Charlie put his arms around Lillie to keep her warm and she scooted close. They sat in silence for a few minutes, and then he leaned in and kissed her at the base of her neck.

Lillie melted into him. The passion running through her body was so overwhelming she barely heard her father calling for her from the porch. The weeping branches of a large pine tree hid them. Lillie jumped up when she realized he was calling to her. Charlie stepped back and took a deep breath before accompanying her to the house.

"There you are. I was getting ready to send a search party out for you two! Charlie, your mother is growing tired. I think she would like to be going home shortly."

"Of course. I'll go and get her ready." Charlie walked into the house, and Lillie was following him when her father stopped her.

"Lillie, walk with me a moment, will you?" Her father put his arm around her to shield her from the chill in the air.

"Sure, Dad." Lillie held her breath and quivered. She wasn't sure if he had seen them kissing or not.

"You and your mother were everything to me and when I lost her. I made a promise to myself that I would always keep you safe. I think this relationship with Charlie is much more serious than you have let on, and I want to be sure you are thinking your life through. He's a great boy, but you are very young. Don't rush. Take your time to be sure and maybe experience a few things first. I know this is the kind of talk you would have rather had with your mother, but I'm afraid you're stuck with me. What I'm trying to say is, you don't have to decide on any long-term choices right now. Enjoy your time together and let that be enough."

Lillie paused. Maybe he was just concerned, but she knew she had to be adult about this or the situation could become difficult. He was still her dad, and even if she felt there was no need for protection from Charlie or their relationship, he would do what he thought best for her, even if she didn't agree. "I understand what you're trying to say, Dad, and I love you for it. First of all, I'm not 'rushing.' And yes, it would have been nice to have Mom, but I have you and that's what matters.

"You have always been there for me every step of my life, and I hope you will always be there, but I love Charlie. Dad, I know you think I'm young, but I'm the same age as Mom was when she met you. But you're right, we don't have to rush. We have time. I'll be staying home now, and that will give us the opportunity to get to know each other better."

Even though I already know I will spend the rest of my life with him, she thought. "Don't worry, okay?" Lillie gave her dad a hug and then a kiss on the cheek.

Her father chuckled. "I don't know how you do it. You certainly have a way of turning me around."

"I don't know what you mean. I haven't done anything but engage in a little conversation with my dad." Lillie giggled and went into the house to see Charlie and Ellen about to leave. She hadn't even given Ellen her gift yet!

***

Lillie ran and grabbed it from under the tree and placed it in her lap. "This is for you. Merry Christmas." She placed a kiss on Ellen's cheek. Ellen's face flushed and a tear emerged from the corner of her eye. She motioned for Lillie to come closer. Ellen pulled her arm up, gave her a hug, and whispered in her ear. Lillie looked into her eyes and nodded.

Charlie watched all this unfolding, perplexed. "Okay, time to get you home, Mom. It's getting late and tomorrow's Christmas Day. Mrs. Russo wouldn't be very happy with us if we slept through the Christmas dinner she has prepared." Lillie accompanied them as Charlie wheeled her out to the car and placed her in the back seat. "I had a really fine time tonight. What did my mom say to you back there?"

"I'll tell you someday, but not now. When the time is right."

Although anxious to know, Charlie knew Lillie would tell him when she was ready. "Not going to say, Miss Whitman? I'll let it go for now, but you promise eventually you'll tell me?"

"Yes, I promise. Merry Christmas, Charlie Murphy. I love you."

Charlie kissed her gently on her lips. "Merry Christmas, my beautiful Lillie."

***

She watched as the car drove away. She missed him already. Once back inside, Lillie spent time with Claire and Bastian. They really were right for each other. They would get in the most heated discussions. Politics, women's rights, the impending war—if it was a current topic, they could go back and forth for hours, but they seemed to thrive on it. Claire looked so happy and Lillie was thrilled for her. She had found someone who truly loved her for who she was and would grow with her. Lillie sensed their future would be spent together and with true purpose.

It was getting late, and everyone was slowly going home. Bastian went to get their coats. This gave Lillie some time alone with Claire.

"So," Lillie said anxiously.

"So...So what? I don't know what you're getting at." Claire was playing coy.

"We don't have much time. You know *exactly* what

I'm talking about. How about this dress, for one? You don't wear dresses!"

Claire laughed."I saw it in the window at a boutique in town and thought I might wear it for the party. It really isn't much. Don't make such a commotion. Why don't you like it?"

"Of course I love it. You look sensational. The color is gorgeous on you, and I think you know already that it looks good or you would have never worn it. Honestly, Claire, sometimes you just exhaust me!" The two girls looked at each other and started laughing. By then, Bastian had returned with their coats.

"Looks like I missed the joke." He helped Claire with her coat.

"No, just silly girl stuff. Nothing you'd be interested in." Lillie giggled.

"You'd be surprised at what interests this boy." Claire kissed him on the cheek.

"Merry Christmas, you two," said Lillie. "Claire, I'll see you on Saturday for breakfast, right?"

"Yeah, I'll see you then. When are you telling Charlie about your decision?"

Lillie paused. "I was planning on Saturday night after dinner, maybe in the garden. I'll see how the evening goes and then decide the right time."

"I'll see you Saturday morning. Merry Christmas Lils."

Lillie went in to admire her chair again after her father brought it up to her room. She ran her fingers over the edges of the trim and the carvings. Charlie's hands had touched this and created it. It seemed as if his scent were soaked in the wood. She sat it in with a blanket. It was like she was back in his arms. Her thoughts wandered to the perfect evening and their time in the garden, the heat she had felt from his body, and the longing she felt when they were together. She rocked in her chair until she fell asleep with visions of them together.

Chapter Thirteen

It was a morning of great frustration for Claire. She had agreed to meet with Gwen for a dress fitting for the wedding. After the dreaded appointment was over, she couldn't wait to go over to Lillie's to let off some steam.

"Honestly, Lils, you have to see the dresses Gwen picked out for us to wear. They're hideous in this peach and yellow taffeta with purple things all over it. We are getting along better lately, but this frock is testing my good nature."

Lillie laughed. "Your 'good nature'? I thought when it came to Gwen, your good nature went on an extended vacation."

"I deserved that, but I really don't deserve the dress."

Dinner with Charlie that evening called for a new dress and perfume, so the girls were off to Sherman's Department Store, the only place to go for the latest in fashion. Claire wasn't interested in shopping that day after her morning of pain, so the only things she bought were the latest issue of the *New York Post* and a new hat to hide her face when she tried on the dress. Lillie walked Claire to the bridal shop, where she congratulated Gwen and peeked at Claire's dress for the wedding.

"You're right. It is hideous," she whispered in Claire's ear. Claire glared at Lillie, who laughed as she kissed her goodbye and ran out the door.

***

The dinner setting was exceptional. A table was placed in the garden with a white cloth accented by ruby rose blooms and candles. The flames cast a mellow glow that gave new meaning to love being in the air. The evening was chilly, so Lillie had one of the groundsmen create a fire pit near the table so they could feel warm and toasty during dinner.

Charlie barely noticed anything but Lillie the entire evening. They spoke about their plans for the future, their dreams, and their desires. They discovered they both had very simple wishes for their lives: to be together, to raise a family, and to share a life filled with love. At one point, Charlie looked around at everything that was Lillie. His eyes took in the large house, the beautiful garden, and her stylish, new clothes. Lillie caught the look in his eyes and reassured him it all meant nothing without him. After dinner, they decided to stroll around the garden.

"Charlie, can we sit for a moment? There's something I've wanted to tell you, and I haven't been exactly sure how to do it."

Charlie felt a pain in his stomach. *What could she want to tell me that is making her so anxious?*

"I don't want you to get upset," Lillie continued. "Just listen to me first, okay?" Charlie nodded nervously; he felt a little sick. "I'm not staying in school. I'm going to—"

Charlie jumped up. "What? What do you mean, you're quitting? No, you can't! Lillie, you always wanted this. Please don't do this because of me."

"What happened to waiting until I was finished explaining? Besides, you couldn't be more wrong. I'm not doing it for you; I'm doing it for me! I've been growing unhappy at school. I've changed, and yes, maybe that does have something to do with you, but it's not everything. I want different things than I did before, things that I just can't get at Princeton or any other school. You can't talk me out of this. I have made up my mind, and if you feel the need to rant for a while then by all means, rant away. But just know when you're done. Nothing would have changed. I'm not going back."

Charlie took a moment to let this all settle in his head. He knew she was serious. Part of him, most of him, was so happy he thought he would just explode, but there was a small portion that was not only guilty, but also sad. He had changed her, even if were just a little. He had taken something she had wanted all her life. And although she seemed perfectly content, he wondered if one day she might have regrets, and he couldn't live with the thought that he had done anything to make her unhappy. But he knew he couldn't argue with her about this; he would have to deal with that issue if it ever arose in the future.

"Lillie, I understand what you're saying, and I've so wanted you here with me, but are you sure? Very sure?" He swept her hair over her shoulder.

"I am completely sure. I've been thinking about volunteering at the hospital. I'm sure they could use the help."

Charlie kissed her on her cheek. He was so proud of her. With everything she could do or have in her life, she always surprised him with her choices. She was not an ordinary girl, and if it were possible, he was falling deeper in love with her each passing day.

***

On Sunday, Charlie invited Lillie over for dinner. Mrs. Russo had prepared a large pot of gravy and pasta and kindly brought it over to the Murphy house. They all ate until they felt they would burst. Mrs. Russo wouldn't accept just one helping, and with her hearty cooking, there was never a reason to turn her down.

After the dishes were cleared, Charlie put his mom to bed and said his goodbyes to Mr. and Mrs. Russo. Charlie and Lillie walked off the feeling of fullness in their stomachs. As they were passing Duffy's Bar, he asked if Lillie wanted to go in and have a glass of brandy to warm up. Once inside, Charlie saw John McDougal and William Duffy sitting in a booth. John had his fiancée, Margaret O'Rourke, next to him and they were laughing and lifting their glasses in a toast. John had been dating Margaret since high school and just recently proposed to her. She was a cute girl with long dark hair, freckles and brown eyes. She had been born in Ireland, but her family moved to the United States when she was only six. If you listened, you could hear a slight accent when she spoke, something that seemed to amuse John even after all the years he had known her.

"Hey, Charlie, come and sit with us." William turned to John. "Is that Lillie Whitman with Charlie?"

"Aye, they've been dating for some time now. I think since the summer."

Margaret put her head on John's shoulder. "She's very pretty."

"Not as pretty as my Maggie."

"Always my hero." She kissed him on the neck.

"Hi, guys," said Charlie. "Margaret, this is Lillie. What's going on?"

John raised his glass. "We were just toasting Pete. I saw Deidre today, but she had sad news. His mom isn't doing so well."

Charlie and Lillie sat down in the booth. "I should go by and visit. I've been so busy with work and my mom, but I'll make time this week." He ordered two drinks for himself and Lillie.

William nodded. "That would be a fine idea. It might help for her to see you."

Lillie whispered to Charlie, "Pete was your friend who was killed in Mexico?"

"Yes, and we grew up together. He was the closest thing I had to a brother. We were always together...inseparable." Charlie raised his glass to his friend. "To Pete, may he be safe and well, wherever he is."

They all clinked their glasses together and talked about Pete for a while. It was getting late, and Charlie knew he should be bringing Lillie home or Mr. Whitman might send out more than just a search party. They wished everyone a good night and had made plans to get together again soon.

***

On the way home, Charlie and Lillie held hands in silence. When they reached her house, Charlie walked her up to the door and kissed her. When they pulled away, she looked in his eyes.

"Charlie, promise me something."

"Anything. What is it?" He held her close to keep her warm.

"This is very serious. I want to make a request." Lillie squirmed a bit and then moved closer to him.

"You can say anything to me. What is it? Tell me."

"Promise me you won't leave me, ever."

"What? Where is this coming from? I'm not going anywhere. I would never leave you."

"It's just that with what's going on in Europe, all the guys are signing up and I know how it affects you. I've seen the look in your eyes. Look what happened to Pete. I couldn't bear to lose you; I would lose my mind. I'm pleading with you. Don't leave me, please?"

Charlie hugged her tightly and whispered in her ear, "I'm not leaving you. I'll never leave you." He put his hand on her chin and kissed her lips. Lillie melted into him for a moment longer and then went inside.

Why don't I believe him?

***

Monday, Lillie knew Charlie was speaking with her Dad about his future in furniture. She decided to plan her trip to Princeton to collect her belongings and break the news to Caroline. She owed it to Caroline to tell her in person, so after the New Year, when everyone returned to school, she would go back with Claire. Claire was speaking with her boss today about it. Thankfully, the congressman was an easygoing fellow, and Claire told Lillie she shouldn't have any trouble.

They'd go up on a Friday. This way, Claire would

only miss one day of work and they could get back by late Sunday afternoon. Most of her belongings would fit in a few trunks, with the only large item a mirror she had purchased in a nearby town. She would give it to Caroline; it eased her guilt about leaving school.

***

Charlie agreed to produce two chairs a month, and Mr. Whitman agreed to let Charlie take four paid hours each day to compensate for his time. Mr. Whitman would also make arrangements with Anderson & Sons, a furniture store, for Charlie to place his chairs in the window. He was confident Charlie would be producing more furniture very soon.

Charlie couldn't believe he was actually going to be working for Mr. Whitman. To celebrate, he went by the flower shop on the way home and bought two bouquets, one for his mom and the other for Lillie. When he got home, Lillie was waiting on the porch and his mom was taking a nap. She ran over to him and wrapped her arms around him, kissing him on his lips.

"What was that for?" Charlie smiled.

"Maybe I'm being a bit presumptuous, but I think one of those is for me, correct?" He smiled even wider. "No, I don't think so. These are for another beautiful girl, but I'm sure they're not for you."

"Charlie Murphy, you're impossible!"

He couldn't stop laughing as Lillie huffed. He handed her the flowers and they walked hand-in-hand towards the house. Mrs. Russo had sent dinner over again, and Lillie set the plates on the table while Charlie woke his mom. He gave her the flowers and she grabbed his hand, brought it up to her face, and kissed it. The three of them sat and ate while Charlie told them about the day and his meeting with Lillie's father.

"Charlie, that's wonderful," said Lillie. "I do have the best dad, mind you, but he also knows talent when he sees it."

The trio spent the evening listening to a new record that Lillie had brought over. The words were in French, but the music was lovely and Ellen seemed to enjoy it the most. When the evening was over, Charlie walked Lillie home and kissed her good night. Tomorrow was going to be a big day.

***

Charlie started building his two chairs and by the end of the month, they were proudly displayed in the store window of Andersons. He brought Lillie by to see them, but when they got there the chairs were already gone. Perplexed, he went inside to speak to Mr. Anderson. His son Kevin was at the counter, whom Charlie had known from school. He was two years older, and Charlie had heard that he'd just signed up for the army. He was supposed to be leaving for training in a week.

"Hey, Charlie, Lillie, how are you?" Kevin shook Charlie's hand.

"We're doing well, thank you. Kevin, do you know where my chairs are? They were in the window this morning?"

"Sure, they're gone. Not more than an hour after we placed them in the window, we had three buyers. That's what these orders are: they're for your chairs! Charlie, they loved them. Mrs. Crenshaw wants to know if you could make a dining room table and chairs, and Mrs. Meyers ordered four of your rockers, two for her and two for her daughter in Connecticut. Oh yeah, and the Olsens also ordered two chairs.

"I guess your father was right, Lillie. I heard him speaking with my dad. He said that Charlie had excellent craftsmanship, and your furniture would be a great success, I think today definitely proved him right. My dad's going to want to speak with you, Charlie, about carrying more of your pieces."

Charlie was astonished. He never thought he would get this much interest, especially not this quickly. He had hoped for a chair here and there, maybe a side table, but a dining room table and chairs and six rockers...He was about to get very busy. Perhaps Mr. Whitman would give him a few more hours each day. He was going to need it.

He felt exhilarated and nervous at the same time, and he couldn't help but fret. For now, people were ordering his furniture very quickly, but what if it all just stopped? What if people were to suddenly change their minds and choose to go to another furniture maker? What then?

"Charlie! Where are you? I've been calling you for several moments." Lillie looked concerned.

"I...I was just thinking. Can you believe all the orders, Lillie? I didn't think this would happen to me, that I would be doing this well."

Kevin smiled. "Maybe one day you'll have your own furniture store with all of your own creations."

Charlie just nodded. He was still stunned from his good fortune.

That evening he spoke with Mr. Whitman, who arranged for Charlie to spend six hours a day on building his furniture and the rest on house framing. In the morning they would go and speak with Mr. Anderson. Mr. Anderson had phoned Charlie that afternoon about expanding, and since Charlie was new to the business, he had asked Mr. Whitman if he would accompany him. Everything seemed to be falling into place. Life was indeed looking up.

Chapter Fourteen

It was mid-January, and Lillie felt it was time to return to school. Claire came over in the early morning hours with her driver, Henry, who took them to the train station.

On the trip to Princeton, Claire was quiet. The long train ride gave her the time she needed to think about the changes in her life without distraction. Her relationship with Bastian had been getting serious, and she wasn't sure if she wanted that kind of commitment in her life just yet. After all, she wanted her career. It was very important to her. But she did love him; maybe they could compromise. If they could be together for now while she built her career, there would be time later for family and the "white picket fence" sort of life most men seemed to want. Believe it or not, it was the life she could see herself having with him.

I hope he agrees, she thought.

Lillie, on the other hand, was already thinking of walking in the garden with her and Charlie's children. Her dream included a family that would have dinner with her dad several times during the week, then making the short trip home, putting the children to bed and cuddling with Charlie on the couch, exchanging stories about their day.

Both girls were so deep in thought they never felt the train stop and didn't hear the whistle for departure. The conductor came and tapped Claire on the shoulder. She was startled and jumped up, as did Lillie. He apologized, but they had reached their stop.

***

When the girls reached Lillie's dorm room, Caroline wasn't back from classes yet. They began packing Lillie's belongings in the empty trunks she had brought. They were almost finished when Caroline came bolting through the door.

"Mercy, you're here. I was getting worried. I was

going to get a telegram out to your dad this weekend if you hadn't shown up. Where have you been? You're late for classes. Oh, what's wrong with me? I'm sorry, is everything okay? Of course not, why else would you be so late? And you brought Claire. Lillie what's wrong? Is it your dad? Is it Charlie? Tell me."

"Slow down and take a breath." Lillie sat down on the bed and motioned for Caroline to join her. "First of all, everything and everyone is fine. Thanks for your concern. I'm sorry I didn't let you know I was coming late. I should have sent a telegram or letter. I wanted to come and tell you in person—I owe that to you. Caroline. I'm leaving school and before you become upset, let me explain."

Lillie explained everything to Caroline. How she had been feeling lately, how she missed Charlie so much it made her life miserable, and how, for the first time in her life since her mother passed away, she felt complete. She explained how her father was happy to have her home and how Charlie had reacted when he she first told him, but then how he had finally understood. She expressed her need to work at the hospital and her dream for a future with Charlie, including having a family with him. And finally she talked about his new furniture business and his mother's great improvement. When she was done, she waited for Caroline's response.

Caroline's eyes had misted up, and she hugged Lillie tightly. Then she stood up and walked across the room to a little silver box on her dresser, pulling out a beautiful dainty pin. It was a silver leaf with tiny diamonds running along the stem. She handed it to Lillie. "I will miss you terribly, Lillie Whitman. Please take this to remember me by."

Lillie started to cry.

"Caroline, I don't need a piece of jewelry to remember you by. It's beautiful, but I just can't accept this. I know we're going to stay in touch. You'll be at my wedding. Even though Charlie hasn't asked me yet, I know he will."

The two girls began to laugh while Claire rolled her eyes. "No, please, I want you to have it. It will make me happy to know you have this." Lillie walked over and gave her friend a hug.

"There is something I had wanted you to have as well. Will you please accept this mirror? I know you've always admired it and it would make me happy if you did."

Caroline cried again and Lillie gave her another big hug.

Lillie and Claire had a few hours before their train left for home, so the three girls went into town to have dinner. Caroline chatted about the boy she was dating, the one she had met right before the holidays. His name was Eric Richman and he was majoring in finances. He was from South Carolina, a Southern boy, which made her parents accept him even more quickly. He was warm and kind and treated her as if she were a precious, delicate work of art. She couldn't be more happy. She felt sometimes as if she fell into a dream that couldn't possibly be happening to her.

Lillie was thrilled for her friend. Caroline was such a kind person and deserved someone who adored her.

When the car arrived to take the girls back to the train station, there were tears again and an exchange of hugs and kisses and promises to write. As they drove away, Lillie saw her friend standing alone and felt a knot in the pit of her stomach. Caroline was the one thing about Princeton she didn't want to leave behind.

Chapter Fifteen

Over the next few months, Charlie was so busy building furniture and filling orders he barely worked with the construction crew. The more pieces he made, the more in demand he was. Mr. Anderson was so elated with the sales that he gave Charlie a space of his own in the store to display his furniture. It wasn't too long before the word spread to a few neighboring towns and they had to hire another driver to do deliveries.

On Friday morning, Mr. Whitman called Charlie into his office at the construction site.

"Please come in and sit down."

Mr. Whitman waved Charlie in and motioned at a leather chair across from his desk. His office was modest and didn't have the luxurious furnishings of his home, but it was filled with photos of Lillie and Elizabeth, which made it feel very comfortable.

"Your furniture is becoming more successful by the month. The work you do is outstanding. Your designs are not only beautiful, but also practical. I think it's time you were doing this full time. What do you think?"

Taking a breath, Charlie couldn't believe his dreams were coming true so quickly. Just a few months ago, it felt as if the whole world were caving in, but now everything he could have hoped for was at his feet. He felt like shouting from the top of the building.

Suddenly, Charlie was shaking James's hand so hard he nearly squeezed off his blood supply. James laughed and asked if he'd go and tell Mr. Anderson what they had discussed and that he was in agreement. Charlie tried to calm his excitement and ran all the way back to the store. He had been thinking about some new designs, and now he would get the chance to try them out. When Charlie got there, Mr. Anderson was almost as excited as he was. He had a bottle of single-malt Scotch out on the counter ready to toast.

"To you and your talent. You're a fine boy, Charlie Murphy. You deserve all the riches of the world that come your way."

***

Lillie was in town shopping for candy at Millers' Sweets. Easter was Sunday, and her young cousins were visiting from Chicago, so she wanted to make them baskets filled with sweet treats. Claire was meeting her for lunch before heading out to a rally with Congressman Meyer. The diner was crowded, and the girls decided to sit at the counter instead of waiting for a booth. The weather was warming up and the ladies in town were wearing brighter colors with new spring hats. The smell of flowers and freshly cut grass lingered the air. The feeling of spring in the air seemed to lighten the spirits of all. Winter was ending and everything was waking up.

"Isn't it lovely out?" Lillie smiled. She felt so alive today.

"It is a glorious day for the rally. We should get a good turnout. Congressman Meyer said many of the women in town were coming today. It makes me so proud to be working for him." Claire was beaming with delight.

"It would be something if we could win the right to vote. I'm glad you work for a man who is so open-minded and conscious of our plight for the future. You really have gotten yourself the perfect job."

Claire was still beaming and nudged Lillie with her shoulder. "I was very fortunate, but so was he. After all, I am a great asset." She chuckled at her own praise.

"There is no other as capable as you, Claire." Lillie winked and the two of them burst into laughter.

The girls were just about finished with their lunch when Charlie came barreling into the shop. He almost passed them up, he was whisking by so fast. Lillie shouted his name and he stopped at the counter. He was out of breath, so he sat for a moment before explaining everything that happened that morning. As he spoke she could see the pride in his eyes, but she also knew how humble he was; he was truly grateful to both men for the opportunity.

Claire finished her lunch and left to go meet with everyone for the rally. It was more crowded than she had expected. It seemed as if all the women in town, and those in the next one over, had come to hear Congressman Meyer speak. Claire was standing by his side when he asked her to say a few words.

Lillie reached the crowd just as Claire was struggling for words. It was the first time in her life that she had seen her friend genuinely speechless. After a few seconds, though, Claire gathered her thoughts, and began to give one of the most powerful speeches that Lillie had heard. She was so passionate and believed so deeply in what she said that her strength and conviction had the crowd shouting in agreement. Her beliefs ignited them, gave them the desire to embrace the new definition of a modern woman. They cheered and the energy was infectious. It spread from each person until the heat from the crowd could be felt just by standing nearby. Claire was a powerful and overwhelming force that would not stop until what she stood for was put into action.

Afterward, many of the women signed up to help in any way they could. Whether it was handing out pamphlets or standing on a soapbox of their own to spread the word, the cause was definitely growing.

***

"I'm going over to congratulate Claire. Would you like to join me, Charlie?"

While they spoke, Charlie looked around at all the women and the lingering crowd of progressive men. He spotted an older woman who was there with someone who could have been her granddaughter. She was lovingly admiring her younger companion as she chatted with a group of other women in the crowd.

Similar to Claire, the young woman displayed an attitude of self-assurance and focus, but with her it seemed more subtle. When she spoke, it was quietly commanding, her speech gently persuading rather than igniting a fire. Her beauty came with a refined elegance that made it nearly impossible to turn away.

"That's Hanna Pittman, and the older woman is her aunt," Claire said. Charlie looked over at Claire, who continued, "She's a true supporter of the cause. Her family is ridiculously wealthy and she's a main contributor. She goes out and speaks as well. She's outstanding."

Lillie grabbed Charlie's hand and held it tight. He realized what she was doing and gave her a kiss on the cheek. Hanna was beautiful, but there wasn't any one who compared to his Lillie.

"I was watching how she quietly brought them in closer to listen to her. It was brilliant." Charlie put his arms around Lillie's waist and held her tightly. "Claire, have you thought about joining forces with her? You'd be an unbeatable team?"

"I don't know. I usually work alone, except for Congressman Meyer. I don't know if we're a good match. She is effective, but I'm more of a bee than the flower, if you know what I mean."

Charlie chuckled. "Yeah, I think I do."

The three chose to wait, and after a few minutes went over to Hanna so Claire could introduce Lillie and Charlie. The closer they got to her, the more Charlie could see how truly beautiful she was. Her hair was the color of honey with streaks of gold that glistened when the sun caught it. She had a slender figure and long legs, making her quite statuesque. Gliding her arms in the air as she spoke gave her an air of elegance and grace. When he got closer, he saw that her eyes were the lightest blue he had ever seen; they almost appeared transparent. But it was her smile that lit up everything around her.

"Claire, how are you? That speech was magnificent!"

"I'm well, but look at you! You're like the Pied Piper—everyone just following you around. It would be best if you don't get too near a cliff."

Hanna laughed. "Who are your friends?"

"I'm so sorry, that was rude. Hanna, this is my very best friend, Lillie Whitman, and her beau, Charlie Murphy."

Hanna put her hand out to shake theirs. "Lillie Whitman? As in, Whitman Construction?"

"That's my father, James. You've heard of him?"

"Actually, he's a business associate of my uncle. You have that beautiful garden at your house, don't you?"

"How did you know about our garden?"

"Lillie, everyone for miles away knows about your garden. I'm told it's lovely. Your father took my uncle for a walk through it a few years ago. He said he had never seen such a beautiful place. It really made an impression on him."

"It's quite magical. Maybe one day you could drop by and we can have lunch on the porch. I'm sure we could persuade Claire to join us. What do you say, Claire? Lunch in the garden?"

"That would be fine."

"What is it that you do, Charlie, in addition to accompanying this beautiful lady to rallies such as this?" asked Hanna.

Charlie stumbled on his words for a moment, conversation not being one of his stronger points. "I make furniture." He looked down at the ground and then nervously away at a passing crowd of people.

"When you say furniture, what do you mean? Do you make single pieces or do you work on entire rooms, perhaps sets for the bedroom or parlor?"

"Yes, both."

"Well, aren't I the lucky one? I've been searching for a new bedroom set, and I can't seem to find anything that suits my taste. I'm so glad to have made your acquaintance today."

"Hanna, you have got to see Charlie's work," said Lillie. "It's like nothing you have ever seen. I'm sure you'll find something you'll love. He has a few display rooms at Anderson & Sons. You should stop by."

"That sounds perfect. I'll stop by tomorrow. Charlie, can I put in a special order if need be?"

Lillie grabbed his arm. "Of course you can. He's the best in New York. You won't get finer furniture!"

Hanna smiled and then apologized. She had to say her goodbyes. Her aunt had a dinner engagement and they needed to be on their way. Hanna had asked Claire to ring her for a date to have lunch and then wished them well before she left.

***

Charlie walked over to sign them up to help with the congressman's next rally. When he was a distance away, Lillie turned to Claire. "She's very pretty."

"Now, there's nothing for you to worry about, Lils. Not only does Charlie love you and only you, but I think there's something you should know about Hanna. She would probably be more interested in you rather than Charlie."

Lillie stopped. She had to process just what it was that Claire was saying. "Are you saying what I think you're saying? Does Hanna prefer girls to boys?" Lillie was astonished. She had heard there were people such as this, but not here, not on Long Island. She didn't know what to say. Hanna was so pretty and feminine. Maybe Claire was mistaken. "Are you sure? She seems so...not what you said. Maybe you heard wrong or were given the wrong information?"

"She told me herself about a year ago. She thought she was different, but it wasn't until she went on a trip abroad that she figured out just what that difference was. Listen, Lils, she's a lovely girl, and this doesn't change anything. I've known her for a long time and I don't care who she wants to love. She's my friend just as you're my friend. I wouldn't stop being your friend if you suddenly told me you're actually a two-hundred-year old alien from Mars and your family crashed here a century ago. I would be shocked, of course, but I wouldn't judge you and I couldn't ever stop loving you for who and what you are."

Lillie stared at her for a moment and then burst into laughter. "An alien from Mars...A bit extreme, wouldn't you say?"

"I was just making a point. You know what I meant." Claire gave Lillie a shove.

"I know exactly what you mean. She's an impressive girl. Let's leave it at that."

Just as they closed the subject of Hanna, Charlie joined them again to walk into town for coffee at the dinner. They were sitting at a booth when one of the younger boys from town came rushing in, shouting loudly.

It was as if time stood still and willed everyone to stop and listen to the message: the United States was going to war.

Chapter Sixteen

Although Lillie enjoyed being with Claire, she was hoping for some time alone with Charlie, too. Thankfully, Claire had the final fitting for her dress for Gwen's wedding and afterward a dinner with her family, so the two of them could finally be alone. Lillie and Charlie decided to have dinner in the garden. Ellen was improving steadily, enabling Charlie to spend more time with Lillie and less time worrying about his mom.

They had just finished eating and were taking a stroll to look at all the new blooms and budding trees. Lillie was holding onto Charlie's arm and trying to work out how to ask Charlie about Hanna without sounding jealous or petty. She decided the straightforward approach would be best.

"I was wondering, Charlie. This afternoon, you were staring at Hanna before we met with her. By the look on your face, it seemed you already knew her. Does this have anything to do with how pretty she is? I'm not saying I'm jealous, just awfully curious."

He quickly grabbed her and held her close. The kisses began playfully but soon turned into the kind that left knees weak and put heads into the clouds. She thought she might collapse on the very spot they were standing. When he finally pulled away, she was flustered and her face felt warm, as if it had been showered by the sunshine.

"My silly girl, you should know by now I don't want any other girl. I only yearn for you. Lillie, no one can take my heart like you have. It's yours forever."

Lillie was embarrassed; she knew how he felt. *Why did I act so silly?*

Charlie took her hand. "You were partly right. I had met her before. I wasn't sure until Claire told us her name. She had looked familiar, and that's why I was staring at her, trying to place her." Lillie nodded. "When I was seven years old, her mother hired my mom to help around the house while she recovered from some sort of surgery. Unfortunately, she never did recover and passed away after a few months. My mom would take me with her on the weekends and after school. Hanna was a few years older than me. I don't think she would remember a young boy who was only around part of the time. My mom told me she went to live with her aunt and we never saw her again. She was a sweet kid, a little peculiar, but sweet. It seems she's overcome a great deal and has grown up just fine."

"What do you mean by peculiar?" Lillie burned with curiosity.

"I don't know. She was just different from the other kids I knew. One day I found her sitting on the floor in the kitchen cutting out the models from the fashion part of the magazine."

"There's nothing peculiar about that. All little girls like to look at the clothes in a magazine."

"No, she wasn't just looking at the clothes; she was talking to the pictures and kissing them as if she liked them. I didn't ask her what she was doing. I just ran out of the room. It was all too weird for me. After her mom passed away, her aunt took her to Paris, I think. Over time, I had just forgotten about it, until today, that is. When I realized who she was, that peculiar memory resurfaced. It was so strange."

Lillie decided that Hanna's secret was better kept. It wasn't hers to tell. She reminded Charlie that it was long ago when Hanna was a young girl. Maybe her odd behavior was a way of coping. Losing a parent was devastating, but losing two was horrific. Charlie agreed, and they didn't bring Hanna's name up for the rest of the evening.

***

Later that evening, Hanna was lying in bed, reviewing her day. The rally had been more successful than she had imagined and they had gotten a great deal of women, and surprisingly some men, to sign up to help.

Then her thoughts wandered to Charlie Murphy. He hadn't seemed to recognize her. She hoped he hadn't. She had known who he was immediately but had kept quiet. Maybe he didn't remember the kitchen incident. They had been so young. Her aunt didn't need to hear about another scandalous story involving her attractions. Having her leave Paris, a place she had loved, had been enough.

No, she would spare her aunt any further grief. She did enjoy seeing Claire again, though; she would have to ring her for lunch one day soon.

***

Easter Sunday arrived with cotton clouds and blue, blue skies. Lillie enjoyed watching her younger cousins call out shapes they imagined in the clouds and trip over each other in boisterous excitement. She made sure each child was given a basket filled with chocolate and sweets, but only if they promised to hunt for the elusive holiday eggs. And boy, did they! What fun was had by all. Charlie and his mom came for a late Easter lunch, and the whole family dined in the garden. It was so alive, with green buds bursting forth and flowers blooming in all their finest colors.

Her father had also invited some of the guys from his crew who didn't have family in town. One man in particular was very far from home. John Winston was from England and his brother, Eric, had been sent to the front lines near the German border. He had joined the British army and had been stationed in France. John brought a letter Eric had sent to him recently so he could read it to her father, who had been following the war and England's efforts to end the terror.

Charlie was telling John about his friend Pete, and Lillie's father suggested if he didn't mind, that John read the letter to everyone. John was more than happy to share his brother's letter; it was obvious that he was proud that

Eric was being honored for joining up to serve his country.

Eric's letter was short but poignant. It spoke of a country in shambles and its people, who were suffering. He compared it to his life at home and declared his love not only for his family, but also for the freedom and protection he had enjoyed, growing up in such a country as England. He also wrote how most of the guys were not really prepared for what they had begun to witness and the conditions they were enduring. When he finished the letter, John excused himself for a moment, and the somber mood was laid to rest with the welcome change of serving dessert.

The children were running to the tables for ice cream and cake and the adults had tea and pastries. Afterward, they all went inside to sit in the parlor and listen to Aunt Emma play the piano. The day went quickly and before she knew it, Lillie was hugging and kissing her family goodbye. Charlie had taken Ellen home; it was late and she was getting tired. It had been one of the finest Easter Sundays ever.

After everyone had gone, Lillie joined her father in the kitchen for a last cup of tea before bed. "Dad, what do you think will happen now that we've joined the war, too?"

"I don't know, honey. I think we might be there for a while, but it's not for you to worry about. Whatever happens, you'll be safe here." Her father kissed Lillie on the forehead.

"I'm not worried about me. It's Charlie. I know if he could, he'd join now. He feels as if he should be with his friends, especially now that we are going to war. He wants to defend his country and fight by the sides of the people of this town and the rest of the U.S. Honestly, Dad, sometimes it keeps me up at night, and I worry so much about him. I don't know how I could go on without him, I love him so much. You know what that feels like, having loved Mom the way you did; completely, and with your heart wide open. I know he feels like he's not doing his part, and I think it's only his obligation to his mom that keeps him from joining. I know he loves me, but in his mind he feels he would better protect me if he left to go fight. If his mom were completely well, my nightmare would become a reality."

Lillie's father took her hand protectively and smiled. "Whatever happens in the future, no one knows, but you have your life with him now. Don't waste time thinking about 'what if,' my darling daughter, because 'what if' will always come. It may not be tragic or devastating, but eventually all things change, and of that, you have no control. I know the boy loves you deeply, and you have told me many times how you feel for him. Please, make that be enough. Learn to hold that close to your heart and cling to the present, for that is the secret to true happiness."

She stared at her dad for a moment and gave him a tight hug. "How did you become so brilliant?"

"Luck, I suppose."

Chapter Seventeen

The next few months were fairly uneventful, and although the war pressed on everyone's conscience, Lillie's days passed in a calm, almost mundane repetition that made life predictable but safe. Charlie was busier than ever with the furniture business, and Lillie was volunteering at the local hospital.

Ellen was improving at such a rate that Charlie didn't need Finola as much. Her schedule was adjusted to three times a week part time to help out, but Ellen was usually capable of getting through the day on her own. There were some functions that still troubled her: cooking and speaking being the most challenging. Yet despite it all, her progress had been nothing short of a miracle, something she reminded Charlie of every Sunday when it came time for church.

There had been a few times that he had missed Mass because he was working overtime to complete an order. And on those days, the Russos had been kind enough to bring Ellen with them. This did not sit well with her. Missing Mass to work on Sunday was not a valid reason in her book, the Bible, and she gave Charlie a very disapproving look when it happened. It was something he dealt with but dreaded. He did not want to disappoint her, but there were responsibilities and obligations to those who had supported his dream when he needed it the most. God would understand. He was sure of it.

***

With the wedding coming and the re-election, Claire was busy juggling her days. She had lunch with Hanna a few times to discuss a campaign strategy and the new projects they wanted to tackle if Congressman Meyer's re-election was successful. She enjoyed spending time with Hanna. They had the same ideals and goals, and it made the grueling process of campaigning much easier to endure.

Her only issue, one she had a hard time trying to understand, was Hanna's apparent dislike of Bastian. She had never said anything directly to Claire, but every time Bastian came over, Hanna found some excuse to leave. She would have liked to talk to her about it but decided that if Hanna really wanted to, she would bring the subject up herself.

Saturday was Gwen's wedding and the Whitmans were amongst the invited guests. Claire's mother would not pass up an opportunity to have James Whitman attend one of her functions, and since she and her husband were giving Gwen her wedding for a present, the guest list was hers to influence. Naturally, Lillie had asked Charlie to accompany her. She had persuaded him to buy a new suit, and she had bought a lovely, pale pink dress with a matching hat that made her look as if she had stepped off the cover of one of the latest fashion magazines.

The wedding ceremony was at First Presbyterian, the church that Claire's family attended. There was an explosion of flowers everywhere and the arrangements were breath taking. The bride was a vision and the groom was fidgeting with nerves, it was perfect.

Afterward, the reception was on the lawn of the Dumont house. Crystal vases filled with peach and white roses graced all of the guests tables. The same delicate roses were strung along the front of the bridal table and laid around the wedding cake. The bridesmaids wore pale peach dresses adorned with tiny flowers encircling the waist. Claire, as the matron of honor, wore a soft yellow dress dotted with pale peach flowers and lace trim. Gwen was in antique white. Her dress was a vision in layers of tulle, creamy lace and floral beading all along the bodice. Claire couldn't help but think how uncomfortable she looked. The wedding ceremony was traditional with a full Mass. A horse-drawn carriage took the newlyweds to the house while the wedding party followed in two chauffeured cars.

So very posh indeed. It was the event of the season; Claire's mother would have it no other way.

The food was plentiful and rich, with Claire's father hiring a chef from a well-known restaurant in Manhattan. A sixteen-piece orchestra played on their spacious back lawn. Claire didn't know how much this cost her parents, but when she looked at how thrilled Gwen was, it somehow didn't matter. She and her cousin were getting along so much better lately. Perhaps it was because she had resigned herself to the fact that she and her mother never really got along, and that wasn't Gwen's fault. Whatever the reason, she was truly happy for her cousin.

***

The heat of the day gave way to a cooling night sky that twinkled with just the right sprinkling of stars. Thick glass lanterns lit with candles were laced throughout the property. An assortment of candles in varying sizes garnished the tops of each table. It was an evening of such magical proportions that romance was denied to no one. The bride and groom just glowed. Lillie and Charlie danced all night long, unaware of anyone else moving around them. They glided through each moment; they belonged to eternity and the world was theirs alone.

Looking into her eyes, Charlie realized something he hadn't noticed before. Lillie had a small, teardrop-shaped cluster of freckles in the corner of her left eye. They were so faint; maybe that's why he hadn't noticed them before. He took her hand and gently glided his fingers over them. He put his hand under her chin and lifted her face up to his, then he kissed her little freckle cluster and brushed her hair from her face. They didn't speak; they didn't need to. He could feel her relax and melt into him.

When the evening came to an end, the bride stood in the center of the lawn with her bouquet and asked all the single girls to come and stand around her. She put her back to them and threw her bouquet over her shoulder. It glided up and came down right on Claire! She hadn't even tried to catch it, not like the other girls, and yet there it was in her hands.

Bastian bounded over with a huge smile on his face. "Calm down. Not yet, but someday soon, Miss Claire Dumont, you will be mine for always."

He drew her closer, and kissed her cheek. They danced for a few minutes before going over to say goodbye to the parting guests.

***

On Sunday morning, the sun rose especially bright. Ellen decided to wear her large brim hat to protect her eyes when she went to Mass. Charlie had stayed home to accompany her, knowing it would make her happy.

Today they were riding with Mrs. O'Leary and Deidre, who was visiting from Manhattan. Ever since Pete had died, Deidre made it a point to come out to Long Island more often to visit with her mom and make sure she was holding up well.

The mass was longer that day. There was a visiting priest, Father Feeney from Culion Island in the Philippines. His stories were extremely interesting but disturbing. He had been living there for five years now, where he helped care for the three thousand or more lepers that had been sent there when the Island was designated in 1904 by the United States.

As Charlie listened to the priest describe the daily horrors that these people endured, he felt ashamed for some of the things in his own life that he would have worried about in the past. These people faced true hardships: the loss of limbs, isolation from loved ones and the prospect of never recovering from such devastation. Somehow they woke each morning and fished for the food that took care of their families and friends. He was extremely touched by their devotion and strength, and when Mass was over, he went up to the priest to speak with him about helping them in some way.

After a few minutes Charlie returned to the car, where Ellen and Mrs. O'Leary were waiting. Deidre wasn't far behind; she had stopped to talk with Patrick Matthews, and a friend from school she hadn't seen in a while. As Charlie got into the car, he was especially excited. It seemed the priest, Father Feeney, was organizing a carnival at the church next Saturday, and all the profits would go to a fund for the people on Culion Island. It would greatly help with medical supplies and daily needs. Charlie had volunteered to help and told Father Feeney he would speak to some friends as well.

When they got home, Charlie rang Lillie and explained the Father's plight. Lillie quickly placed calls to many of her friends. By day's end, between Charlie and Lillie they had organized thirty people to join in the carnival's effort to raise funds. Charlie couldn't wait to tell the Father the good news. He was overjoyed and thanked him repeatedly before saying good night.

***

The week was busy with work and the preparations for the carnival. Lillie's father was able to obtain a Ferris wheel for them to use. He had a friend who traveled with the circus, and they were performing in a neighboring town. He lent it to them for the evening as long as they had it back for their next show on the following Friday night. He even sent his crew to set it up and take it down the next day.

Sunday night, the land around the church was packed with people from the town. Everyone showed up to help support Father Feeney's cause and enjoy a night at the carnival. Lillie and Claire worked the candy apple and popcorn booths, while Charlie volunteered to take a seat in the dunk tank. The two girls watched and laughed hilariously each time Charlie was dunked underwater by a boy who had a great throwing arm and could land the bull's eye. Bastian helped with the Ferris wheel and the rest of their friends worked the various booths and food tents.

For most of the people in town the evening was a few hours of sanctuary from the worries of their daily lives and the constant weight of the war. At the end of the evening, Father Feeney thanked everyone for coming and giving their support. He blessed them and closed with a short prayer.

Chapter Eighteen

Charlie was at work on Monday morning when Father Sullivan stopped by to tell him the good news about the carnival's success. He would make an official announcement on Sunday, but he thought Charlie deserved to know first. The little town had helped raise over one thousand dollars. Charlie thanked Father Sullivan for coming over to tell him personally and promised he would see him in church on Sunday. After dinner, he took Lillie for pie and tea and they ran into Hanna, who was out having a bite to eat herself. The three decided to share the table.

"Charlie, that was quite the carnival last night. I heard you were a big part of making it so successful. Great job. We could use more people like you on the campaign."

"Thanks, but Lillie and many other people helped as well. I didn't do it alone."

Thankfully, the waitress brought their pie just as the silence became awkward. Lillie pretended to be distracted by a couple arguing outside the window, which forced Charlie and Hanna into an already strained conversation.

After a moment Charlie delved in and asked Hanna if she remembered him.

"Yes, Charlie, I did remember you. You used to come to my home with your mom to help my mother while she was ill. You hadn't said anything to me, so I thought you didn't remember me. I knew that wasn't long after your father had passed away, so I didn't want to bring up sad memories for you."

"I remembered you, too, but I was thinking the same thing. I thought you didn't recognize me, and I didn't want to upset you with any of those memories, either."

They both hesitated for a moment and then simultaneously broke out in laughter, laughter being the medicine needed in such situations. They were never awkward with each other again. They both realized they shared a common bond; a great loss that gave them a new understanding of each other. The rest of the evening, they shared stories of their childhood and the years following. When they left that night, they waved goodbye with promises to get together again very soon.

Charlie walked Lillie home, and they sat on the porch for a few minutes.

"I really enjoyed Hanna's company tonight, Charlie. I'm glad I've gotten to know her a little better."

"Yes. I had a good time too."

They enjoyed a few more minutes of solace before a sweet kiss good night.

***

It was already late, so Ellen was asleep when Charlie got home and he went straight to bed. He had a busy day ahead of him tomorrow and needed his rest.

The following morning, Charlie woke and lay in bed for a few minutes. Usually at this time, he would hear Ellen moving about. *Maybe she decided to sleep in,* he thought. He got up to wash his face, get dressed, and thump down to the kitchen to make a simple breakfast.

Mom's still not up yet. That's odd.

He didn't want to wake her. Maybe last night had been painful, one of her bad nights. He truly hoped not, but sometimes she did need to sleep in. He left a cheery note before he dashed off for work.

It was busy just as he thought it would be. Hanna came to visit as promised to discuss the bedroom set she fancied, and being no exception, there were a few tweaks to the order she placed. Charlie noticed each customer wanted what they chose to be unique. Of course, that always took additional time, and he made sure Hanna understood that she must wait. He would begin on her set the following week.

By the end of his work day, Charlie was so tired he

couldn't wait to get home and relax. Lillie was going to see one of her father's friends for dinner. He had come in for the week from Chicago, and she and James were joining him and his wife at the restaurant in town. So he was on his own tonight. He would have liked to dine with Lillie and the others, but he knew he wouldn't be able to keep his eyes open. It took some getting used to, how busy he had become at work, but it was all worth it. It was a good kind of tired.

Charlie stopped abruptly in the front of his house. He stood there, not wanting to move. His heart beat faster and his insides raced to keep up, It was completely dark. This was not like his mom: she always put the lights on, no matter what. He stepped inside and was faced with total silence.

"Mom, Mom!"

He edged towards her bedroom and carefully reached out to turn on her lamp. Even before he glanced over at the still figure in the bed, he knew, she was gone. He reached for her hand. It was cold. Trembling, he clasped it in his and knelt down beside her. He sobbed uncontrollably until he had no more tears left.

Charlie didn't know how long he was there at his mom's side; he must have fallen asleep. For a second he thought he had just had the most horrible dream, but with light beaming through the window, he saw his mother's face again. It hadn't been a dream. She had passed away yesterday, and he hadn't even realized it when he left for work.

Why didn't I go and check on her? he thought. He looked away at the morning sun coming through the window. Any other day this room would be familiar and calm, but today it just held tragedy.

As he went to ring Doc Clarkson, he looked back at his mother's face. She was so peaceful. Her face was somehow softened and content, as if she had been relieved of every worry she'd carried in this world. She seemed to be smiling. Was that possible? Somehow this thought eased Charlie's grief. *Maybe she's happy because she's with Dad,* he thought. *Yes, she is with Dad.*

Doc Clarkson thought it was probably another stroke. "Unfortunately, these things happen," he said. "I know she was improving, but too often, that is the calm before the storm. With this kind of condition, the outcome can be very unpredictable."

Charlie barely heard a word that anyone spoke all day; he couldn't grasp the world around him until Lillie stood by his side. She was his strength, helping with everything he could not do alone. She aided with any decisions that had to be made concerning the funeral, the house, and other financial issues that needed to be addressed. Being strong was something Lillie could give with all her heart, and it was what he needed the most. By the end of the day, neighbors had begun to drop by, one by one, to offer condolences and bring food. More food than Charlie had ever seen.

"Why does everybody cook so much food when someone passes away? The last thing you feel like doing is eating." Charlie could hear the disgust in his voice.

"Charlie, the reason everyone cooks is really to make themselves feel better. Remember, Ellen had many people in this town who adored her. They are feeling a loss too. Certainly not as much as you, but they want to know that they are helping in some way, and cooking helps to occupy their minds for a while. They want to feel like a part of the process, the mourning, and to help comfort you."

Charlie looked into Lillie's eyes. Tears streamed down his face. This was the first time he had allowed himself to cry that day. Exhaustion overwhelmed him, and he collapsed into her open arms.

The funeral was accompanied by a full Mass. Ellen

would have wanted that. The church was standing room only. Father Sullivan had the altar boys open the doors and put extra chairs outside to accommodate everyone who attended. Charlie was amazed. He didn't realize how many lives his mother had touched. They came from everywhere in town and beyond. These were the families whom she had helped with food occasionally when she had extra. Here were the people for whom she had worked over the years, close friends and even family that came in from neighboring states. Father Sullivan spoke of the kind of woman Ellen was: strong, caring, thoughtful, generous, and stubborn.

"Yes, stubborn," he said. "She had a strong Irish will that no man could break once she made her mind up." Everyone chuckled. They knew he was right.

Afterward, close friends and family went back to the house with Charlie to eat, drink and share memories. It was a long, memorable day. By the end of the evening, there were still many who volunteered to help clean dishes and store food in the icebox so Charlie wouldn't have to attend to it.

After the last guest had left, he sat with Lillie in silence for a few minutes until a car came to pick her up. There were no words left to be said in that moment there was only the loving kiss she left on his lips.

Charlie went into his mother's room and looked at the empty bed. It was made up so neatly, he thought. Mrs. Russo must have done that. She had come earlier to straighten the house before everyone had arrived. It looked so normal, as if her room were patiently waiting for her to come in and go to sleep, just as she had done every night for the past twenty-five years. He turned, walked into his room and collapsed onto his bed. It cradled his body and allowed him to fall into a dreamless sleep.

It was the next evening when he finally woke up again. He had slept away a complete day.

Chapter Nineteen

Charlie lost himself in his work and only saw Lillie a few times a week for dinner or quiet walks in the garden. Being with her was the only way that he could ignore the thoughts that clamored for attention in his head. He couldn't forget how he had failed his mother, how he had never checked on her that fateful morning. He blamed himself for all the time he had spent with Lillie and how he left Mrs. Russo to do what was his responsibility.

He imagined his mother alone in the dark, unable to call for help and wondering where he was. His nights were tortured; he would wake up from nightmares, too ashamed to tell Lillie and too tired to try. He was falling apart inside and didn't know what to do except work.

***

Lillie was growing increasingly concerned; she knew Charlie wasn't himself. He had grown very quiet over the past few weeks and she had hardly seen him. When they were together, he was somewhere else, another place far away where she couldn't go, or he wouldn't let her go. She wasn't sure how she was supposed to help him. She had tried every way she knew, but she wouldn't give up. He was isolating himself and barely speaking to anyone, claiming that he was "just tired." Perhaps if she spoke with her father, he would have some suggestions on what to do.

One could only hope.

After dinner that evening, her father retired to his study to catch up on reading. Lillie made two cups of tea, placed them on a tray with few cookies, and brought them into her father's favorite room. She placed the tray on his side table and sat down in one of the plush chairs across from his desk. Her father looked over at the tray of tea and cookies and then back at Lillie. He put the newspaper down and waited.

A moment passed before she burst into tears. James

got up and went to Lillie's side and, trying to comfort her, he patted her back. When she had calmed down a bit, he kissed her on the forehead. "Lillie, darling, what's wrong?"

Despite her shaky voice, she was able to explain to him how Charlie had been acting lately. She told him she didn't know what to do for him and that she was scared because he was plummeting deeper into sadness. She felt it went beyond the loss of his mother, and she didn't know how to help him. He just wouldn't speak to her about it. When she tried, he attempted to appease her with more excuses.

"Dad, he works all the time. He gets up early and stays up to all hours of the morning. He's not sleeping, and I can tell he's losing weight. I don't think he's eating. I know the depth of sadness he must be feeling, but there's something else gnawing at him, I know it. He won't talk to me. He just seems to move through the day without really being awake. I don't know what to do. I feel like I'm losing him and I can't stop it." Lillie started sobbing again, and her father pulled her into his arms to comfort her.

"Would you like me to speak to him?"

"Would you, please? Maybe he'll talk to you, I don't know. He doesn't have any one else he feels close to, except maybe Mrs. O'Leary, but I know him. He wouldn't want to burden her with his problems after all she has been through."

"I'll talk with him first thing tomorrow morning. He is dropping by my office to discuss business ideas. We'll speak then." Lillie's father gave her a comforting hug,

Lying in bed, Lillie had a hard time fighting off the tears. She was so worried about Charlie. Eventually, her body succumbed to exhaustion, and she drifted off.

***

Early that morning, Charlie got up and dressed quickly. He had a full schedule of work that day and needed to visit Mr. Whitman before he got started. He had developed a few new ideas he wanted to share with him and ask his opinion on. Mr. Whitman had been so good to him; he gave Charlie complete freedom with his furniture designs, and he respected Mr. Whitman for that. It wouldn't be right if he didn't discuss his latest ideas with him. Charlie valued his advice; his boss was a smart businessman. He knew Mr. Whitman would steer him in the right direction.

When he arrived at Mr. Whitman's office, his boss was sitting at his desk drinking tea. He motioned for Charlie to come in and sit down. He offered him a cup of tea and Charlie accepted out of respect, tea not being one of his favorite drinks. They spoke for a few minutes about Charlie's ideas and Mr. Whitman approved.

After they were finished with their business, Charlie pushed his chair back and got ready to leave.

"Wait." James stood up and walked over to the door to his office, shutting it. Charlie was perplexed. What was this all about?

James eased himself into a chair next to Charlie. "Charlie, Lillie has spoken to me about you. She has been very concerned about your behavior as of late. She tells me you're working excessively and she thinks you might not be eating. She also told me you're not sleeping very well. Is there something you would like to talk about?"

At first, Charlie felt a little angry with Lillie for going behind his back and speaking with her father about him, but after a moment, he calmed down. It was her love for him that was causing her to worry. Now he felt guilty.

"I'm fine, sir, just tired. I've been working long hours due to several new orders that came in, and I don't want to miss my deadlines. I know everyone has been patient, especially after my mother's passing, but I do want to hold up my end of our business. I don't want to disappoint you."

Charlie hoped this would appease Mr. Whitman.

How could he tell him how he was really feeling? He was a man, and he should be able to act like one. He shouldn't be falling apart; that was unacceptable. He couldn't help what was going on inside himself...no matter how hard he tried to ignore it. He didn't want Mr. Whitman—or even worse, Lillie—to find out. How could she feel safe and secure if he fell apart? He needed to take care of her. That's what real men did: they stayed strong for their families. And Lillie was his family now.

"Charlie, you know you can talk to me. I won't judge you. I haven't yet, have I?"

"No, sir, you haven't, but there is nothing to say. I am just tired."

"If you say so, then I will let it go, but if you ever feel you need to, you can turn to me, son, okay?"

"Thank you, Mr. Whitman."

"Please call me James. I think it's appropriate at this point. Oh, and slow down, take some time off, maybe shorter days." He stood up and patted Charlie on the back.

"Thanks, Mr. Whit—I mean James, I promise I will slow down with work. Tell Lillie not to worry and that I'll see her later in the garden." Charlie was relieved to leave the office.

Later that evening, Charlie walked over to Lillie's and found her waiting for him in the garden. She didn't hear him come through the gate; she was sitting and gazing at the fire thorns, deep in thought. He admired her for a moment. She was incredibly lovely, and it had been quite some time since he allowed himself to just look at her without the distraction of his guilt. He felt as if he would never get over the blame he'd placed on himself for losing his mom.

Lillie had been strong all throughout this, but she had a very giving, sensitive side to herself that must be hurt over how he had been treating her. She didn't deserve this. So much had been going on inside his own head that he didn't realize how those closest to him were being affected. He needed to do something. He couldn't hurt her any more than he had already. She deserved more; she deserved everything.

As he went to walk towards her, he froze. A fiery heat consumed him. He looked down at his sweating palms as his head started pounding. Air forced itself through the narrow tunnel of his throat down into his gasping lungs. Everything around him faded to gray, then black. He had to get out.

He bolted from the garden out through the gate and onto the lawn. He sat down for a moment and tried to steady his heavy breathing. After a few minutes it became normal again and the heat in his chest went away. He put his head in his hands.

What's wrong with me? He couldn't let Lillie see him like this. The only thing left to do was to go home.

As he turned at the corner, he saw three of his friends waiting for him on the porch. Mr. Russo sat tense and hunched on the steps. The conversation had to be serious, judging from his somber expression. *Oh no,* he thought. *What now?*

"Hey, Charlie boy? Where you've been? We've been waiting for you for about an hour now." He hadn't seen Frankie Dalo and Jason Chambers since graduation.

"Charlie, Charlie, did you hear what I said? We've signed up. We're shipping out on Thursday and we wanted to come over and say goodbye." John was waving his hands in front of Charlie's face, trying to get his attention. "Hey, are you in there?"

"What do you mean, you ship out Thursday? Why so soon?" He couldn't believe three more of his friends were going. *How many does that make?* he thought. *Ten, no, eleven including Pete.*

"I said, we're leaving Thursday because they want to begin training us right away so we can be sent to Europe as soon as possible. The army needs as many of us as they can get signed up. It's really getting bad over there."

"I didn't even know you joined up," said Charlie. "This Thursday? I can't believe it. What did your family say?"

Frankie stepped down and put his hands in his pocket. "Well, our fathers seemed proud, but our moms, they weren't too happy about it."

"You should have seen Frankie's mom." Jason looked over at Mr. Russo. "She cried enough for two people. Carried on about Mother, Mary, and Joseph. We weren't quite sure what she was saying. There was too much wailing going on."

Frankie shook his head. "My mom can get pretty emotional."

John chuckled. "So, this is it. We wanted to be sure we saw you before we shipped out. I also wanted to tell you again how sorry we all are about your mom. She was a good lady. Tough break, Charlie boy."

The three boys left and Charlie sank down next to Mr. Russo. For a moment he thought about everything that was happening around him. His friends were leaving, his mom had passed away, and he was pushing Lillie further away from him each day. He loved her so much, but he couldn't be there for her right now. He would only continue to hurt her.

"Mr. Russo, can I talk to you about something? I need your opinion."

Charlie explained how he had been feeling lately. It wasn't easy, but he had to share it with someone, and Mr. Russo had been there for him many times over the years since his dad had passed away. If anybody knew him almost as well as his own mother, it would be either Mrs. O'Leary—and he didn't want to burden the already overwhelmed woman—or the Russos. The Russos had been like surrogate grandparents over the years, helping his mom when she needed it and staying with Charlie when she sometimes had to work at night. He told him about his excessive work, avoiding Lillie, and the episode that had happened to him that night in the garden. He shared his feelings about wanting to go and serve his country even before his mom had passed away and how then, he wouldn't have left her. He didn't want to leave Lillie, but he thought staying was only hurting her.

Mr. Russo listened to every word Charlie had to say and when he was done, he put his arm around Charlie's shoulder. "Charlie boy, if you're asking me if I think you should join the service and serve your country, I can't make that decision for you. You are the only one who can answer that question. I can say this to you: if you feel this burning within you and your heart is guiding you towards that duty, then you already have the answer, don't you?"

Charlie shook his head yes.

"Mrs. Russo and I don't want to see you leave, and I know your mother would have been very worried, but I know she would have been very proud, too. You are a good boy, and you will get through this thing that is eating at you now. It will just take some time. But if you're truly serious about going, do it for the right reasons. Don't just run away because I'll tell you this: your problems will just go along with you. So be sure of all the reasons why you want to do this."

"Thanks, Mr. Russo, I will. I'm going to bed. I'm exhausted."

"Goodnight, Charlie."

"Goodnight, Mr. Russo."

Charlie went home and lay in bed thinking about their conversation. He had made a decision, and he hoped it wouldn't cost him Lillie.

Chapter Twenty

Lillie couldn't sleep that night. She couldn't believe Charlie never came over. She had tried to ring him, but there was no answer. He would never miss one of their dates. Not unless there was a good reason, and certainly not without telling her. She was sick with worry, something must have happened to him. With first light, she was out of bed and dressed. After ringing Claire and telling her what had happened, she ran out the door.

Claire had agreed to meet her in front of the house with the car and have Henry drive them over to Charlie's house. Walking was far too slow for today.

They both ran to Charlie's front door. At first they just knocked, but after several minutes their knocks turned into a series of loud thumps on the solid wood. There was no response; he wasn't home. Lillie just stood there, paralyzed with shock; while Claire went next door to see if the Russos knew anything. Mrs. Russo was home, but Mr. Russo had already left for his shop.

"I can't tell you anything, I'm afraid," said Mrs. Russo. "Why don't you check in at the shop? Maybe Charlie went in to work early."

On the way they blew in to Charlie's workshop only to find him absent. Then it was a race over to the furniture store, but Mr. Anderson hadn't seen him, either. Lillie's heart was skipping beats, and her breathing wasn't cooperating either. Claire had Henry stop the car.

"I knew something was wrong lately," said Lillie. "He kept telling me he was tired, but I knew it was more than that."

"Lils, he just lost his mom. He's not going to be normal, and it's going to take a while. Don't you remember?"

"Of course I remember what it felt like to lose my mother, but this is different. He's hiding something, I know he is; I just don't know *what* it is."

Henry knocked on one of the doors to see if anyone was at home for a glass of water to calm Lillie. After a few houses he found a sweet, elderly woman who was more than happy to assist them. She brought out lemonade and cookies, convincing them the sugar would help Lillie feel better much faster than just water. It worked, and after only a minute or two, Lillie was much calmer and thanked the woman for her help. They decided to continue on her journey to Russo's Butcher Shop and to check with Mrs. O'Leary on the way.

Mrs. O'Leary hadn't seen Charlie in a few days, and she didn't know where he would be other than work. When they arrived to the butcher shop, Mr. Russo was busy helping several customers. He saw them rush in and asked them to wait in the back room. Lillie became more nervous when Mr. Russo came in mumbling and rubbing his hands on his apron.He pulled up a chair and sat next to Lillie.

"Mr. Russo," began Claire, "we've been searching for Charlie all morning. He was supposed to meet Lillie last night, but he never made it. Lillie is a wreck, as you can see. We've checked everywhere we could think of. Your wife said maybe you've seen or spoken to him recently. Have you?"

Mr. Russo cleared his throat and spoke in a soft voice. "Yes, I have. I spoke to him last night and then again early this morning. Please stop worrying. He's fine. He had something he needed to do, but I'm sure he will come and speak with you later."

"Something to do? What do you mean?" Lillie became agitated. "Is he all right? Does he need help? Where is he? Mr. Russo, please tell me what's going on!"

"Lillie, I'm sorry, but I cannot. It is not mine to tell. Charlie will speak to you himself. But until he does, once again, I'm sorry. You will just have to find comfort in knowing he is fine and will come to you later with his news."

"Come on, Lils, let's go home," said Claire. "You need to eat something...I need to eat something."

Lillie was silent in the car for the entire ride and when they arrived home, she went straight up to her room and closed the door, leaving Claire to hurry after her upstairs.

***

Charlie had anguished over his decision, but after discussing it with James in the study, he knew it was right.

"Thank you for listening to me, James. I know Lillie's going to be upset, but I feel this is something I must do."

"I understand my boy. If I were a few years younger..."

Footsteps sounded, and the door creaked open.

"Claire?"

She was standing in the middle of the room, her face red with anger. Charlie knew this was going to take some explaining, but he'd rather James work on that one. He had Lillie to deal with: one angry female was enough. Besides, judging by her flaring nostrils, Claire was going to be the harder one of the two.

***

Charlie stepped slowly up to Lillie's room. He could hear her crying. He gently rapped on the door, and she asked who it was, but when he said his name he heard silence. He stood there, waiting for her to respond, but she still didn't say anything. He lowered his head and leaned heavily on the door.

"Lillie, please open up so I can explain why I didn't come over last night and where I've been all day."

Nothing. "Lillie, please. I'm so sorry for what I did to you. Please.

"Charlie, are you hurt? Are you okay?"

"I'm fine, but..." He settled down on the floor.

"Lillie, open the door." Charlie was desperate; he needed to set things right with Lillie before Thursday, before he left. A few seconds passed and he heard the key turn. He stood up.

When she opened the door, Lillie looked pale and fragile. Her eyes were swollen and red, and her body was trembling. His heart plummeted to his stomach. Looking at her and knowing he caused this...He felt as if he would be sick. He put his arms around her and brought her close to his chest, holding her tight. He kissed the top of her head and stroked her hair. He was afraid to let go for fear she might collapse. After a few minutes, she calmed down. Her body was still and her breathing had returned to normal. He tenderly took her hand. He knew where he must take her: they had to go the garden.

***

She hadn't asked him what had happened last night. Maybe if she didn't, it would all just go away and Charlie would return to the man she knew and loved.

They slowly made their way over to where the fire thorns grew. They seemed to be reaching for each other but were still a good distance apart. Sitting down where she had waited, however, just made her feel worse.

"Lillie, there's something I need to tell you. First, I am so sorry for last night. If I could take it back and do it over again, I would. The one thing I never wanted to do is hurt you, which is one of the reasons I've made the decision I have. I feel lately that all I do is hurt you."

"Wait." Lillie jumped up. "What do you mean? No, no, you haven't. I've been worried about you, yes, but you have never hurt me...Not until last night. I don't know what you've done, Charlie, but I think your reasons are deeper than that. Something has been bothering you a great deal, but you refuse to tell me. Whatever it is, that is what has caused this change, not me. Tell me what it is!"

Charlie pulled her next to him and told her

everything. He explained how his guilt had been consuming him, how he couldn't think clearly anymore, and what had happened to him when he had come over last night.

"You were here, in the garden?"

"Yes, but I couldn't move. Everything was turning black. I couldn't let you see me like that."

"Why? I'm stronger than that, Charlie. You think of me as fragile. Haven't I proven that I'm not? I could have helped you if you had only let me."

"No, I'm supposed to take care of you. I'm the man. I'm the strong one."

Lillie finally realized why he had shut her out lately; it was his pride, misguided though it was. She grabbed his face with both of her hands and kissed him firmly on the lips. "We take care of each other, and we are strong for each other. This is not a sign of weakness, but of trust. Charlie, when you love someone deeply, you trust them to be there for you always. We are two people growing together. But there has to be trust."

"Lillie, there is something else. I joined the service. We ship out on Thursday. I don't know when I'll be home again."

Lillie heard the words but couldn't make sense of them. Her ears buzzed as if bees were swarming around her head. She saw the look on his face. He was waiting for her to say something, but how could she? What could she say to that? He was leaving. *He doesn't know when he'll be back. He may never come back; that's what he's really saying.*

"I know this is not what you want, but I need to do this. Everyone I know is going to fight for our country while I stay here and make furniture! It's just not right. While Pete was risking his life and losing it, I sat at home sanding wood. No, Lillie, I can't stay. I love you so much and I want a life with you when I get back, but it just can't be now."

Lillie's eyes once again filled with tears. "What about your business? What will you do about all the people who have placed orders?" She was clinging to anything she could think of.

"I've already spoken with Mr. Anderson and your father. They will explain and give the customers the option of waiting or going elsewhere."

"So that's it. You have it all figured out. Everything is taken care of." Anger and hurt consumed her. Her body raced inside and her head was swimming. Desperation took over and her breath became shallower with each word.

"Lillie, please try to understand. I leave in two days. Can we just be together, please?"

Charlie held her tight and started kissing her, first her forehead, then her cheek and then her lips. She wanted to be mad but couldn't hold on to her anger any longer. She was in his arms and he was kissing her. Heat rose through her body and she snuggled against his chest. The longer he kissed her, the more she forgot about last night and earlier today. She was in his arms and that was enough...for now.

***

He stroked her hair as her head lay on his chest and she drifted off. Charlie watched her as she slept, trying to memorize every angle of her face. He would take that memory with him, wherever he was sent.

The next day they were each other's shadows, spending every waking moment together. They packed his things together and had lunch in town. He left a key with Mrs. Russo, who assured him she would attend to the house while he was gone. He wanted to tell her not to worry about him, but he knew better than to argue with a hardheaded Italian woman. Then time lurched forward and he had to say his goodbyes. Mrs. O'Leary tried to put on a brave face, but despite herself broke down in a storm of tears. Charlie felt the need to promise her he wouldn't go and get himself killed, but they both knew it was a promise he might not be able to keep. Even with that said, she brought a smile to her face and hugged him tightly in a silent farewell.

He was going to spend his last night home at Lillie's house. James had arranged a car to take them to the train station in the morning. They stayed up almost all night, that final night together before he was to leave. They strolled through the garden, where they felt like the only two people in the world. It gave them the strength to know their love was up for the miles placed between them. Somewhere around two in the morning, they moved into the kitchen to share a sandwich. They made plans for his return and how they were going to celebrate in the garden. How special and beautiful it would be.

But time crept up, as it always does, and ended the night for them.

***

When they arrived at the station, they only had a few minutes before the train left. How Lillie wished they could both just turn around and go home. As they walked out to the platform, Charlie grabbed her and held on tight. He took her hands and brought them up to her face, cradling the soft contours of her cheeks. In a blur of tears they kissed. In its brief intensity, it sealed their love forever.

Lillie pulled away first. "Do you have your compass?"

"I do, and the knife too."

"Good. If you get lost, you know how to find me."

"I will always find you, no matter where I am."

Just then the whistle blew and Charlie had to board the train. He gazed deeply into her eyes, the kiss of the soul, and jumped onto the train as it began to move. Lillie ran at its side, the platform quickly narrowing and shortening, all the while throwing kisses and shouting.

"I'll love you forever," she yelled.

“I’ll come back. I love you. Look for me in the garden...”

Chapter Twenty-One

Three days had passed since Charlie had left, and Lillie was fading deeper into despair. She hadn't gotten out of bed since Friday and she barely ate anything the cook prepared. Claire had visited several times but even her persistence failed.

Mrs. O'Leary and Deidre came for dinner on Sunday. Lillie had enjoyed their company in the past, but wasn't happy about accepting guests. And although she kept up the air of being gracious and accommodating, it was a contrast to her inner hollowness.

After dinner, Mrs. O'Leary asked Lillie for a tour of the garden. They were walking for several minutes when Mrs. O'Leary sat down on one of the benches in front of a lovely oak tree.

"Forgive me, Lillie, but I must rest for a minute. I'm not as young as I used to be. Age just suddenly creeps up on you. I think back to the days when the children were small and Mr. O'Leary and I would take them for picnics on the beach. We would be out playing with them all day. I had unending energy back then, and now I get tired from just walking in a garden." Mrs. O'Leary smiled. Lillie chuckled and then stared blankly out into the garden. "You know, dear," she continued, "you have to keep your strength up. For Charlie. What will he think when he gets back and you've grown pale and weak? He will blame himself. Do you want to burden him with that, especially after he's fought a war?"

Lillie looked over at Mrs. O'Leary. "No, I don't."

"I should say not. If you love him as much as you say, then there is no time for indulgence and self-pity. He needs you to be strong and healthy. You will need to take care of him when he gets home. He will rely on you to be there for him and help him become reacquainted with society.

"Lillie, he is in a very different place right now. Coming home is an adjustment for any soldier, but this time is especially difficult. I've read that many boys going home in England are terribly ill mentally. I'm not implying Charlie will end up like that—he is a very strong-willed boy—but he will need time and attention once he's home. What if you're not well? Then how will you be able to give him what he needs?"

"I understand, but I feel dead inside. It's as if someone has ripped out my heart. My stomach hurts all the time and I can't sleep anymore. My head is constantly buzzing. It's an effort just to get out of my bed in the morning. I want to be strong for him. I used to think I was a strong and capable woman, but lately I don't feel that way at all." Lillie put her head in her hands and started to sob. Mrs. O'Leary put her arms around her and patted her back.

"Hush now, honey. It will all work out, but you have to try harder for Charlie's sake and for yours."

Lillie picked up her head and wiped her tears away. She looked at Mrs. O'Leary for a moment. *Is this what my mother would have said?*

Somehow, having someone as maternal as Mrs. O'Leary helped her feel hope again. The woman just seemed to know how she honestly felt, that despite the pain she could get up every morning and live through the day and function. Perhaps it was because of the loss of her son and husband that she could understand the magnitude of pain, or perhaps it was that she was a mother and knew how to take her child's pain and lift it away, almost making it her own.

"I know what you say is true and Charlie will need me, but how do you do it? How do you get up every day and act as if nothing has changed?"

"You don't, Lillie darling. Of course life is different. But it's up to you how you face your days. You can whither up and just blow away, or you can fight. When you love so deeply you take on all of it, the bad as well as the good. You don't allow it to defeat you or your right to a future together. Fight, Lillie Whitman, and be the strong, capable woman that you know you are, the one that Charlie is counting on." Mrs. O'Leary stood up and took Lillie's hand. "Now, child, let's go in and have some dessert. Your father mentioned something about apple pie."

They both laughed and Lillie wiped her face, took a deep breath, and gathered herself to go in.

After dessert, James drove Mrs. O'Leary and Deidre home. Claire went with Lillie up to her room, where the girls settled in for a long chat. It felt just as it did when they were in high school, something Lillie needed and Claire thoroughly enjoyed. It was very late and the girls were getting sleepy, so they decided that Claire should spend the night and leave in the morning.

"Hey, Lils, are you okay?" Claire asked as she climbed into bed.

"No, but I'm getting there. I'm determined not to crumble."

"That's the spirit. I knew you had it in you. Good night, my dearest friend."

"Good night, and thanks."

"For what?"

"For being my friend in a time such as this."

"You know I can handle adversity. Just think about my mother and you'll understand how I survived childhood."

Lillie laughed and then drifted off to sleep with thoughts only of Charlie.

***

On Monday, Claire was having lunch with Hanna to discuss campaign strategies. Claire had asked Lillie to join them, but her friend had decided to go to Connecticut and visit with her cousins for a few days. They were having a birthday party for their youngest daughter, and Lillie thought it would help lighten her mood if she got away. Claire agreed with her and had dropped her off at the train station before joining Hanna at the diner. She was also going out with Bastian after lunch and had asked him to meet her at the diner later in the afternoon.

When Claire arrived, Hanna was already seated at a booth by the window. Hanna got up and greeted her with a hug and a kiss on the cheek. When the waitress came over to take their order, Hanna ordered eggs with toast and bacon, which Claire thought was funny. She had such a big appetite for such a skinny girl. Claire was content with her much lighter choice for lunch: a small cup of chicken noodle soup and crackers.

While they were waiting, they discussed the possible men they could approach for campaign contributions. Congressman Meyer was extremely liberal, and this didn't sit well with some of the older businessmen in town. They would have to be careful whom they approached, as they didn't want to create any unwanted issues before election.

During lunch they put business aside for a while and decided to catch up on their personal life. Claire told Hanna about Lillie and Charlie and the sheer terror he had put Lillie through by signing up for the service and leaving for the war. Hanna listened intently, hanging on to every word. At first, Claire just thought it was out of concern for the couple, but as the conversation changed it was evident that no matter what she spoke about, Hanna was riveted. Claire wasn't sure why, but she was flattered that someone other than Bastian and Lillie was interested in her. Maybe it was because Hanna had been out of the country for so long that it was refreshing to have a conversation with an American again, but whatever the reason, Claire discovered she liked the attention. Hanna had a way of making her feel important.

After lunch, the girls lingered over tea while

discussing business a little further. A few minutes later, Claire noticed Bastian entering the diner. As soon as he arrived, Hanna abruptly ended the conversation, wished them well, and left. Claire was annoyed. *Why does she keep doing this?*

"I don't think she likes me very much. Every time I come to meet you, she leaves so fast you can feel the air whiz by." Bastian frowned at Claire. "I'm going to have to ring her later and find out. This is getting ridiculous."

But Claire soon forgot her annoyance. Bastian had planned a surprise for her. They were to go a new picture show, *Rebecca Of Sunnybrook Farm*, starring Mary Pickford and Eugene O'Brien. Claire marveled at the people on the screen and the story itself coming to life; it all mesmerized her. She had read the novel by Kate Douglas Wiggin, but this was just exhilarating. How could images be projected on a screen and make a story unfold right before one's eyes? And such actors! Mary Pickford with her bowed lips and sharp, bobbed hair was delicate and powerful at the same time. In a way, she reminded her a bit of Lillie. Then there was Eugene O'Brien. He was so handsome and elegant, but she knew she shouldn't say such things to Bastian.

After the movie ended, Claire didn't want to leave. She could have watched the moving picture all night long, but instead they headed over to the diner for a quick supper before Bastian walked her home. Full of energy, Claire wasn't ready for sleep yet, so she decided to ring Hanna. She just had to find out what was troubling her about Bastian. Could she really dislike him so? He had barely spoken to her, and they'd only met a handful of times. What could it be?

She went into the kitchen and pulled a chair close to the telephone. Before she dialed, she checked the time. It was only eight in the evening. No wonder she wasn't tired. Hanna stayed up fairly late, and her aunt was out of town for a few days, so she didn't have to worry about disturbing her. She rang the operator and requested the Pittman residence. Hanna answered and sounded surprised to hear Claire's voice on the other end. They chatted for a few minutes until Claire felt comfortable enough to ask her the burning question.

"Hanna, there is something I wanted to speak to you about. It's Bastian. It might be just my imagination, but it seems like every time he comes near, you choose to leave." There was a long pause and Claire could hear Hanna's breathing through the telephone.

"Hanna, are you there? Did you hear what I said? Hello?"

"I'm here. I was just surprised by such a seemingly silly question. It isn't anything personal against Bastian. I barely know him. I'm a very busy person with the campaign. There just aren't enough hours in a day! Really, Claire, you have put me in a very uncomfortable position, and I don't appreciate being attacked like this."

"Attacked? I just asked you a simple question. You're the one who's got herself in a tizzy. Hanna, what's wrong?"

"You wouldn't understand. I'm not sure even I understand."

"Understand what?"

"I'm saying it would be better if I tell you in person. Can I come over or is it too late?"

"No, it's not too late. I'll make us tea."

"Tea sounds wonderful. I'll be there in a few minutes."

By now Claire was completely perplexed. *What could she have to tell me?* She put the water on for the tea and waited for Hanna, who arrived nearly twenty minutes later and looked as if she had been crying. Claire sat at the kitchen table and motioned for her to join her. Hanna took a sip of her tea.

"Firstly, I must say I don't hate Bastian. I don't have anything against him other than his relationship with you."

"With me? What are you saying, Hanna?"

"It isn't that I don't get along with Bastian; it's because he has something I want and I can't bear to see him have: you. When I see him with you, the jealousy is too much."

Claire sat speechless. She had known Hanna was different but had no clue that Hanna's feeling were for her. . . There weren't any words she could muster up, no matter how hard she tried. She wanted to say that it was okay, that she understood, that they were friends and they would always be friends, but never anything more. Instead, Claire remained silent. Hanna jumped up and ran out of the house. Claire sat alone for a few seconds, stunned and still, but she knew she must go after her.

"Hanna, wait. Don't leave. Please let me talk to you."

"Why? You are obviously so repulsed you can't say anything!"

"Repulsed? No. You misunderstood. Surprised, yes, but not repulsed. You are my friend. That doesn't change. I just didn't know what to do with what you said. I love Bastian. I can't feel about you the way you say you feel about me, but it doesn't mean I don't still love you. Please understand, this will take me a little while to sort out, but I will always, always be your friend."

Hanna started to cry and Claire put her arms around her. "Come on, let's go back inside and finish our tea."

"No, but thanks. I think I'd rather be on my way."

"Are you sure? We could speak some more about this."

"I'm drained. I'd like to go home and go straight to bed."

"But are you all right? Is there anything I can say,

anything I can do?"

"No, I'll be fine, Claire. It's been a rough evening, but I'm sure I'll feel better tomorrow." Hanna started to walk across the lawn.

"Wait, Hanna. I meant what I said. I do love you."

"I know you do. That's what hurts the most."

Claire watched her friend walk down the street and felt sick inside. She now understood how much she had hurt Hanna tonight.

Claire couldn't wait for Lillie to come home. She needed advice, and she was certainly not going to ask her mother or Bastian. Three days went by, and they felt like years, but Lillie finally arrived. Claire practically ran over. She went straight up to her room to tell her everything that happened. Lillie was as speechless as Claire had been at first, but then she was able to give her the advice and comfort that only Lillie could.

"Stay in contact with her, Claire. Give her a little time and keep being her friend. She'll come around. Time will heal her wounds, and she will need her friend by her side. She constantly lives in fear and can't let anyone know who she really is. Friends, true friends, will get her through."

"Boy, when did you become so insightful?"

Lillie smiled. "I think I've gone through a few changes this past week. Some good, some I wish I could forget. But I think it's pushed me to see what's inside and around me differently, perhaps a little clearer."

The girls lay down on Lillie's bed, staring at the ceiling.

"Claire?"

"Yeah?"

"Where do you think Charlie is now?"

"I don't know. Maybe training in South Carolina."

"Maybe. I hope so."

Chapter Twenty-Two

Large weeping willows and overgrown green grass was the landscape passing by from the bus window. Charlie kept running the last words to Lillie over in his head. *I'll come back*. But he knew they were empty; he had no way of knowing the truth. He closed his eyes and laid his head back—it was going to be a long ride.

Charlie arrived in South Carolina with John McDougal, Frankie Dalo, and Jason Chambers. They were enlisted for seven days of training. Even though they were young and active, the long days were grueling. They were exhausted by sunset and their bodies ached. The living conditions were crude at best, still being constructed because of the urgency that the United States had taken to war. They trained mostly with the bayonets on dummies constructed of corn husk. And despite their additional training on rifles, they hadn't seen the main portion of the artillery that they were expected to use on their real enemies.

After the seven-day stint, they were sent by train to Philadelphia. From there, they boarded the *Henderson*, a Navy vessel that would take them to France, where their training would continue under the now more experienced French army. Their trip across the Atlantic was long and cramped. Charlie had never been out in the ocean; few of the new recruits had. And though the ship was enormous and could take the battering of the waves, they still felt extremely ill with nausea. They were miserable. After a few days, however, their sea-sickness started to subside, enough for them to function and perform their daily duties. At night the boys lay in their bunks and reminisced of home and their days in high school. They talked about Pete and how much had changed in such a short time. Their lives were different now, and sometimes the past seemed merely a nice dream that they all shared.

The boys began making new friends on board almost immediately. One by the name of Luke Dempsey had befriended Charlie during the first week on the ship. He was from Chicago and had signed up right before they had started the draft. His brother, Kevin, was already in France. They came from a poor family and the boys had decided the army would give them an opportunity to make things a little easier at home, with two less mouths to feed. Their mother had been hysterical with grief when she found out, but their father had understood.

"Fathers usually do," Luke had told Charlie. "Mothers, they're the top worriers. They worry about you from the time you're born through your whole life. And it never matters how old you become. You could be eighty years old, and she's one hundred, and she's still going to worry about you. It's their job. But dads, they handle all the tough stuff. They know we have to fight, and you know that deep down inside they're worried just as much, but they'll never show it, no siree."

Luke was easy for Charlie to talk to, as he didn't know the strain of Charlie's past few months at home. It was liberating to talk to someone about things other than his mother's death or his relationship with Lillie. Charlie basically told him about his furniture business and how he had gotten started in it.

Without Luke, the trip would have been dull. He had a way of making the tasks on board go more smoothly. He was funny, and the other guys thought he was a stand-up kind of guy as well. By the end of their first week at sea, the five new friends were inseparable.

After what seemed to be an eternity, they arrived in France.

Before they could catch a breath, they began training with the French army. For the next two weeks they ate, slept, and drank warfare. It was not as complete as it should have been, from what they'd been told, but time was of the essence, and fresh troops were needed out on the front lines. The English, French, and Russians had been fighting with Germany for three long years, and they were worn down and disillusioned. They had all thought the war would end in a few months of it starting; no one believed that it would go on as long as it had.

Then the boys finally received their orders: they were going to the Western Front. There had been a trench stalemate there for the past three years, and the leaders felt the fresh energy of the Americans could possibly be what they needed to end the fighting. Major battles had been fought there each year, and each one had been bloody and long.

The night before they were to leave, the friends gathered and spoke to each other about what they wanted to send to their loved ones if they didn't make it home.

John wanted his mom to know he was never afraid and because of her he stayed strong. He also needed for Margaret to know that he had always loved her, but that, without guilt, she should go on living and someday meet someone else to spend her life with.

Frankie wanted his kid sister to have his book collection. He loved to read and so did she, but he would never allow her to borrow his books. For that he was so sorry.

Jason just wanted his dad to know that he had made the right choice, to not think he pushed him into enlisting, and that he loved his mother very, very much.

Since Luke was not from New York, he made Charlie promise to take the trip to Chicago to deliver his message if necessary. Charlie agreed. Luke wanted nothing but for Charlie to just go and tell his family that he had served his country with honor and to try to remember him without regret. Oh, and to make sure to kiss his younger siblings and tell them not to forget their brother.

When it came time for Charlie to reveal his wishes,

he handed John a letter for Lillie.

"What would you like me to tell her?"

"Nothing. Just give her the letter. It says everything. Please don't forget, and whatever you do, don't lose it."

"I won't forget, Charlie. Don't worry, I won't lose it. But you'll be giving it to her yourself."

"Thanks, John."

The boys talked for some time before turning in for the night and their last day of peace for a while.

The next morning they were up at dawn being loaded up and transported on to large trucks. John, Charlie, and Frankie were with one convoy with Luke and Jason on another. It had been the first time the five friends had been separated since they'd left Long Island and it was an uncomfortable, eerie feeling. They sped across bumpy, mud-covered roads, the truck sliding excessively from a lack of traction.

Even under the horrible circumstances, Charlie was too frightened to notice. Bombs exploded the distance, and with each minute they seemed to be getting closer. He glanced over at John and Frankie. They had the same fear in their eyes that he was sure he had.

Although the sergeant was shouting loudly, they could barely hear him over the explosions. They watched him as diligently as they could, hoping to catch a few words here and there. If they kept an eye on the men up front, they could take their lead and hope it would pan out well. One thing was for certain: they made a pact to stick together no matter what.

The booming grew louder. Each explosion rattled in Charlie's chest. He could barely breathe, and his palms were clammy and cold. Frankie kept rocking his body back and forth every time they heard an explosion, and John was silently praying; Charlie could see his lips move as he crossed himself periodically. He thought about his mom and how he wished he could see her right now. She could always calm his fears.

It seemed they had been driving for hours when suddenly the truck stopped.

As soon as they jumped down from the convoy, they were guided to a long maze of trenches. Gunfire and explosions surrounded them as they ran through blinding clouds of smoke and ended up directly in the center of their first battle.

There was no time to think. Instinct kicked in and each soldier started shooting. Caught up in the frenzy, the men had no time to look for the others. Frankie lost his footing in the thick mud. John grabbed him by his arm, first lifting and then dragging him along. Charlie kept firing at whatever it took to keep them intact and alive. Soldiers were screaming, their shouts lost in the curves of whizzing bullets and bursts of shrapnel. Somehow, in the heavy, charcoal haze of battle, he saw a group of British soldiers waving them forward and pointing where to go next. Charlie shook uncontrollably. His gut was on fire. John and Frankie fought by his side, zigzagging and staying low, taking cover wherever possible.

The band of brand-new soldiers, the boys from the United States, became men in a matter of minutes.

***

Covered in mud, sweat and blood, the three men plodded on in uniforms as heavy as their hearts. The bone-chilling European cold tore through their bodies like shards of glass. They were almost at the trenches when suddenly Frankie stopped and Charlie with him.

John was a few feet ahead and didn't see that his friends were no longer beside him. His aim was for the trenches and the platoon in front of him. Settling in the deep hole of safety he looked up, expecting to see his buddies right behind him, but they were nowhere to be seen. John raised his body up to survey the still-active battle when an unfamiliar soldier in British uniform grabbed him and yanked him down.

"Are you a nutter? You don't just stick your head up like a damn bull's-eye. What the bloody hell is wrong with you?"

John was paralyzed with fear and couldn't answer. All that ran through his head was the promise he had made to his buddies to stick together. But they were missing already. Missing! It didn't matter that he had made it to the shelter; they were still out there somewhere.

"I have to go. Let go of me!" John shouted.

"You can't go back out there. Just settle down for a moment. Come on, solider, you'll be okay. You're new here. I should have known; you look too healthy." The soldier chuckled.

John was flabbergasted. *My friends need me, and this guy thinks it's funny because I don't look pale and gaunt like the rest of them.*

"What the hell's wrong with me? What the hell is wrong with you? Look, my friends are still out there and I need to go and help them. I don't expect you to go with me, but if you don't let go of my arm, I'll break yours! You understand?"

"Hey, it's your life, mate. Do what you must. I was only trying to keep you alive. But if you feel the need to act like a target, then by all means, have at it." The soldier released John's arm.

John slowly raised himself up to take a look around. He spotted what looked like Charlie and Frankie about ten yards away. Frankie was just sitting on the ground and Charlie was trying to pull him up. He took a big breath and jumped out of the trench, heading for his friends. A stream of hot air rushed by his face followed by a sharp burn on the tip of his right ear. He kept running, and it wasn't until he reached them and heard Charlie gasping that John realized a bullet had grazed him. He could now feel warm blood trickling down the side of his face, and the burning on his ear was getting worse. He looked first at Charlie and then at Frankie. They both seemed fine, but neither one was moving.

"What the hell are the two of you doing out here? Come on, get on your feet. We've got to get out of here!"

"What do you think I've been trying to do?" Charlie yelled. "He won't move and I can't get him up. The mud is too thick for me to get solid footing."

"What's his problem? It doesn't look like he's been shot or anything. Why can't he get up?"

"Not can't, won't! We were running and he just sat down. He said he doesn't want to go on. He just wants to go back home."

"Charlie, look around. We don't have time for this. Let's get him to the trench. We can deal with his breakdown then."

Charlie nodded. The two guys got on either side of Frankie and hoisted him up, practically dragging him the whole way. Finally they descended into the trench. Out of breath and shaking, they sat there for a moment before assessing what had just happened.

***

"Good to see you made it back," said a soldier in British uniform. Charlie looked at him. "I presume these are the chaps you were searching for. Well, it's nice to meet you. My name is Hugh Templeton. Your buddy was awfully serious about going back for you. He even threatened to break my arm if I didn't let go of him. Glad to see it all worked out and with only a minor injury. Here, let the medic have a look at you. You're still bleeding."

After a few minutes, John was bandaged and Charlie was still trying to calm Frankie. Hugh was listening to their conversation and tapped Charlie and John on the shoulder, asking them to come with him for a minute. They both got up and told Frankie to stay put—not that he made any effort to move, but for safety's sake it had to be said.

Hugh took them a few feet away to a lower part of the trenches. It seemed as if they went on forever.

"Look, mates." He motioned for them to sit down. "I've seen this happen before many times. Either your buddy will wake up tomorrow and be fine, his mind having have had time to adjust, or he's never really going to be right again. But there's nothing you can do about it now. You'll just have to stick with him and hope that through the night he comes back."

Charlie and John looked at each other and then back at Hugh. He seemed to have been here for a long time. His shoulders were broad and he was fairly tall, but his body was stick thin and his hair was matted and filthy. His pungent odor suggested there hadn't been any bathing for a while as well. Lice crawled both in his hair and on his body, and when he took his boots off to dry, his feet looked as if someone had put them through a meat grinder. Hugh noticed the boys staring.

"Trench foot."

"Trench foot? What's that? How did your feet get so bad?"

Hugh kept drying his feet and then applying a thick grease to them before putting on a clean, dry pair of socks. "It's called trench foot. It's from our feet constantly being in the water and mud. It used to be worse, but we found that drying them after exposure and changing our socks several times a day helps. The officers have even begun a mandatory check once a day, and if you're not keeping up with it there's hell to pay. But I don't know why any bloke wouldn't want to keep his feet dry. At any rate, my feet are improving. You should have seen them before."

Charlie and John exchanged a glance of horror but didn't utter a word.

Then Charlie heard an unusually loud roar in the sky. He looked up to see two bi-planes soaring overhead. He could tell they were British by the paint on the wings.

They made several passes over the trenches before releasing hundreds of papers that floated down like fallen clouds. John looked at him and Charlie shrugged; they were both confused.

"What the hell are those planes doing?" John asked.

"Sending us coded messages for our new orders. It's the only way for us to receive the information as quickly as possible. If they came by road, it would take too long, or who knows if they'd even make it. Not exactly an easy trip."

"Tell us about it. We had no idea what to expect, but none of us could ever had dreamed it was like this. You hear that things are bad, but you don't know until you've seen it for yourself." Charlie patted John on the shoulder.

Hugh leaned in so the boys could hear him over the noise. "Just keep down, do what you're told, and always, always pay attention. I've seen more blokes get hurt because they forget and don't think. All it takes is one split second of forgetting and the next thing you know, you're lying on the ground wishing for your mum, or worse. So head down, follow orders and never stop thinking. We sleep as much as we can during the day, as most activity is at night. We're in 'stand-to' at dawn and dusk. Those are the times they're most likely to attack."

"What's 'stand-to'?" Charlie felt foolish asking, but he was sure John didn't know, either.

"It means we're in combat assembly. That's when you want to be very alert. You never know when those Krauts might attack."

The night seemed to go on endlessly, but mercifully Frankie slept for most of it. The fighting had stopped by morning, and Charlie had gotten very little sleep. All he could think about the whole night through was Lillie. He tried to picture them sitting in the garden, but couldn't. It hadn't been that long since they were there together, but everything about home seemed hazy. He couldn't bring her face to his mind. Hugh said it was because his mind was in a bit of shock and had to settle down before he could think clearly again. That sounded right, but how could he forget Lillie's face? He never thought that could be possible, but then again he had never been in a war before. He would have to trust that Hugh was right and hope his mind snapped back soon.

When Frankie woke, it was quiet, certainly better than the day before. Charlie was starving and waited impatiently for the food to arrive. The cooks were preparing the food behind the lines so it could be packed up and sent to the front. By the time they got it, it was no longer hot, but it was food. They had corned beef and biscuits, which Hugh said they ate often, and canned stew as well. After breakfast, Charlie watched Hugh and some of the other guys take candles and cigars and run the flame along the seams of their clothing. Hugh noticed Charlie watching them and held up his shirt.

"It kills the lice, but not the eggs. So it'll be better for today, but we'll just have to do it again tomorrow."

Just then John jumped up and yelled.

"What the hell is that?" Charlie grabbed his friend and yanked him down.

"John! Get down. Are you crazy? Didn't you listen to what Hugh said?"

"I know, Charlie, but what is that?" John pointed at something scurrying along the wall of the trench. It was almost the size of a cat, but it didn't move like one.

"Oh, that's a rat." Hugh pointed at the creature, which kept running.

"A rat? More like a horse! That's the biggest rat I've ever seen." John crossed his arms and sat with his back to the trench wall. There wasn't much else to do that day but sit and wait and try not to become too anxious with the silence. Frankie had sat up and joined the conversation around midday, and when dinner came he ate his entire meal, to Charlie's relief. The guys tried to look down the trenches to see if they could find Jason and Luke, but they were nowhere in sight. They hoped later they would be part of the incoming men, either from battle or just lost and wandering in.

The rats were worse at night. They hadn't noticed the night before because they were still in shock, but they definitely saw them that night. And they were everywhere. At night, if you were lucky enough to fall asleep, you were often rudely awakened by a set of tiny feet running across your face. But the rats were far from the worst that could happen to them. Hugh told them about how after battle, sometimes the men wounded in the field became tangled up in the barbed wire that had been set up as a barrier between the Germans and the Allies.

"To go out and do a rescue is insanity. It's very dangerous, with the dark being the blackest you can imagine. Leaving means getting killed or worse, getting stuck out there yourself. You can hear the stranded moaning through the night, with the rats hungry and nibbling at their flesh. And if that isn't enough for you to cry for mum, there are the gases...

"Phosgene gas creeps over the ground, and the effects come on slowly. First your eyes and throat burn, then your lungs start to fill with liquid, and finally after about forty-eight hours of drowning slowly, you die. Mustard gas is just as brutal when it comes to death, but it takes much longer to kill you. Most blokes exposed at a lethal level can take up to four or five weeks to die in sheer agony. The Krauts are a sneaky bunch. They shoot the gas over to our side when the temperature falls. Initially it's a brown liquid that encases the skin within minutes. Most men run into the tunnels of the trenches to avoid further dousing. Once inside, the temperature rises and turns the liquid into gas, covering every poor bloke in its radius. It's a sight so horrible you hope you never, and I repeat never, have to witness."

The guys just stared at Hugh in silence. No one knew what to say, especially Frankie, who had begun to rock back and forth again.

Days turned into weeks, and life in the trenches was wearing them down. The conditions were cramped outside, and when you were able to go further underground into the tunnels, your stay wouldn't be very long. The tunnels were used primarily by the officers, and it was where the strategies were forged. However, a make-shift shower was constructed, and as primitive as it was, it lifted Charlie's spirits to be clean for a while.

He also wrote to Lillie every week. Daily he waited for the mail and a reply from her, but he hadn't received one yet and began to worry; he had left her so abruptly. Guilt weighed down his shoulders. Could he have pushed her too far? Was it possible he had driven her to someone else's arms—someone who wasn't in the service? The regret rattled him to despair and the absence of letters just escalated it.

***

The next morning started out just like each of the last thirty-five. They knew that at any given moment, the enemy could start bombarding them with mortar and this monotony would end. But that was an alternative no one wanted to have.

At dawn they were in combat assembly, where they were granted a bit of peace and quiet. Breakfast was served while the men told jokes they had heard from the last set of marines who had passed through.

Charlie was laughing heartily and then suddenly stopped, straining his ears. It was a faint, keening whistle coming from the distance and moving in very quickly. He had no time to act. A boom crashed around him. It threw his body several feet. The bodies of the other men were thrust into the sky only to come down like unlucky cards thrown down in a losing bet. It was a sound that shattered the air into pieces, leaving a gaping hole of silence. Complete and total silence.

Charlie looked down at himself and began testing his limbs. He seemed to be fine. Upon sitting, he could see some men trying to get up, some already scrambling, and others just lying immobile on the ground. He was watching their mouths move, but no sound came out. The blast had been so loud it had rendered him temporarily deaf.

He stood and started to search for his buddies, but there was so much confusion he couldn't begin to find them. As he faced forward, he saw several of his fellow soldiers raising their rifles and firing. He grabbed his gun and started shooting over the rim of the trench. The sergeant was motioning to some of them to go over the top, and Charlie was still firing when John came up beside him and just sat down. Charlie was running on adrenaline and instinct and didn't even notice the look on John's face. He just kept firing until one of the other guys came over and pulled him away to stop. He slid down the trench with his back up against the wall.

As he started to look around, he saw only disaster. The bodies of dead soldiers were everywhere, scattered broken dolls and streaming blood, red and thick. Of those that lived, Charlie could see their mouths opening and screaming in agony, but he was almost thankful he couldn't hear a thing or move to action.

John was not moving either, but where was Frankie? Charlie tapped on John's shoulder.

"Frankie—did you see him?" John just shook his head yes, and then Charlie saw the flood of tears streaming down his face. Charlie began shaking him. "John, where is he?"

John pointed to a soldier lying in the mud about fifteen feet away, unmoving and covered in blood. Both of his legs were gone and a large piece of shrapnel was lodged in the side of his head.

"John, are you saying that the poor bastard over there is Frankie?" Charlie ran over to the dead soldier, and when he reached him, he dropped to his knees and sobbed, watching the other soldiers piling the dead in a mass grave. They took off their dog tags and other personal belongings, holding on to them so they could be sent home for their families. The soldiers had come over and started to pick up Frankie, but Charlie jumped up and stopped them.

"Don't touch him! You take your hands off him. I'll do this." He scrambled to his feet, pulled off Frankie's dog tags and removed what was in his pockets. What he found was the true Frankie. He had courage, he had a heart, and certainly he had a fine brain. He displayed all the traits of his friends from the tiny book wedged tightly in his back pocket: *The Wonderful Wizard of Oz*.

"Frankie loved this book," Charlie said, half crying and half chuckling as he grabbed Frankie's St. Christopher medal and a letter from his sister. He rubbed the blood off of his face and wrapped Frankie's belongings in a hanky.

Then, as with all the other boys that were killed that day, and thousands of miles away from home, Frankie Dalo was laid to rest in a mass grave in a foreign country.

Chapter Twenty-Three

It had been three months since Charlie left home, and Lillie had written him faithfully every week. She had received a few letters from him, but from the contents she knew he must not have received any of hers. The last letter he'd written was filled with despair. Usually he tried not to be so serious, but this letter was different. She felt helpless. He was so far away and there was nothing she could do. Perhaps if he had gotten her letters, he might have something to hold on to.

She decided to speak with her dad. James knew a great deal of people, many of them influential. Maybe he could find out what had happened to her letters.

She could hardly wait for her father to arrive home after work. As soon as he entered the house, she dragged him into his study. She explained about her letters not reaching Charlie and began to read him his last letter. He agreed that Charlie needed to be in touch with his life at home and that what he wrote in this letter mentioned nothing of what he knew he would be missing. James promised Lillie he would look into it and see what he could do.

Several more days went by, and Lillie hadn't heard anything from her dad yet about her letters. She was restless and depressed. She knew Charlie was in trouble and there wasn't a darn thing she could do about it! Needing a distraction from her pain, Lillie phoned Claire and the two girls went out for something to eat. When they arrived at the diner, Hanna was there having dinner with a few of hers friends from the campaign.

"Claire, go over and say hello to her." Lillie gave Claire a little shove. Claire frowned, but went over to Hanna's table. Hanna introduced Claire to her friends, and they chatted a few minutes before Claire left and sat down with Lillie.

"So, what happened? Was your conversation with her awkward?" Lillie whispered.

"She seemed fine. She even asked me to join her for lunch on Friday and I agreed. I do want Hanna to know we are still friends, and it just seemed like the right thing to do."

"It was the perfect thing to do. You are a good friend, Claire. Hanna's lucky to have you and so am I."

"You can stop being mushy. What's been going on with Charlie? Any news from your dad yet?"

Lillie gazed out the window at the children playing outside. "No, he hasn't said a word. I'm so scared, Claire. Charlie's in a bad way, I can feel it. Not having any word from home must be torturing him. I just want to scream at the top of my lungs. This horrible, horrible war! Just as we fell in love with each other, he's taken away from me. I know I sound like a selfish child, and I do understand serving your country, but I don't think he realizes how much we are all still here, waiting on and missing him. Imagine letters coming every day and not one of them being for you. He must be lost." Her eyes were heavy with tears.

"Why don't we go find your dad after dinner and see if he's made any progress? And if he hasn't, tomorrow morning we'll go talk to the recruitment office in town. Perhaps they can offer us help." Claire rubbed Lillie's hand. "Don't worry, Lils. We'll find a way. He'll know; we'll make sure of it."

Lillie gave Claire an encouraging smile as the waitress came and took their order.

After dinner, the girls went back to Lillie's house and found James in the kitchen, stealing a piece of leftover cherry pie.

"Lillie, I was looking for you. I have some news you'll be interested in hearing."

"Is it about Charlie? Did they find my letters?"

"Partially. It seems it wasn't just your letters that weren't getting through. The same thing was happening to many of the other soldiers in that area of Europe. Several weeks of letters were delivered to the wrong platoon. It's taken them a few weeks to sort out the problem, but they told me that all the mail is finally being routed to the correct destination. Charlie should receive all the back letters you've written to him. They also said your letters should be getting through fine now, but you know darling, that depends on the conditions."

"I know. Thank you, Dad. I knew you could do it." Lillie gave her father a big hug.

"Now, wait a minute. I didn't do anything. I'm just the messenger."

"I don't believe you. You worked a little of your Whitman magic and don't try to deny it. I know better."

"If my daughter thinks I'm magical, who am I to argue? This is good news, though. It should give Charlie hope again, knowing you are indeed waiting for him."

Lillie and Claire walked out to the garden and sat on the bench in front of the fire thorns. Lillie closed her eyes. *I'm here, my Charlie, and I'm waiting. However long you take, I'll be here.*

***

That Friday, Claire went to lunch with Hanna. Everything went smoothly. Hanna seemed to be her vibrant, wonderful self, and Claire breathed a sigh of relief that everything had gone back to normal. Hanna even asked Claire if she would accompany her to the florist. One of her friends had taken ill and Hanna wanted to bring her flowers. Claire agreed and the girls strolled over to Wilson Flowers.

"How are you and Bastian? Is he treating you well?"

Claire wondered where this was going. "Yes, he treats me well. Excellently, in fact. I love him because he's the best kind of man for me. He loves me for who I truly am. He doesn't question my character or feel threatened by my academic and career pursuits. And most importantly, he doesn't harp on the subject of marriage. We both know we want to be with each other for the rest of our lives, but at this time we are not quite ready." Claire was pleased with her response to Hanna.

"I'm not sure I understand. You say that you love him, that you want to spend the rest of your life with him, but you don't want it to begin right now...Can you be certain what you're feeling is love? I don't understand postponing or putting love on a schedule. Shouldn't sharing your love and being together every day be the priority?"

Claire let out a screech and then huffed. With a closed fist, she thumped the table. It was enough trying to explain how she felt to her mother, but to Hanna, this was ridiculous. Why was she saying such things? Didn't she know it would upset her? Then Claire thought, *Wait a minute.*

"I know what you're trying to do Hanna, and it's not going to work. Not only will I never doubt my feelings for Bastian, I will never doubt the woman that I am to him. And quite frankly, it's none of your business. I wanted to mend and continue on with our friendship, but that you question the love between Bastian and me is all wrong. I can't believe how intentionally mean you are being! Well, I guess you're truly not my friend after all, which of course means I can't be yours. Now go pick out your own damn flowers." Claire stormed off toward home, leaving a speechless Hanna behind.

***

It was early in the evening, and Lillie and James had just finished with supper. He had work to do, and Lillie wanted to get a start on writing her latest letter to Charlie. It was so peaceful at this time of the day. Gathering her stationary and ink, she went out to the garden. It always made her feel that much closer to Charlie. She had only been there for a few moments when one of the housekeepers, Lenore, came out to tell her that Hanna Pittman had come to pay a visit.

Lenore brought Hanna out to the garden and she sat down next to Lillie on the bench. Lillie was curious and somewhat apprehensive. What could she possibly want to talk with her about? She knew Claire had lunch with her earlier, but she hadn't yet heard back from Claire. She took that to be a good sign that all had gone well.

"Your garden is beyond words."

Lillie smiled. "Thank you, Hanna. I am happy you came for a visit today, but is there something you may need from me, or my father perhaps?"

"Did you know I had lunch with Claire today?"

"She told me she was meeting with you. Did something happen?" Lillie was fiddling with the edges of paper.

"Yes, she's fine. It's just that, well, she is extremely angry with me and I don't know what to do. I apparently said something hurtful towards her, but for the life of me, I don't know what it could be. I've reviewed our lunch together over and over in my mind. That's why I'm here. Lillie, I haven't been friends with you very long, but I need you. You're the only one who knows Claire well enough."

"Let's start from the beginning. Tell me everything that happened today."

Hanna explained everything to Lillie while she intently listened.

"Now I understand what happened today. Claire is very different than most women. She stands up for herself and others without a thought to convention, and constantly tests the barriers put up by society. Some people—men, mostly—aren't comfortable with that. Over the years, Claire has had to put up with their foolish innuendos and whispered slurs, yet she has managed to forge ahead and stay strong. But when you approached her today, I think it caught her off balance. You questioned how and why she loves Bastian. And that my dear, is not acceptable to her."

Lillie smiled, knowing how stubborn her friend could be. "Bastian makes her feel feminine despite what others have considered her excessive boldness. He appreciates all the qualities that she has had to suppress in order to be taken seriously in what is unfortunately still a man's world. When you invited her to lunch, she accepted, thinking it would be the perfect way to repair your friendship. But unknowingly you pushed her away by not trusting in their love for each other. Can't you see, especially you, Hanna, that for a woman to truly be herself in this day and age is nearly impossible? Bastian is the kind of man that will not be threatened by her. Rather, he's the opposite. He loves her even more for her independence, and you attacked that very security he gives her."

"Lillie, I never wanted to hurt her. I have, well, I don't know how to say this, but I..."

"I know, Hanna. Claire told me, and I know you would never want to hurt her."

"How will she ever forgive me?" Hanna put her head in her hands and started to cry. Lillie put her arms around Hanna and held her for a few minutes until she had calmed down. "Lillie, what am I going to do? I don't want to lose her friendship."

"Don't worry. She's upset now, but we'll talk with her tomorrow."

"We'll speak with her? Oh, I don't know, Lillie. I don't think she wants anything to do with me. Can you try speaking with her first and then we can all talk after?"

Lillie hesitated, but then realized that it might be a better idea to talk with her first as Hanna had suggested. "I'll ring her in the morning and then later we'll stop by your house. It'll be fine, you'll see. Once she calms down, she will forgive you. I just know it. Claire has a heart bigger than anyone else I know."

Lillie didn't have to wait until the next morning to fix her friend's relationship. Lenore came into the living room to tell her Claire was on the telephone. Lillie took a deep breath and took the phone. After several minutes of listening to Claire's version of the story, Lillie asked if she would come over and speak with her in person. Claire sounded perplexed, but agreed and told her she'd be over in few minutes. Lillie would have gone over to Claire's house, but she knew they would never have any privacy with Mrs. Dumont hanging on to ever word spoken. Honestly, Lillie thought it was out of sheer boredom that she eavesdropped and was a bit of a gossip, but nonetheless, this wasn't a subject for her mother's ears.

She prepared tea and placed the freshly baked cookies on a tray. A little sugar could go a long way in sweetening the difficult visit. She brought them up to her bedroom and waited for Claire to arrive. She mouthed the words she would say to Claire about Hanna and genuinely hoped that practice made perfect, as the saying went. Words had to be chosen wisely; if Claire felt even remotely "ganged up on," she could become hot-headed. The last thing Lillie wanted was to make matters any worse.

Just then, Claire's feet pounded up her steps. As she entered the room, Lillie could see she had been crying. Claire sat down on the bed as Lillie began to pour the tea.

"I'm here, but for the life of me, I don't know why. What was so important that we speak in person?"

"I'm going to say things that you may or may not want to hear, but whatever I tell you, I want you to promise not to leave in a huff. Are we clear on this matter?"

"What's going on here?"

Lillie stood up and paced about the room. "Hanna came to see me earlier this evening and we spoke about what happened today."

"What? Hanna came here, and you spoke with her?

How could you? Lillie, did she tell you what she did? I never want to see her again."

"Calm down. I understand why you're so angry, but she really feels awful and wants to apologize. She doesn't want to lose your friendship."

"Too late!"

"Claire, I know you're better than that. You believe people deserve second chances. She knows what she did was wrong and she is sincerely remorseful. You should have seen her. She was so distraught. I know what she said was terrible and her motive, whether it was a conscious one or not, was equally as bad, but what would you do if you truly loved someone and they didn't return those feelings? She's asking for you to just hear her out."

After her emotions settled down, Claire agreed to meet with Hanna the following afternoon. Lillie could finally take a deep breath. Her work for today was done. Sometimes friendships could be very challenging, but in her heart she knew Claire would be open for discussion.

***

They decided on Hanna's house at two o'clock. Claire needed Lillie at her side from start to finish and was grateful for her ability to drive. When she drove up to Lillie's house, Lillie was already waiting on her porch for the short trip over to Hanna's.

As soon as Claire stepped through Hanna's front door, her body stiffened with anger. This was not going to be easy, but out of respect for the friendship she had shared with Hanna, she would listen to what the other girl had to say.

At first it was hard to sit quietly and allow Hanna her explanation, but eventually, Claire settled in, knowing there was no other way of dealing with their differences. She could see in Hanna's eyes that her remorse was genuine, and when she admitted that maybe her motives had been selfish, Claire was surprised by her honesty. That took true courage. She was beginning to feel the hard edges of her heart soften. When all was said and done, she stood up and walked to the other side of the dining room. She sat on one of the side chairs and rested her elbows on her knees, her chin in her hands.

"Hanna, I respect that you were honest with me. What I don't appreciate is that you would hurt me for your own gain, but once again, I thank you for your honesty." Claire looked up at Lillie, then to Hanna. "You asked me, Lils, what I would do if I felt that way for someone and they didn't return the feelings? And my answer, my honest answer, is *I don't know*. So, Hanna, I don't agree with what you did, but I do understand it. You are my friend, and I would like to remain friends, but you need to understand that we will never be anything else. I love Bastian, and even if I didn't have him in my life, I could not return the same type of feelings you have for me."

Hanna smiled broadly and wiped the tears from her eyes. "I understand, I do, and I am so sorry, Claire. Truly, I am. It will never happen again. To have your friendship is more than enough for me. I will never take advantage of that again, ever."

They both walked towards each other with arms extended. In the hug they gave each other was the promise of a friendship that would last the rest of their lives.

Bastian was waiting in the front of Claire's house when she arrived home. His arms were crossed tightly over his chest and he was pacing along the bottom step. He looked up and his cheeks were stained with dried tears.

Oh no. What now?

Chapter Twenty-Four

Charlie awoke to another day without a message from home. It had been so long since he had heard Lillie's voice or looked into her loving eyes. If he would just get a letter...Something must be wrong. She wouldn't do this intentionally. There has to be a reason she hadn't written to him, but what? What if something terrible had happened? He would have no way of knowing. What if she needed him? He had been foolish to leave her. What had he been thinking?

"Charlie, Charlie," John was yelling at him. "They're here. Jason and Luke are here!"

Charlie looked up and saw Jason coming down the trench with Luke right behind him. He got up and ran to his friends. The boys all hugged and patted each other on the back.

"We didn't know what happened to you guys. We had no idea if you had made it here or not. Everything has been so insane. Where have you been?" Charlie was rambling. He couldn't believe his friends were actually there.

"When we first started out on the convoy, our truck was struck by mortar and we had to make a run for it. We ended up in a trench due east of here. Our captain moved us down here because we got word the Germans might be planning an all-out attack and they wanted reinforcements," said Jason. "Hey, where's Frankie? Don't tell me he's down in the tunnels taking it easy on some cot. When I see him I'm going to give him hell for not being out here!"

Jason laughed and then looked at the expressions on John's and Charlie's faces. "Seriously, where's Frankie? Guys?" Charlie put his head down. "Now you're officially scaring me. He's okay, right?" Jason shoved Charlie. "Where is he?"

Charlie looked down at the ground and whispered,

"He's gone. Frankie's gone."

"What? No! Come on, not Frankie." Jason gasped for breath as Charlie told him about the attack and the bombing. Charlie was kind and left out the part about their friend being blown apart.

Jason collapsed on the floor. He and started to cry and the other guys sat with him for a few minutes in silence.

"Frankie was such a good guy. He never hurt anyone. He came here to help and fight with his buddies to defend his country. We never thought it would happen to one of us, not really. What will we tell his mom?" Jason was trying to stop his tears.

John tapped his helmet. "We'll tell her and the rest of his family what he wanted us to tell them. We'll tell them he died fighting to protect them and everyone else back home. That's exactly what we'll tell them." The others nodded in agreement as they sat waiting for the night to come. There was always the possibility of another attack and the reality of losing another friend.

The darkness came on suddenly. The quiet of the calm night air hovered around them, giving a feeling of uneasiness. Every man was in combat assembly and waiting. No one knew if the Germans would attack or when, but everyone would be ready if they did.

The glow of the stars made the sky almost look peaceful. It was as if they were back home and sitting on the front porch of Charlie's house. Any minute, Mr. Russo would come out to sneak a puff or two of his cigar while Mrs. Russo was fast asleep on the sofa. Sometimes a moment could feel so normal, but then with one look around came the reality that there was nothing normal about this. Just listening to a few men praying, or with many of the others frozen in silence, snapped a soldier right back to where he was: sitting in a deep ditch and hoping against hope that his time wasn't up yet.

Later on in the evening, everyone allowed themselves to relax, but not too much: a soldier always had to be alert. It had been calm and they couldn't hear any movement from the other side. A few men were ordered to scout around beyond the trench, but they found nothing new to report.

Charlie leaned in close to John. "Hey, do you have my letter to Lillie?"

"Yeah, buddy, right here in my pocket."

"Thanks. Just checking."

"Nothing's gonna happen to you, Charlie. Nothing!"

Charlie knew his friend's words were just meant to comfort him. There was no way any of them could be sure.

***

The temperature had dropped since early evening and they could see their breath in the air. Every soldier was rubbing his hands together to stay warm when coffee arrived from the ramshackle kitchen they had constructed in the tunnels. The grumpy cook had a heart after all.

The night lingered on, and when they saw the first flicker of dawn, they thought they had made it through without an attack. Charlie was about to tell a story he had remembered about Frankie when they began to hear the now-familiar popping exchange of gunfire.

Then all hell broke loose.

The men scrambled, positioning themselves and their rifles to fire back. The captain was ordering men to go over the top and fight. Charlie cautiously peered up to look at the battlefield and was horrified at the sight. Soldiers were dying where they stood, some having to witness pieces of their own bodies scattered on the ground. There was a chorus of screams and continuous fire. The boom from the shells was deafening. Everywhere he looked was chaos.

Charlie took position and started to fire. Once he started, he couldn't stop; he shot off round after round in a mad frenzy. There was only one thing he could focus on: killing. With each loud pop and recoil of his body, he thought, *This is for Frankie.* His friend was gone, his face unrecognizable, his body damaged and re-arranged from this hell of a war. No, Charlie couldn't bring him back, but he could make damn certain he'd take down as many of the enemy as possible.

Charlie saw men frantically running and jumping into the trenches, covered in brown liquid and yelling as they ran down into the tunnels. The officers and soldiers, the many wounded, and the one cook were all tightly packed in, waiting for what was coming next. Constantly exploding shells competed with screaming rifle fire, making it impossible to hear anything. And so Charlie didn't hear the twenty soldiers and officers who emerged from the underground tunnels until they plowed into his body, furiously hacking and coughing and grabbing at their swollen eyes. The soldiers were covered in mustard gas. Anyone inhaling the toxic fumes was a dead man. There was nothing anyone could do other than rounding up the victims, keeping them calm and getting them sent to the nearest hospital behind the lines. This had been the first war that such horrible weapons were unleashed. Who could have been prepared? After the quickly rising body count, the answer was clear: no one.

Later that brutal morning, the Germans sent rounds of another poisonous gas toward the men fighting in the fields: phosgene gas. The wind seemed to be blowing in their favor when the Germans made their decision to do douse the Americans, French, and British with this treacherous and merciless killer.

Then something happened that neither side could have planned on nor known was coming: after the Germans fired their artillery filled with the poison, suddenly there was a shift in the wind. When the shells holding the gas landed and exploded, the cloud of gas that was crawling along the ground reversed. The enemy was about to be poisoned by its own hand. Everyone could hear the screams of pain and chaos coming from the other side.

Charlie looked on in disbelief. It was not only the gas that was killing the enemy, but artillery and ground fire as well. Bodies from both sides were dispersed across the field, separating the two trenches. The field swam in a thick, life-sucking clay that looked as if it came from the from the devil's workshop, with its deep rivulets of blood turning the ground a murky reddish-brown. Bodies were fractured, blown apart, or hanging from tree branches. Many soldiers moaned or begged to be killed, lying on the ground, their bodies no longer whole. As Charlie looked on in horror, he thought, *This must be what hell looks like, because nothing here could come from God.*

The captain waited until most of the gas had dissipated and called for volunteers to go over the top. Any time a soldier was to "go over the top," there was a good chance he wasn't coming back. He was out there face-to-face and in the open without the protective shroud of the trench. His chances for survival were slim. Sometimes this was the only way to gain ground and push the enemy back. Most of the time, the orders were just to go, but given the recent events, this time the captain preferred to have volunteers who chose their fate.

Charlie couldn't stay in the trench any longer. He needed to be out in the open and fighting. He needed to feel adrenaline surge through his body to confirm that he was alive. All the death and destruction surrounding him made him feel as if he were already dead, the kind of death that didn't come from poison gas or gunfire, but from the defeat within. But he couldn't just sit and wait trying to guess when they might finally overtake their hold; he had to move *now*...even if it meant confronting the enemy up close and very personally.

"John, I'm going to tell the captain I'll go over."

"What? Damn it, Charlie, are you crazy? Do you see what's going on out there? Those guys who left, they're not coming back. You can't do this. Think of Lillie."

"I have, but right now I have to think of everyone here. They need me. Someone needs to stop this madness. We can't keep going on like this. How long do you think we'll be here? Look at those poor guys." Charlie pointed to the British and French soldiers. "How long do you think they thought this would last? Do you really think they expected to be here for three years? No! I'm sorry, John, but this is something I have to do. I'm dying inside anyway. I'm going."

He got up and told the captain, who nodded for him to join the other men who were preparing to go. Charlie was checking his pockets and pulled out the knife and compass that Lillie had given him. He kissed them both before slipping them back in. Then he saw Jason running over to him.

"Charlie, you've got to rethink this. You can't go. I know you're going screwy here—we all are—but this is suicide!"

"Thanks, Jason, I really needed the pep talk."

"This isn't even close to being funny!"

"I'm not laughing, and I'm still going."

"Then I'm going too."

"Now who's being crazy? This isn't what you want; don't do this just because you feel like you have to stick by me. Think. John and Luke need you. Please take care of them, okay?" Charlie gave his friend a quick hug and a bump on the helmet.

"Charlie, come back to us, okay?"

"I'm gonna try my best. But if I don't, make sure John gives Lillie my letter, okay?"

"I will, but you'll be giving it her yourself."

Charlie smiled and then looked back at John and Luke, who were staring in disbelief. He waved to them and they nodded in return. There was one last thing to do. He closed his eyes so he could hold the picture of them in his mind as he got up and went over the top.

Chapter Twenty-Five

John, Jason, and Luke had been firing at anything that resembled a German soldier, trying to block the constant shelling. Their captain ordered a maneuver down east of the trench, where they needed the extra firepower. Jason loaded all his ammunition and John grabbed another rifle from a dead soldier. Luke moved with the two boys, following closely, when an incoming mortar exploded in a fragmented burst not far from where they stood. They heard the whistling in their ears, and John gave Jason a look of horror before everything went silent.

Jason didn't know how long he had been out, but when he awoke he saw John lying next to him, or at least he thought it was John. The shell had come down directly beside him and torn his body completely apart. There was a partial torso and what looked to be a leg, but nothing else remained. Jason scrambled to his feet and looked around. Maybe he was mistaken. Maybe this wasn't John at all. After all, he couldn't tell who it was with what was left of this body, but then he saw something that proved undeniably it was John. Five feet from him, partially covered in mud and turned upside down, was a helmet with the name John McDougal written inside. Jason dropped to his knees and vomited. Overcome with shock, he lay down in the mud and nearly stopped breathing.

***

Hours later it had quieted down, the enemy having failed once again to gain ground. The men in the trenches were gathering all the dead bodies of their friends and piling them up to be put in a mass grave later. In the confusion, helmets, boots, and other personal belongings that were left were shuffled around. Each dead soldier had to have their pockets cleared and dog tags taken for identification to send back to their loved ones. When they reached the body of one particular young soldier, there were no tags. The private checked what was left of the pockets in his shirt and pulled out a letter, miraculously intact. It had been addressed and sealed.

"Sir, there are no tags on this one, but there is this letter. It's addressed to a Miss Lillie Whitman in Long Island, New York, and it's from a Charlie Murphy."

The captain looked down at the ground and whispered to himself, "Oh, Charlie. I'm sorry, boy. Be happy where you are now. You're safe." Then to the soldier, he said, "I will write the letter to his girl myself. Hand it over, Private."

***

Bastian's older brother, Spencer, had been overseas for a few months now. He had left a few weeks before Charlie and the others. He had been writing to his parents as often as he could, but they hadn't heard from him recently and his parents were beginning to worry. Bastian had been at home when the telegram came for his father:

Dear Mr. Penfield,

We regret to inform you that your son Spencer was killed while engaging in battle. We are deeply sorry for your loss. At this time, take comfort in knowing your son died defending his country and the men who served with him.

Regretfully,
Captain James Kelvey
U.S. Marine Corp.

The body was being shipped home. Spencer would be buried in the family plot at St. Mary's Roman Catholic Church. There were people who actually told the Penfield family that they should consider themselves lucky; some families never saw their loved ones' remains.

What a stoke of good luck that was, Claire thought sarcastically. Bastian lived in the next town over from

Claire, so it didn't taken her long to get there, but by then the entire Penfield family had already arrived. Claire felt awkward, not knowing any of the family, but her concern for Bastian kept her by his side throughout the day. His mother was so grief-stricken by the news that Doc Clarkson had to sedate her, and his sister wasn't doing much better.

Bastian's sister Emily was tall, slender, and blond. Every man in town wanted to be given a chance at dating her, but she only had eyes for one man: David Jameson. David was the complete opposite of what Emily's parents felt she should have in a potential husband, but he treated Emily as if she was the only woman on this planet for him, and she adored him for that. Emily had wanted both her brothers present when she walked down the aisle, and David was more than happy to do anything that made her happy. Now that could never happen.

Claire tried to keep Emily calm while the boys helped Mr. Penfield with the guests. Everyone who had heard the news had dropped by to pay their respects. The crowd grew by the minute. People were bringing food, and Bastian had the housekeeper set up tables in the dining room for the mourners to eat buffet-style. David sat beside Emily, holding her hand and holding her close. Her eyes were red and swollen. Every time she looked like breaking into tears he would gently kiss the top of her head and whisper words of comfort.

Claire looked at the couple and felt sorrow. This should have been one of the happiest moments in their life together, a passionate romance and the promise of marriage, but instead it would be remembered with great pain. Then she looked over at Mr. Penfield. Here was a successful man with a lovely wife and family who adored him, a man who worked hard for his wealth and had turned that into a beautiful home and a thriving business. Yet, for all his good fortune, she was certain he'd trade it all in just for the chance to have his son back safely home, but that was never to be.

The more Claire looked around, the more she thought, *I have been so silly. I've been telling Bastian we need to wait to get married because I'm not ready. But what if I wait too long? What if we miss our chance because I'm being so darn stubborn?*

Bastian sat down next to Claire, breaking her train of thought.

"Bastian, can we go somewhere to talk? It will only take a moment. I wouldn't want to keep you from your family."

Looking puzzled, he stood up and put out his hand. They decided to go outside to the back lawn. The Penfields' garden was smaller and with less blooms than the Whitmans' wide array, but it had a charm and warmth that was all its own. They sat down on a double swing hanging from a giant oak, which gave off a large umbrella of shade on a hot summer's day.

Claire looked into Bastian's eyes and just blurted out what was on her mind. "You must think I'm completely daft, but let's get married. I know my timing is horrible and I am not trying to be disrespectful to your family, or most of all you, but Bastian, I took a look around today and I've been wrong. The time to share a life with you is now. I know I've told you we should wait until I have my career secured, but the truth is that's all a bunch of rubbish. I think I was just being nervous. I've never felt love for another man as I feel for you, and frankly it's been perplexing. I've always known myself as a woman of ambition and intelligence, but now when I think of you, I understand there is so much more to who I am. There will always be time for both. I can be with you completely in heart and still have my career. I finally realize that."

After a pause, Bastian got down on one knee. Claire started to shake as he looked into her eyes and said, "My beautiful, passionate, headstrong Claire, will you make me the happiest man to walk this earth and marry me?"

As he stood up, she threw herself into his arms and kissed him. Each kiss cemented the trust, respect and love they had for each other. And as for passion...that desire was finally allowed to grow untamed.

They both spoke for a while and agreed this would not be the time to announce their engagement. Even though Claire and Bastian knew it would a happy occasion for all, they needed to grieve for Spencer, and his family needed time to heal.

It took a few weeks for Spencer's body to arrive home. His casket was closed and draped with the American flag. The funeral honored Spencer in a way that brought both tears of pride and sorrow to everyone there. Afterward, family and friends gathered at Spencer's favorite Italian restaurant.

Claire was filled with mixed emotions. Part of her was grieving for Bastian and his family, but the other part of her was bursting with the secret of their wedding plans. She felt guilty for having this happiness at such a solemn occasion, but she knew the proper time would come soon to tell his family. They had agreed to wait and she would never break that promise. She hadn't even told Lillie. As somber as dinner was, it still warmed her heart to be with Bastian's family. She enjoyed their company and was thankful they all got along so well even through this trying time. Even David seemed to fit in despite the initial coldness of Bastian's family.

After dinner, Bastian brought Claire home and lingered at her front door. Today had been extremely emotional, and the kiss he gave her told its own story: intimate, passionate, and filled with a deep love. Claire's legs threatened to collapse. As she entered her house, she stumbled a bit and Bastian caught her. Once again she swooned, and she quickly hugged him and closed the door.

Claire pressed up against it and took a moment to

close her eyes and feel that last kiss a moment longer. Then she ran into the kitchen to ring Lillie. She couldn't tell her about the engagement, but she could certainly tell her about that kiss!

***

Lillie was enjoying her work at the hospital. Lately, volunteering was the only thing that got her through her day without thinking of Charlie every minute. At least with volunteering, she only had to think of him only every other minute. The work was hard but very rewarding; she enjoyed reading to the soldiers who came back wounded, and she especially liked it when she could write their letters for them. They felt better knowing their loved ones were connected in some way, and Lillie felt closer to Charlie being around them.

Lillie was sitting with one of the soldiers when she heard a loud commotion come from the hallway. She jumped up and ran to see what was happening and couldn't believe her eyes. The floor was lined from head-to-toe and shoulder-to-elbow with injured people. There had been an accident at a large construction site on the outskirts of town. Being short-staffed that day, the head nurse had the receptionist try and ring every person she thought could help.

The resident doctor struggled to attend to everyone. The nurses were trying to calm the victims that were conscious and move the ones that weren't. Fortunately, there was a young visiting doctor on call as well that day, and he worked very hard to keep up with the seasoned resident, yet he was clearly overwhelmed.

Lillie dashed over to him to see if there was any way she could help. She hadn't gone to a school for nursing, but she had learned a few essentials working with the staff each day. She grabbed a tray and stocked it with the medical basics: scissors, gauze, tape, saline, peroxide, alcohol, cotton balls, and a local anesthetic with syringes and sutures. Then she stood beside him, making sure he had what he needed for each patient.

After what seemed like hours, other staff members finally started to come in. Lillie saw that her help was no longer needed and went to the bathroom to clean up. When she came out, the young doctor was waiting for her.

"Hello, I don't think we formally met. I'm Doctor Fredrick Miller. I want to thank you for coming to my rescue today. I must admit, that was the first time I have been in such chaos."

Lillie smiled. "You're welcome. I'm Lillie Whitman. It's a pleasure to meet you."

"Well, Miss Whitman...It is Miss, isn't it?"

"Yes, it is."

"Well then, thanks again and have a good evening."

"You too."

Lillie watched the doctor walk down the hall and thought, *Evening? How long have I been here?* When she finally looked at the clock behind the front desk, it was seven p.m. *Twelve hours!* No wonder she was exhausted. When she got home, the cook had saved dinner for her, but she was too tired to eat and went straight to bed. James knocked on her door just as she was settling under the covers.

"Lillie, honey, can I come in?"

"Sure, Dad."

James came in and sat on the edge of her bed. "Honey, you were at the hospital for a long time today. Is everything all right?"

"There was a large construction accident outside of town, and there wasn't enough help to go around, so I stayed. I had no idea how long I'd been there, though, and I'm so tired."

"I see. I was just concerned. I'm very proud of you and how much you want to help, but promise me you'll attempt do other things. Spending every day in a hospital for twelve hours is not the life for a young woman, all right?"

"I promise. Don't worry. I'm fine, but very tired, so can I get some sleep now?"

James chuckled. "Good night, my sweet daughter."

Lillie decided to go in a little later the next day. She spent her morning in the garden, where she could do her own healing from yesterday's shift at the hospital. Life had been so hectic lately and she hadn't been out for a visit in a while. Maybe part of her was avoiding it; the last thing she had wanted lately was time to think about what the garden meant to her and Charlie. But today she needed the sanctuary it provided her. Yesterday had been a glimpse into complete chaos.

Was that what Charlie is experiencing right now? She could only wonder. Her heart ached at not knowing where he was or if he was safe. Her imagination could be such a cruel tool. She looked over at the fire thorns. They were growing so close, but they weren't touching just yet.

Lenore came and brought her a blanket. Lillie hadn't even noticed it had grown colder.

"Thank you, Lenore.

"You're welcome, ma'am. Is there anything else you require?"

"Yes, actually, there is."

"Ma'am?"

"Would you be so kind as to sit with me for a moment? I could use the company."

Lenore looked surprised but sat next to Lillie on the bench. "Ma'am, would you mind if I spoke what was on my mind?"

"No, not at all. I would appreciate it if you did."

"Ma'am, I've known you since before you were born. You are so much like your mother beautiful just like her, but also extremely sensitive and caring. Maybe a little too caring. Sometimes we have to learn to let go because if you don't, you can become consumed with worry and you miss everything else.

"Now, I'm not saying to forget Charlie and the danger he must be facing, but know he is loved by you and that will give him the strength he needs. And you must wait for him with hope and the thought that you will be together again someday soon. He needs that from you, and you need it for yourself. You know your mother always worried about you and your father; she loved you both so much. But too much worry can get in the way sometimes, and when she grew ill I think she realized that. When she let go and decided to enjoy all your moments together and the precious memories you made along the way, it was then that she had truly lived, even if it was for only a short time."

Lillie smiled warmly and patted her hand. Lenore had always been such a comfort to her all these years, and today was no different. The women sat there for a while before the cold forced them to retreat inside.

***

Lillie arrived at the hospital mid-afternoon. There were new arrivals that had been shipped home from France that needed her attention. Gathering a few books, pens and several pads of paper, she went to go see them. While she was at the nurse's desk, Doctor Miller came over to say hello. Lillie didn't hear his approach and jumped as he startled her.

"Miss Whitman, I'm sorry. It seems I've frightened you."

"No, I'm fine. I just didn't hear you coming. I suppose I was deep in thought. There seem to be several new boys back from battle."

"I'm afraid so. They wound them and we patch them up, or so we try. I fear there are some that we won't be able to put back together."

"I don't think I understand what you mean."

"What I'm trying to say is that some of the boys that come back have more than just injuries to their bodies. There are the injuries of the mind, and those I can't heal. I know there are doctors, psychiatrists, who attempt it, but there is still so much we don't know yet about the human brain. Some of these boys are lost to us forever. One of the new boys is such a case. He arrived late last night and we've patched his bodily wounds, but he hasn't said a word. I've sent a telegram to Doctor Williams in Manhattan; he is supposed to be very skilled in his field of psychiatry. He rang me this morning and will arrive in two days. This unfortunate boy is catatonic; he's not just silent, he's gone. Whatever horror he witnessed has gripped the very core of him and won't let go."

Tears filled Lillie's eyes and she tried to keep her composure in front of the doctor. "Which room is he in? Maybe I could go and read to him."

"That would be lovely, Miss Whitman. Let me double check." Doctor Miller grabbed the charts for the new arrivals and flipped through it. "Lillie, I would like to ask you...Well, I'm new to this town and I don't really know anyone outside of the hospital. I was wondering if you might... if you might have dinner with me some night?"

Lillie's face flushed and her palms began to sweat. As men went, Doctor Miller was handsome and seemed to be very kind and caring toward his patients, but there wasn't anyone who could fill the void of Charlie's absence, and honestly, she wasn't looking for it to be filled.

"Thank you for such a kind offer, Doctor Miller, but I'm afraid I must decline. I am waiting for my own soldier to return and I couldn't possibly consider..."

"I understand. Let's find you that room number. Here it is. He is in room number forty-nine and his name is Jason Chambers." Lillie grew white and put her hand over her mouth as if she were getting ready to vomit. "Miss

Whitman—Lillie—what is it? Are you all right?"

Lillie looked up at the doctor through tear-filled eyes. "I know him. I... know that boy."

Then she turned and ran down the hall, headed for room forty-nine.

Chapter Twenty-Six

Charlie Murphy was running faster than he thought possible. Everywhere he looked there were bodies, and the yelling—they were the wails of the damned. Some men surrounded him, shooting, while others were also trying to avoid the incoming bullets. But most frightening of all were the soldiers who wandered in a blank haze, unaware of the flying bullets or any form of attack. He'd barely finished high school a few months ago—how could life change so much in such a short time? His days of comfort in Long Island, New York had come to an end. He could only hope it wasn't permanent.

Charlie could not stop to help; he searched for life-saving cover and waited to advance on the enemy. He spotted a disabled truck a few yards away. He dodged and dropped, trying to keep low. When he got there he was frightened; his adrenaline was in overdrive and he was short of breath. He lay on the ground, furiously searching through the haze of apocalyptic chaos.

What he didn't notice were the three German soldiers still trapped under the truck, or their buddies, who were running his way to see if they could release them. A patch of land to his left seemed clear. Cautiously he got up and looked around before firing. As he pivoted, he heard a hailstorm of fire and something incredibly hot hit his chest.

He looked down. A pool of red seeped through the hole in his shirt. He had been shot. He grabbed his chest and tried to keep running, but the mud was slippery. Pain seared through his body and consumed him, a branding iron pressed against the gaping hole in his flesh. He fumbled through the pocket in his coat for the compass. His hand clasped it, squeezing it tight and close to his body.

Collapsing, he sank into the mud. His eyes, clear of the muck, looked skyward, where he thought he saw Lillie's face. The very last thing Charlie could remember was the hazy vision of the woman he loved and the compass that would get him home. Then his world went completely black.

***

When Charlie opened his eyes, it seemed he was in a hospital, but none like he had ever seen before. The room was a large tent lined with cots filled with injured soldiers. His throat was dry and burned when he tried to speak; there was little to nothing left of his voice. He struggled to get up, but a nurse came over and laid him back down. She was speaking in another language, perhaps French.

Another woman in a white uniform came over to him and said, "Okay, soldier, you have to lie still. That's a nasty shot you took to the chest. You're lucky to be alive." Once again, Charlie struggled to speak. "Don't try to speak. Your throat is parched. I'll go get water to try and fix that. In the meantime, you have to rest so you can get well."

Charlie looked up at her face. She had kind eyes and a warm smile. She was much older than the other woman, but he could tell she had been very beautiful in her younger days. Her silver hair was neat and perfectly styled, her uniform crisper and whiter than most of the other nurses' uniforms. He tried to give her a smile, but the corners of his mouth cracked painfully and he could only nod instead. In a few minutes, another young nurse brought the water and a thick lotion to rub around his mouth. He drank a few sips and felt better. After several small glasses of water he could muster up a few words. "Where...am I?"

The older nurse was fixing his blankets and bed sheets and came over and sat down beside him. "You're in a hospital in Basoilles. You were very lucky your friend found you in time. You could have bled to death out there or been captured."

Charlie was confused. "My friend? What friend?"

"Why, the one that rode here with you. He insisted on staying with you, wouldn't let anyone else bring you here. He needed to check in, but he'll be back shortly. Now

I've told you, what you need is rest."

"But..."

"No buts. You must rest." Although she was warm and attentive, he could see that she meant business. Charlie kept that in mind as he turned his head and went back to sleep.

***

Charlie stirred awake. He opened his eyes and saw a nurse standing beside his cot, holding a few large pills for him to swallow. She gave them to him with a glass of water while another brought soup. They propped a few pillows behind him and fed the soup to him with a spoon. It was hot, and it felt good to eat something that didn't come out of a can.

"You're looking a little better today. Your friend came by, but you were fast asleep, so he said he'd see you a little later."

"How long was I out for?"

"Well, that was yesterday morning, and it is now three o'clock in the afternoon, so a little over a day."

"Over a day. It felt like I closed my eyes for only a few minutes." A whole day had gone by and he'd missed it!

"I told you, you were very lucky. Your injury was serious and your body needed the rest. Now finish your soup and maybe by then your friend will be...Oh, here he is." Charlie peered over to see who it was, then beamed with delight as Luke walked over.

"Charlie, you're awake, buddy. Boy, you really scared me! I thought we'd lost you there for a while."

Charlie pushed the spoon away; he'd had enough.

"Okay, son, but you will finish this later."

"Yes, I promise. So Luke, what the heck happened?"

"Don't you remember, Charlie? You were shot by the Germans, and they were getting ready to finish the job when I spotted you."

"No, it's all blank. I do remember running and hearing a loud series of pops, then nothing. I remember being there and ending up here with no memory of the middle."

"Good God. Charlie, they were standing over you, guns ready, when a couple of our guys and I saw you. We fired and none of the other soldiers made it out; you were barely holding on, so we loaded you into the nearest truck and drove you here. The hospital here wanted me to leave immediately, but I couldn't. I had to make sure you made it here all right. Look at you now. You look great. You'll be better in no time. And you know what this means: you have a one-way ticket back home. So sit back, buddy, and soon you'll be seeing that lovely girl of yours."

Charlie patted his friend on the back.

"Luke, I don't know what to say. I can never thank you enough for saving me and staying by my side."

"Hey, that's what we do, right? We watch out for each other. How the hell else are we gonna get out of this place?"

Charlie smiled and squeezed his friend's arm. "What about John and Jason? Are they here, too?"

Luke looked away. "Charlie, I'm sorry. John is missing and Jason is on his way home. He's really messed up. I don't know what exactly happened, but he's really in a bad way in his head."

Charlie's stomach went queasy, and he had to fight to keep down the soup. He sank back into the bed and covered his face with his arms.

"Luke, do you mind? I'm feeling a little tired and need some time alone."

"Sure...Sure thing, buddy. I'll come back a little later. The nurses tell me they're shipping you to the hospital in Château Guyon in a few days, but I'll make sure I see you before you go." Luke patted Charlie on the shoulder and left.

Charlie lay there, thinking about his friends. *Frankie's gone, John is missing, and Jason is messed up in his head.* He shuttered and crawled deeper into the covers before turning and going back to sleep where he didn't have to think at all.

That night Charlie dreamed of Lillie, and for the first time in a long time, he could see her face clearly as if she were right there with him. They were in the garden and she was nestled up to his chest; he could feel the warmth of her body, and he was kissing her soft skin. The sun was shining and they were in front of the fire thorns, which had grown together and were now touching. Suddenly, a loud noise interrupted their kissing. Lillie jumped up. He was no longer in her arms and she began to frantically yell, "Charlie! Charlie!"

Charlie could see Lillie but he couldn't seem to reach her. His arms ached to hold her, but she just slowly slipped away until she disappeared. Lillie was gone. He furiously looked around the garden; everything was turning black and shriveling up. The fire thorns had wilted on the vines and were dropping off the wall. All around him was an incessant booming. He was screaming for Lillie when he turned and saw something curled up in the grass. It was vaguely round, covered in dirt and blood, and there was something oddly familiar about it. He was afraid to walk over and see what it was, but he felt compelled to do so. As he stepped across the grass, the rest of the garden began to disappear into the blackness, and he wasn't sure if he would reach the rounded shape. But he did reach it, and when he saw what lay in front of him, he shook uncontrollably. In terror he bent over and rolled it over.

No, Lillie!

It was Lillie that was covered in blood and dirt, which had now turned to a thick, cold mud. Another loud boom went off when he heard someone calling his name once again: "Charlie, Charlie. Wake up! We have to move fast and get you out of here."

Charlie opened his eyes to see he was still in the hospital. Everyone around him was rushing to pack what they could and to help move the injured. It seemed the bombing had gotten too close and they were moving everyone to Château Guyon tonight.

"Come on, son. We have to leave, now!" The older nurse was lifting him out of bed. As gentle as she was, he didn't realize how much he still hurt. When she got him to his feet, the pain was excruciating. His chest was on fire, flames of pain radiating down to his gut. They hobbled together in a strange sort of run until she got him to the truck, where the soldiers loaded him in. He lay down and looked up to see Luke standing beside him.

"Hey, buddy. I'm shipping out tonight back to the front. We're gaining ground and they're saying all this should be over soon. But I wanted to see you off like I promised. You take care, and I'll write you when I get home, okay?"

Charlie felt a twinge in his gut; he didn't want to see his friend go back to the front, but he smiled and reached up, patting him on the arm.

"You take care and be safe. When you get home, I'll have to come to Chicago so you can show me around, okay?"

"You bet!" Then Luke jumped out of the truck and closed its doors just as it was getting ready to leave.

The trip to Château Guyon was uncomfortable and long. No matter how hard he tried, Charlie couldn't get the picture of Lillie covered in blood out of his mind. He couldn't wait to get home and hold her. He would never let go of her again, ever.

Chapter Twenty-Seven

Lillie held her breath as she ran down the hall toward room number forty-nine. When she found it, she stopped, took hold of herself, and then pushed open the door. She approached the bed slowly as a frail, pale young man came into focus. Lying on the narrow mattress was Jason. Only his wide-open eyes, staring blankly at the ceiling, identified him to Lillie. She had never seen him this still before. There was a blanket at the foot of his bed and she pulled it over him, as if had he every reason in the world to feel cold. She sat at his side for several minutes before uttering a word.

"Jason, honey, can you hear me?" He didn't move. "Jason, it's Lillie...Whitman. Do you understand me? Jason, please, can you try to tell me where Charlie is? Has something happened to him? Is that why you are so silent? Was it something you saw? Please, Jason, please hear me."

Lillie broke down crying. She tried to hold back her tears, but it was as if a floodgate had opened: there was no stopping it. She put her head down on the bed, shaking and sobbing. Someone gently rubbed her hair and her head shot up in surprise; it was Jason. His gaze was still fixed on the ceiling, but he was stroking her hair. She laughed a little and then grabbed his hand.

"You're still in there. Don't worry, someone is coming who can help. You're going to be all right." She knew that was the best she could hope for today. As she leaned over and kissed his forehead, she remembered to take out one of the books she had tucked in her pocket. She knew she would be reading for quite a while.

Lillie sat for many hours with Jason until Doctor Williams arrived from Manhattan. He was a burly man with a scruffy black beard. Most of his hair had gone years ago. He wasn't very tall, and his clothes looked as if he had slept in them before taking the trip over, but he seemed to be very pleasant and had an excellent reputation for healing many boys who had been affected as Jason had.

Lillie tried to stay out of the way by moving to the corner of the room and quietly watching them. She had hoped if she became nearly invisible, she could stay with Jason, but after a few minutes Doctor Williams saw her and asked that she leave. She paced nervously down the hall, waiting for the doctor to come out. She felt guilty; of course she wanted Jason to recover and resume his life, but there was this selfish piece of her that knew he was her only connection to Charlie, and it consumed her. She had no idea what had become of him, and if only Jason could just snap out of it, maybe he had some information that would help her understand what had happened.

Lillie's back was to the door when it creaked open. Turning, she saw Doctor Williams exit with Doctor Miller by his side. She trailed behind them. Casually, she picked up a stack of files off the nurses desk and pretended to flip through them while they spoke at the other end of the station. She thought she heard the words "war neurosis" and "electroshock," but she couldn't be sure. *Oh no,* she thought. *I've heard of that electroshock. Some boys are worse afterward. Sometimes they never come back and they're never themselves again.* Lillie started to panic, and this time it was all for Jason.

After assisting the nurses with serving lunch, she went back to Jason's room. She sat beside him and once again put her head down on the bed and cried. She just didn't know how to help him! When she looked at him, he was still staring up at the ceiling.

"I'm not sure you understand what I'm saying to you, but, Jason, honey, you have to try. They're going to take you away and do treatments on you that aren't needed. Even though you're silent, I know you're still in there; you stroked my hair the other day. You can do this. Fight, Jason. Fight your way back!" Lillie nestled her head in her arms on the bed. She closed her eyes for a minute and without realizing it, she fell asleep.

When she opened her eyes, it was dark outside. Jason's bed was empty. Frantically she shot up. *Where could he be?* She thought. *He can't even move, let alone get out of bed.* The room was in shadow, and she stumbled to the end table to turn on the light.

There, in a corner chair, sat Jason. He was following her with his eyes. Calmly he said, "Lillie, is that you? I'm sorry if I frightened you. Do you know where we are?"

Lillie was speechless. She collapsed with relief onto the bed and stared at him. "Jason, you know me? You know who I am?"

"Sure, you're Lillie Whitman. Why would you think I'd forget you?"

"Jason, listen to me. You're back home. You're in the hospital. You were wounded, but you're fine now. Everything is going to be fine. You stay right here and I'm going to go and get your doctor, all right?"

"I'm home?"

"Yes, you're home. I'm getting the doctor. Don't move."

Lillie raced out of the room and over to the nurses' station. "Do you know where Doctor Miller is?" One of the nurses nodded and pointed to the large doors at the end of the hallway. Lillie took off and barreled through the doors. There she saw Doctor Miller speaking with another member of the staff. "Doctor Miller, it's Jason. You have to come with me right now."

"Miss Whitman, what is it? What's going on? Is he all right?"

"Oh, he's better than all right. Come with me now, please!" Lillie grabbed his arm and pulled him to Jason's room. When they got there, he was still sitting in the chair, just as Lillie had asked him to.

The doctor looked at him in astonishment. "Mr. Chambers?"

"Yes?"

"Mr. Chambers, Jason, I'm your physician, Doctor Miller. How are you feeling?"

"Well, Doc, I'm feeling a little weak, but I sure could use a sandwich and maybe a glass of milk. I feel like I haven't eaten in weeks."

Lillie clasped her hands over her mouth as tears leaped to her eyes. She had no words, only joy.

"Miss Whitman, would you go and see if you could find Doctor Williams, if you don't mind? He said he was going to catch up on his reading. Perhaps you should check my office." Lillie nodded and went to find the doctor.

It seemed like Jason was with the doctor for hours, but Lillie was not about to go home now. She still wanted to speak with Jason and see if he knew anything connected to Charlie. When they finally came out, the nurse was told to give him a sedative to sleep. Lillie slipped in before the nurse returned.

"Lillie, you're back. The sandwich they gave me tastes great. It sure hit the spot!"

Lillie smiled at Jason; she knew she had to be very delicate with her questions. "Do you remember what happened before you ended up here? Do you know where Charlie or the other boys are?"

Jason's face turned gray, and he put the sandwich down. He shook and tears streamed down his face. "Oh no. God, I'm so sorry."

"It's okay, Jason. Take your time. I'm right here and you're safe. What is it that you're sorry about?"

"John, Frankie, they're dead. They're both dead..."

Lillie was too shocked to cry and sank down on to the bed. "Jason, please, for my sake, do you remember what happened to Charlie...Jason?"

"No, he went over the top. He went over the top and

I couldn't stop him. None of us could. Then we didn't see him, I...I don't know, Lillie. I never saw him again."

Lillie crumbled into a ball as she sank to the floor.

When Lillie awoke, Doctor Miller was standing over her. "Miss Whitman, how are you feeling? Lie still. We've called your father and he's on his way. He should be here shortly." Lillie tried to sit up, but the room was spinning and she just fell back down. "Now stay still, like I told you. You need to rest for a moment. You took quite a knock to your head."

"What happened?"

"It seems you were speaking with Mr. Chambers when you simply collapsed, hitting your head on the corner of the table."

"I fell? What? Oh no, no. Charlie, my Charlie." Lillie was crying and shaking uncontrollably. Doctor Miller asked the nurse to administer a sedative and she drifted into a deep, blank sleep.

***

Lillie woke and was relieved to see she was at home and in her own bed. She cautiously sat up and went downstairs to see her father. He was sitting in the garden having coffee when she noticed the envelope on the table beside him. Tension overshadowed by sadness dwelt in her father's eyes. Lillie knew his expression had to do with the envelope. She reached out, picked it up, and with conviction knew she had to tear it open immediately. It was from the military:

Dear Miss Whitman,

It is with great difficulty that I write this letter today...

Chapter Twenty-Eight

Charlie arrived in Château Guyon full of unanswered questions. He had no idea what had become of John or what condition Jason was in. Luke had to return to the front, and to top off all this misery, the pain from the wound in his chest had spread down toward his stomach and circled around to his back. He longed to be home sitting with Lillie in the garden. He felt further away from her than ever before, and even though he knew being wounded meant a ticket home, he couldn't help feeling as if he was never going to get there.

He was unloaded from the truck on a stretcher held by two enormous marines who looked as if they could single-handedly defeat the better part of the German army. They carried him into the hospital, which bore a striking resemblance to a hotel he had seen once in a magazine showcasing elegant spots in Europe. He remembered that Lillie enjoyed looking at just this type of magazine while she waited for Charlie in the garden or her kitchen. Once inside, it definitely looked more like a hospital, although the exquisite molding and wall décor gave it an air of having once been a destination of relaxation and entertainment. But for now, it was filled with the devastation of a bitter war. A nurse came over and recited something in French, but after seeing the puzzled look on both of the marines' faces; she motioned for them to follow her.

Once in his room, Charlie could tell that at one time it must have been quite grand. The wallpaper was etched in gold and burgundy velvet brocade, and the molding surrounding the ceiling was carved so intricately, it was evident someone had taken great pride in their craft. An elegant chandelier hung above his head, its crystal beads glittering throughout the room. All this beauty was in contrast to the hospital bed and end table arranged with gauze, tape, and other medical supplies.

The marines lifted Charlie and placed him on the bed, a painful task that caused him to wince and the men to apologize. The nurse settled his body and covered him with a thin blanket that was folded at the foot of the bed. She smiled and made a motion that seemed to say someone else would be coming in, or maybe it was just her way of waving goodbye. He couldn't be sure.

After a few minutes another nurse came in, and she spoke English well enough to tell him the doctor would be seeing him in the morning. He asked her for a glass of water and she said she would be back in a few minutes. When she finally did return, she had a pitcher of water and a cheese sandwich. Charlie didn't realize how truly hungry he was until he took his first bite. Cheese and two slices of bread had never tasted this good. He gulped it down, contemplating if he should ask for another, but decided one sandwich was enough. Afterward, he lay back down and the pain medication the nurse gave him started to take effect. As he was drifting off, he hoped that it would be to a peaceful sleep. He had waited months for that to happen.

***

An icy pressure on Charlie's chest jolted him awake. Opening his eyes, he saw a stethoscope held by an older, gray-haired man. From his gestures and white lab coat he had to be the doctor.

"Good morning, soldier. How are you feeling today?" The doctor spoke English with a slight French accent. This gave Charlie relief, knowing he would be understood.

"I'm okay, but it hurts, Doc. I guess that's what happens when you get shot." Charlie chuckled and then cringed.

"Yes, your chest will be tender for quite a while. You're very lucky. A few centimeters to the left and we wouldn't be having this conversation."

"No, not my chest. That's definitely sore. It's my stomach that's really tender." The doctor pulled down the blanket and lifted up Charlie's shirt. He pulled away the bandage to expose his wound and then shook his head. "What's wrong, Doc?"

"I'm afraid you have gotten an infection. This is fairly common. In the rush to make sure you receive basic medical attention, the wounds are not always cleaned efficiently. The first thing we should do is take you for an x-ray to see if it is gas gangrene, so please rest until the orderly comes to get you."

Charlie didn't understand, an x-*what*? But he didn't have the energy to ask. He suddenly felt very weak and tired, so he closed his eyes and dozed off. Before he knew it, he felt someone grabbing his arm and gently moving it.

"Sir, please wake up. We have to take you to the x-ray."

Groggy, Charlie forced his eyes to open. "Oh, okay. Hey, what is this...x-ray anyway?"

"I'm not quite sure, sir, but the doctor will explain it to you later. Right now we need to get you into the wheelchair." The orderly was bald and had a bulky, muscular body. Charlie thought he might have been a boxer before the war, but whatever his history, he was able to pick Charlie up easily and settle him in a wheelchair.

As the orderly wheeled him down the hallway, Charlie passed many rooms filled with soldiers on the mend. Judging by the different uniforms hanging up, he saw American, French, and British boys. Some of them looked to have only minor injuries, and others were severely bandaged from head to toe. *Burns, maybe,* he thought.

As they approached the last door, Charlie saw a soldier sitting in a wheelchair in the doorway of his room. His back was turned to them, and when he heard them coming down the hall, he turned to greet them. Charlie gasped silently: the soldier was missing both legs. This was the first time he had seen an amputee who was alive and not lying on the battlefield somewhere covered in mud. He tried not to stare at his legs and gave the guy a smile. As they passed, the soldier put his hand out towards Charlie. "Hi, how you doing? American, right?"

Charlie was surprised. He hadn't even had a chance to speak. "Yeah, how did you know?"

"You have that look. You know, the one that knows what exactly is going on, and where do I get a hotdog?"

Charlie burst out in laughter. "Charlie Murphy." He put his hand out to shake.

"Michael Camaretti. You have no idea how glad I am to meet you. I've been here for about a week, and all the guys from home are too sick to talk. The British boys are okay, but it's nothing like seeing someone from home, know what I mean?"

"I sure do." Charlie gave him a big smile. "They have me doing this x-ray thing right now, but how about later you wheel over and we can talk? I'd come to you, but..." He pointed to his chest. "It seems they were aiming for my heart. Good thing those Krauts are lousy shots." Both boys laughed and the orderly made the motion that it was time to go. Charlie felt excited—already he would have someone to talk to who made him laugh—but his excitement turned to dread when he entered the x-ray room and remembered why he was there.

After the endless positioning and then painfully sitting absolutely still, Charlie was wheeled back to his room. The nurse gave him a sponge bath, but the cleaning and redressing of his wound was agony. By the end of this ordeal, he was once again exhausted and in pain. He was given medication and drifted off to sleep.

The dream of the garden started almost immediately with his beautiful Lillie sitting next to him. As he turned to admire the fire thorns, they began to blacken and fall off the vine. *No, not again!* He turned to Lillie, but she was already gone and screaming his name. "Charlie, Charlie!" Frantically he searched the garden. "Charlie!"

He turned and saw something on the ground. It was covered in leaves and dirt, and as he got closer he noticed blood. He was afraid to look. Something told him not to, but he couldn't stop himself and he walked closer. He could see her.

"No, no, no!" He ran up to the figure lying on the ground. "Lillie, what has happened? Lillie!" When he bent down to turn her over, he saw her eyes, dark and vacant. A tortured scream escaped his throat and—

"Charlie, buddy, wake up." Charlie opened his eyes to see Michael sitting at his bedside. "Hey, are you okay? It must have been a bad one."

Charlie just nodded; he couldn't bring himself to speak just yet.

"That's okay; lots of guys have really bad dreams here. You can hear them mostly at night. Sometimes it's so noisy at night, it's hard to sleep, but what are you gonna do, right? I feel really sorry for them. They can't seem to snap out of it. They're treated special as mental patients. Their injuries are much worse than ours."

Charlie just looked at Michael and forced a grin. With the bad dreams he was having lately, he was beginning to wonder if he was one of those poor mental patients.

Charlie look forward to having Michael to talk to. He found out that he was from Newark, New Jersey and had been coaxed into joining by a buddy of his. They were stationed at the front, too. He'd made it, but his buddy hadn't. They'd been hit with stray shrapnel from a mortar that had landed too close, cutting his legs in two.

"It's okay, though," Michael looked down at his stumps. "It could be worse. I could be at the bottom of some ditch, so this...Well, I lived, right? My girl is waiting for me back home. Her name is Katherine. Look, here's a picture."

Charlie took the picture from his hands. "Boy, Michael, she's really beautiful."

"Yeah, and sweet, too. I'm a lucky fellow." Charlie couldn't help but admire Michael's strength. *Here he is, with both of his legs gone, and he considers himself lucky.* That was amazing. "How about you, Charlie? You have a special girl back home?"

"I do. Her name's Lillie and she is lovely, but I don't have a picture, I wish I did."

"That's okay. Close your eyes." Charlie closed them. "Can you see her?" Charlie nodded.

Charlie opened his eyes and was delighted with Michael's little trick.. The boys talked for the rest of the day until dinner was being served and Michael had to return to his room. The nurse came by afterward and gave him more pain medication and told him the doctor would be in tomorrow to speak with him. As he lay there, sleep taking over, he prayed that he wouldn't have the garden dream again and that Lillie was safe.

After breakfast, Michael came wheeling into Charlie's room. That made him feel better already about the day. The doctor had been in earlier and told him he had indeed had gas gangrene, but not to worry, as they had a very effective treatment for that, a serum. He would take longer to heal, but the doctor was confident that he would make a full recovery. The nurse came in again and washed his wound with antisepsis and applied a fresh dressing. Charlie wished he could take a bath, but the best they could do was to sponge him down, as the doctor didn't want the wound to become wet and risk further problems.

Michael had gotten word that he was being shipped back home in two days, and although Charlie was extremely happy for his new friend, he couldn't help but feel a wave of depression. The thought of being here alone again brought despair to his already weakened spirit.

To Charlie's dismay, the day did arrive for Michael to leave. Michael wrote out his address and asked Charlie to write. Charlie agreed, and as they wheeled Michael away, sadness turned into desolation.

Charlie stayed in his bed, withdrawn and despondent. Without Michael to fill his days, he retreated deeper into his own boundless depths of guilt and self-pity the nurse who attended to him was normally cheerful and patient, but after a week of his resistance, she became stern. But it didn't matter; Charlie just wasn't in the mood to get out of bed. It should have been quite the opposite. The pain in his stomach had all but gone away, and the wound in his chest was coming along nicely, but it was what was in his head that troubled him. Every night he would have the same dream about Lillie. She felt lost to him forever, and he couldn't do anything about it. And with every morning, he drifted further and further away.

***

The doctor, feeling that perhaps Charlie needed to speak with someone who could help, called in a specialist in this type of injury. He suspected it was "shell-shock." Some soldiers had clear, visible signs: facial and body ticks, continuous screaming, rocking back and forth, or a completely trance-like state. There were others though, like Charlie, who were much harder to diagnose.

Doctor Henry Wellington was a proper British gentleman who was well-educated and aristocratic in nature. It seemed odd that he could reach the emotions of those so damaged by war, yet it was true. His was a rational mind that not only understood but felt compassion. In matters of the heart, he was actually quite tender.

Charlie was introduced to him first thing the next day. In a chair placed beside his bed, the doctor remained calm but alert as he formed the questions that would fill the better part of the morning. Charlie was lulled by his voice into a feeling of safety. Despite his initial thoughts on who some of the guys were calling the "brain doc," Charlie actually liked him. They went deep into his feelings about home, his mother, and Lillie. No one over here seemed as interested in his life as this doctor. When it was time for lunch, the doctor excused himself and said he'd be back tomorrow.

Charlie could hardly eat a bite; he wasn't really hungry. All he wanted was a peaceful sleep devoid of the horrifying dream. But more times than not, he went to that place in his head as soon as he closed his eyes. So instead, he stared up the ceiling. Maybe if he tried to picture his house back home in a way that made him feel good, he could avoid the dream that plagued him. His house was modest with its two bedrooms and one bath, and overall it could use some work, but it was his. He longed to be back in his kitchen, making a sandwich and sitting on the sofa to read the paper. He wanted his own bed in his own room, and the more he pictured it, the further away it seemed to be.

As promised, Doctor Wellington came back the next morning. Charlie was happy to see him; he enjoyed their conversations, although he didn't think anything was wrong with him. He hadn't lost a leg or an arm and he still had all his fingers and toes. Sure, he'd taken a bullet in the chest and that might have killed him, but it hadn't, and it would have no lasting effect. The dreams were probably just the after-effects of battle and they would end soon too. He was fine; he just missed home.

After more talk about his home, the doctor asked Charlie about his friends that had been in battle with him. Charlie was surprised. The doctor already knew about that part of his life. Why did he need to hear it again? He squeezed the corner of his pillow and his face felt hot. "What's to say, Doc. I made it and most of them didn't."

The doctor put his hand on Charlie's forearm. "You

seem angry. Does it make you angry to speak of them?"

Charlie glared at the doctor. This conversation was no longer enjoyable. In fact, it was downright annoying. Why should he have to talk about this? It wouldn't do any good. It wouldn't bring back Frankie or John, and it certainly wouldn't help Jason be whole again. No, he wasn't having this conversation with the doctor or anyone.

"I'm done. This talk is over for today."

"Charlie, I understand you feel angry about what happened, but it's not your fault. You could not have done anything for your friends. Blame the ones responsible, not yourself." The doctor waited for Charlie to respond, but Charlie stared at the ceiling and eventually turned over so he was facing the wall. "Right then, Charlie. We'll stop for today, but I will be back in the morning."

Eventually, Charlie's boredom pushed him to leave his bed. He decided to stroll around in his wheelchair, visiting the other bedridden men, but he felt more tired than he expected. He was going in circles of despair from one room to the next, and there was only one thing left to do: wheel himself back to his room and back to bed. Awaiting him was his nurse, all ready to change the dressing on his wound.

"It's healing nicely," she remarked. As she left the room, silence trailed behind her, filling the space around Charlie. He used to look forward to silence; it was always so noisy working in construction. When he had finally been able to work on his furniture full time, he had appreciated the peace. It had given him time to think and plan. He would picture his life with Lillie and the decades they would have. It would be filled with children, a home of their own, and countless moments of being together. But the silence had changed. It wasn't peaceful any longer; it was torture. He desperately tried to cling to his ideal of life with Lillie, but every time he closed his eyes, all he saw was her body lying on the ground, covered in blood and dirt. And when he slept, it was worse.

Get a grip on yourself, Charlie, he thought. *You've got to get through with this or they'll never let you leave.*

He tried closing his eyes and picturing the last time they were together. They were at the train station and she looked so beautiful. He had left her. He had left her standing there, just like he had left his friends.

Why did I have to go over the top and join the fight? Why didn't I stay and help them? He'd left them all when they needed him the most. He deserved to feel this way. He should have had worse. His body should be lying next to those of his friends.

But it's not, and I don't deserve this life. What makes me better than them? Why am I here? He lay there in total agony before sleep bested him. And then it all turned into sheer hell in his dreams.

***

"Mr. Murphy! Wake up, son. It's me, Doctor Wellington. Snap out of it now!" Charlie was completely covered in sweat. "Charlie, it's me, Doctor Wellington. You're safe...You're safe. You're in the hospital. Do you remember?"

Charlie nodded, calming down. Tears streamed down his cheeks. His body was shaking and he was gasping for breath. "I left them. I left them all to die. They needed me. They needed me to stay with them, but I left. It's my fault they're all dead. It's all my fault..."

Charlie pressed his head into the pillow, still babbling and sobbing. Doctor Wellington asked the nurse to administer a sedative, and after a few minutes Charlie drifted off to sleep. This time wonderfully, mercifully, without dreams.

When Charlie woke, Doctor Wellington was sitting at his bedside again. He turned his head and when his eyes met the doctors, tears began to flow. Doctor Wellington leaned closer and patted Charlie's arm. "Now we get to the root of the problem. My boy, we have some work to do." Charlie nodded.

Doctor Wellington and Charlie spent the next few weeks deep in therapy.

"Charlie, I think I know the reason you're having such horrific dreams of your girl."

"Let me have it, Doc." Charlie scooted up in his bed.

"You feel riddled with guilt. You think you've abandoned her and failed your buddies. But the truth is, you didn't leave Lillie. You have every intention of going back to her. As for your buddies, the war killed them, not you. You are one man. To think that the responsibility of everyone rested on your shoulders, is a task no one could handle."

"I do feel like I left Lillie behind, like I'm not protecting her."

"Protecting her from what, son? She's not in the war, you are." The doctor stood up and paced around the room. He pulled out a memo pad from his pocket and flipped through the pages. When he found what he was searching for, his eyes widened and his mouth raised up at the corners. "You said a couple of sessions ago, that when you see Lillie in your dream, she is covered in blood. Right?"

"Yes."

"That blood is your mind's reference to the guilt you feel for your friends dying. You've coupled it with Lillie and that's the reason for the dreams."

For the first time in weeks, Charlie felt his sanity just might be saved. Doctor Wellington helped Charlie realize that he hadn't abandoned any of his buddies. He had tried to do his best to save them: he'd enlisted and he'd fought shoulder to shoulder down in the trenches with them. He'd honored his belief to come and take his part in this war to help keep Lillie and others back home safe.

It took Charlie a while to understand and fully accept what he begun to explore with Doctor Wellington. This was a different kind of battle he was fighting. His doctor, however, felt that they had made enough progress in the last few weeks to release Charlie as soon as his wound would permit travel, provided he saw a doctor back home. Doctor Wellington would notify the army and they would arrange it. Charlie still had issues that needed work, but the doctor felt the worst was behind him. Admitting his feelings of guilt was a release from the torture that had gripped him; understanding his actions was what he needed to deal with.

Doctor Wellington shook Charlie's hand and wished him well and as walked out the door. Charlie turned and closed his eyes. For the first time in weeks he had a peaceful sleep.

A week went by, and the gray-haired doctor told Charlie he was sending him home. Finally, Charlie was going to leave. Every nerve jumped and danced at the thought of seeing Lillie again. And as for his heart, it overflowed with all the emotions he had left behind on the train station platform, saying goodbye to her. He was, quite simply, overjoyed.

The transport arrived to take him to the ship, and then on to Philadelphia and a train ride home. It was a long trip, and the road was muddy and filled with bumps, but this time he didn't care. He didn't feel any of it; all he could think of was holding her and smothering her in kisses. He longed to smell her intoxicating scent and feel her silky hair brush across his cheek. He could still hear the bombing in the distance. He then closed his eyes and silently said a prayer for everyone's safety.

Chapter Twenty-Nine

Lillie had collapsed. James was in a panic but sent for Doc Clarkson immediately. He carried her up to her bedroom and asked Lenore to place a cool rag on her forehead in the hopes of awaking her. In a few minutes she opened her eyes, but she was completely catatonic, unresponsive to either Lenore's voice or James's. They were extremely worried and hovered at her bedside until the doctor arrived. The doctor asked James to step aside while he examined her.

Never had James felt so hopeless. He stood in the corner and watched his daughter drift away.

"She's in a total state of shock. What did this to her?" asked the doctor. James explained the contents of the letter detailing Charlie's death. "Not Charlie. He was such a fine boy. This war, it has to stop, all the bloodshed. James, we have to be very careful. Something this devastating could be irreversible. She could fall deeper into this trance and may never come out of it. You can help by keeping her warm, talking with her, and trying to feed her. If she won't eat, she won't be receiving the proper nourishment for her body to stay well and we'll have to administer an IV. In fact, we shouldn't take any chances. Let's bring in a full-time nurse and administer an IV so we can be certain that Lillie will have what she needs."

The doctor also instructed James to bring a few of her friends together, especially Claire, and have them take turns coming in and reading to her. Lillie's consciousness had to be reached in order for her to come out of this tragic, dangerous state. The doctor hoped by keeping her at home, and not at the hospital, the familiar surroundings would help her to wake up.

James would not move from his daughter's bedside. If she did come out of shock, he wanted to be the first one to welcome her back to her life. Lenore had to bring his food into the bedroom so he would eat and not lose his strength, but the thought of eating was the last thing on his mind.

***

When Claire received the call, she packed a few essentials for her stay at the Whitman house. She had told her boss, Congressman Meyer, that she would indefinitely need some time away from work and surprisingly, he told her she would have her job when she returned. She was too valuable an asset to lose. From his heart he had wished Lillie the speediest of recovery.

Bastian came by with an armload of books from the library. He was prepared to stay and read with Claire until he lost his voice, if necessary. Anything to try and bring Lillie back to consciousness. The three took turns reading, hoping this indeed would be the spark she needed to come around.

The first few days their hopes were high, but by week's end doubt nagged at them.

"She just lies there. I feel so utterly useless." Tears were rolling down Claire's face.

Bastian sat next to her and pulled her into his arms. "She'll come around. It'll just take time. We need to stay patient. Losing Charlie was the most horrible news she could ever receive, but she's strong. She'll come back."

"I hope you're right. I can't lose her." Claire put her head in her hands and leaned heavily into Bastian's chest.

***

Days turned into weeks with no change in sight. For a brief moment, James thought he saw a glimmer. It was as if she had smiled at him, but it was just a muscle twitch in her cheek. During the day, Doc Clarkson suggested carrying her downstairs to the parlor. He believed that seeing the normal day-to-day activity might help stimulate her and cause her to wake.

It was a beautiful, sunny day and warmth crept

through the windows, making the parlor feel cozy. James thought it would be a perfect time to bring Lillie downstairs. While they were sitting together, a package arrived addressed to a Miss Lillie Whitman. James held it in his hands, contemplating whether he should open it or not, but curiosity won out and he ripped open the top edge of the package's wrapping. Inside was a small wooden box that, when opened, held a knife and a compass. He carefully inspected each object.

Claire gasped. "Oh no, it just can't be." She shot up and dashed over to James, who was now very confused. "It's the pocket knife and compass that Lillie gave Charlie as Christmas gifts."

***

"Claire, Mr. Whitman, I think you need to see this." Bastian was standing by Lillie's side.

"Bastian, hold on. We're trying to see who sent this." Just then James found a letter inside, and everyone's attention focused on it.

"'Dear Miss Whitman,'" he read, "'these items belonging to Private Murphy were accidentally left behind at the hospital. We had your address from the letters he had sent. Could you please see to it that he receives them? Thank you, Doctor Henry Wellington.'"

Claire was astonished. *'Left at the hospital?' 'See to it that he gets them?' What's going on?*

"Claire!"

"What, Bastian? What is it?"

"Look." And he pointed at Lillie. There she sat, staring at both of the gifts she had given Charlie before he had left for war.

James ran to her side with Claire following. "Lillie, darling, can you understand me?" She nodded. "Do you know where you are?" She nodded again.

Claire stroked her hair. "Lillie, honey, do you remember what happened?" Tears pooled in Lillie's eyes as they met Claire's, and instantly all the horror began flooding back into them.

"Take it easy, darling," said James. "Don't leave us again, please."

Lillie turned to him and in a barely audible whisper, said, "Oh, Dad. Charlie...He's gone, isn't he? My beautiful Charlie is not coming back."

"That's correct, my darling. I am so sorry."

"But James, the note—" began Claire.

"Claire, can I see you in the kitchen?" A bewildered Claire followed James into the kitchen. "Claire, we're not clear on what the letter is saying and I can't—I won't—get her hopes up just to see her plummet back into nonexistence. Therefore there will be no mention of the letter. We will only say that the army sent back his personal belongings for her and that's the end of it. Understood?"

Claire didn't agree with the story James had concocted, and it really distressed her to have to lie to Lillie about it, but she stood behind James on this. She knew he was just protecting Lillie. Together they went back into the parlor as if nothing important had transpired between them.

In one hand Lillie held the pocketknife in her lap, while in the other she clutched the compass to her heart. "It didn't work."

Claire went and sat beside her. "What didn't work, honey?"

"The compass I gave Charlie. It was supposed to lead him back to me. It was supposed to help him find his way home."

Claire could only stare at Lillie; she didn't know what to say. Any words spoken would be a sad attempt to make Lillie feel better, and right now nothing could do that. So Claire just sat with her in silence until the light seeped from the room and left them in darkness.

Bastian had gone over to Claire's house to pick up a few more of her things, as she didn't want to leave Lillie just yet. The two girls sat in the parlor with the warm glow of the candle and the crackling of a fire. It was peaceful and they were speaking in a whisper; it seemed to fit the mood, which was both intimate and fragile.

"Lils, what did it for you?"

Lillie blinked. "What did what?"

"What brought you back? I mean, you had been gone for so long?"

"It seems weird and impossible, but I heard Charlie calling me. It was faint and coming from a distance, but I heard my name. And then a second later, I heard you telling Dad about the compass. Do you think that Charlie called my name to let me know that he wasn't lost? That he had found a way to come home to me? Does that make any sense to you?

"These days, what used to make sense to me has been turned completely upside down. So yes, I do believe that you heard Charlie call your name. You know, Lillie, I believe in love and romance even if I don't show it all that much. And I know that no matter what happened out there to Charlie, having the compass to point him to you and the knife to remind him of your bond, kept him whole, no matter what he had to face. Lillie, there's something I have to tell you, even though I'm not certain if I should. John is missing and Frankie is gone." Lillie looked at the floor and took a deep breath. "Lillie, are you okay.?"

"Yes, I'm fine, and yes, I know."

"You know, but how?"

"Jason is in the hospital, or he was. I saw him when I was at work and that's when he told me. Only John isn't missing, he's...dead. Jason was with him when it happened. That's what led to his hospitalization. Seeing John go through that...He just couldn't take it and then he snapped. He must have been in the hospital for a while, because when I last saw him, he seemed to be faring well. His spirits were up. Perhaps we could visit with him in a day or two. Will you go with me?"

"Perfect, but we need to be certain you're strong enough before we go running off for a visit."

For a moment Lillie felt almost like her old self. *Oh, to be normal again.* The moment was not to last, though. As soon as her smile faded, the tears built up. But then she remembered the faint calling of her name and the compass that found its way back to her hands and the tears stopped.

Charlie.

***

James rang Doc Clarkson and he came over after dinner. He checked on Lillie's eyes, reflexes, and temperature: normal. "Well, little lady, glad to have you back. We were very worried about you. It seems your father and friends' constant vigil at your side worked just fine. They were persistent."

"I know, Doc. I have so much to be thankful for. I'm lucky to be surrounded by so many loving people." Lillie gave a half smile, and Claire knew her friend was putting on a good show for the doctor and her father. Doc Clarkson stayed and had a cup of tea with James before heading home to his family. Bastian thought it was best to leave the two girls alone for the evening, so he gave Claire a kiss on the cheek and promised to ring her tomorrow.

Once again, the two friends were in the cozy warmth of the parlor. Lillie spoke and Claire just listened; she knew that's what Lillie needed right now, an attentive ear. Lillie told her of her dreams of marrying Charlie one day and having a family. Maybe they would live in town or possibly move to Connecticut. Charlie would have his furniture business and she would be the perfect housewife and mother. They would have a garden, maybe not as grand as her mother's, but it would theirs and it would be beautiful. And they would be happy because they would have each other. Then Lillie closed her eyes, and a smile appeared on her face.

Claire interrupted her silence. "What is it, Lillie? Why the smile?"

"For a moment, I felt him."

"You felt him?"

"Yes. It was as if he was right here beside me and I could feel his breath on my face just like I do right before he leans in to kiss me. Silly, huh?"

Claire paused to let the notion settle in her brain.

"No. Not so silly, honey, not silly at all." Claire smiled at Lillie and knew tomorrow she needed to take a trip alone; she needed to go see Jason.

***

Claire awoke early the next morning, wanting to be out of the house before Lillie woke up. It would be easier if she didn't have to explain where she was going and why. *It all just doesn't seem to add up. Everyone thought John was missing and not dead, and then the compass and the knife were delivered with that note. What does it mean?*

She didn't know, but she was going to find the answers. Claire had made a promise to James not to say anything to Lillie; she had never promised she wouldn't look into it.

She arrived at the hospital mid-morning, but Jason had been sent home a week ago. After ringing Bastian to tell him what she was doing, she headed over to Jason's parents' house. His mother answered the door, happy to see her. "Claire, come in. Jason is in the kitchen having lunch. Can I fix you a sandwich?"

"No, thank you, Mrs. Chambers. I'm meeting Bastian for lunch."

"How is that fella of yours? I bet you're over the moon he wasn't drafted. Such a shame, him having that trouble with his eyes and all." Bastian had tried to sign up, but when he was administered the eye test, it showed that his vision was badly impaired. Even with special glasses, his eyes were not strong enough for the military and his entry had been rejected. Claire had rejoiced the day they found out, which confused Bastian, but she had explained her happiness to him later.

"Yes, Mrs. Chambers, it is a sad situation with his sight." Claire couldn't help but smile to herself. *Blind as a bat or dead as a doornail. Hmm, I'll take glasses.* She followed Mrs. Chambers into the kitchen, and Jason's face lit up when he saw her.

"Claire! I'm so happy to see you. Did Lillie tell you I was home? Where's she been? I didn't see her at the hospital the last few weeks while I was there. I waited for her to come and visit, but she never showed up."

Claire frowned. "It's not because she didn't want to. I have a lot to tell you." She explained everything that happened: the letter, Lillie's state of mind, and finally the package. She could see Jason fading out when she spoke of Charlie's death. She snapped her fingers. "Hey, did you hear what I said? What do you make of all of this?"

"Make of what? Claire, I really don't know what you're getting at."

"All right, let me try to make this simpler for you. First, you see John die, but somehow the army doesn't know he's dead; they think he's missing. Then Charlie goes 'over the top' and is declared dead. Then Lillie receives a letter from a doctor in a hospital in France asking if she could give him his things. How is that possible if he has been declared dead? It doesn't make any sense."

Claire stepped back and folded her arms. She knew that Jason had been through a lot, but the story was getting stranger by the day.

"First of all," he said, "try to understand that everyone, I mean everyone, who spent time over there was affected. We were all shaken up so badly that mistakes could—and do—happen. I couldn't function for a while."

"I do understand that there must be shock and confusion, but how could they not know John is dead and declare Charlie dead, and we have no body? My God, Jason, this is a serious matter, shock or no shock."

"Claire, stop. I didn't want to tell to you this, but the confusion with John was because...because there was no head. Now do you understand? He didn't have his head! I am sorry to be so blunt, but you were insistent. What most likely happened was that his tags were missing because they were blown off. And men that cannot be identified are laid in a mass grave."

Claire's eyes widened. To think of one her friends dying in such a violent way...Bile rose in her throat, but instead she burst into tears.

"Oh, Claire, just because they haven't shipped Charlie's body back yet doesn't mean very much. Maybe the doc treated Charlie and then in transport he died. That would explain why the doc thought he was alive."

"But the date on the letter that Lillie received from the captain was dated *before* the one from the doctor."

"The letter from the captain? What captain?"

"The one from Charlie's unit. *Your* captain!"

"That's impossible. Charlie went over the top, and the captain was with us. How would he know Charlie had died? That's odd. And if he did know somehow, he would have had Charlie's personal things and would have been the one to mail them back. They would have been sent with the letter. But you're saying the compass and knife were with him at the hospital, and that's all that was sent back? Oh my God! Could it be?" Jason was flapping his arms in the air. "I can't believe this. This is next to impossible!"

"What? Tell me! What's impossible?"

Jason grabbed Claire's hand. "Come on. I need to do something. I think you might be right. Charlie just might be alive!"

On the way into town, Jason explained to Claire about the pact they had all made the night before they went to the front. He told her about the letter Charlie had written and that he had given it to John. John must have still had the letter in his pocket when his body was found. Claire listened intently. *Can this be true? Charlie, alive?*

When they reached town, they went to the local telegraph office. Jason had Claire write down the information that was on the envelope, and with the help of the clerk they sent a telegram to the doctor in France.

"So now we wait." Jason looked hopeful.

"I'm not saying a thing to Lillie. What if we're wrong? It would devastate her. I don't think she would survive another blow like that."

"I agree. Not a word to Lillie until we receive confirmation."

Chapter Thirty

Charlie was assigned a bunk bed in the lower deck of the ship returning home. All soldiers were assigned to these tiny, cramped quarters. It felt as if they were back in the trenches, without the benefit of a sky to look towards, but none of that mattered. They were going home.

Charlie's chest was healing quite nicely, and his disturbing dreams were drastically reducing, but the physical pain still remained. After all this time, he was still mainly put on bed rest. He tried to stay busy during the day by visiting with the other injured men and seeking out odd jobs that wouldn't draw much attention to himself. The last thing he wanted was to be ordered back to his bunk. At night he thought of Lillie and only Lillie. When he let his mind wander and reflect on the past few months, his nights were filled with agony.

Instead, he would work to bring his focus back to Lillie. It was like opening a gift to remember every little feature on her face and the way her skin glistened in the moonlight. He'd trace the curves of her body with his mind and smell her perfume when he leaned in to kiss her neck. This was his therapy, the only one that gave him purpose. Sometimes he'd wonder about the letters, but he'd quickly push that out of his mind. He couldn't bear the thought that she didn't want him anymore, or worse, that something had happened to her.

Adding to his pain was his queasy stomach. The ocean was something he had never quite become comfortable with. This did little for his appetite, but he did look forward to sitting at the tables in the mess hall. There is where he met and made friends with Dennis O'Malley. He actually lived only a few miles from Charlie's town and had gone to a neighboring high school.

It was after lunch, and Charlie hadn't been very

hungry that day. His stomach was overly sensitive, so he decided to lie down on his bunk for a while. He was starting to doze off when Dennis came in to check on him. He took a seat on the bunk across from him.

"Hey, Charlie, are you doing okay?"

"I'm fine, just a little nausea. Boy, will I be glad when we get to dry land."

Dennis chuckled and then rubbed his stomach. "You're not the only one. Say, do you know a Sebastian Penfield?"

"You mean Bastian? Yeah, why?"

"I used to date his sister, Emily, but that was before she met that David Jameson character."

"Well, don't you sound bitter!"

"Have you ever met Emily?

"Can't say that I have, is she pretty?"

Dennis huffed. "Pretty? She's gorgeous. Every boy in school wanted to date her, and I was the only one she said yes to. We were getting along just fine until graduation, and then everything changed. She met this guy and suddenly she's 'in love.' It tore me up, but I think that's one of the reasons I joined up. I needed to get away from there." Putting his arm over his forehead, Charlie whispered to himself, "You weren't the only one."

"What was that you said?"

Charlie propped up his head on his hand. "What was what?"

"You just said something." Dennis sounded frustrated.

"Did I? I guess I said you weren't the only one who had to get away from town."

"Why did you have to leave?"

Charlie frowned. "You know, Dennis, I'm beginning to feel sick again. How about I tell you another time? Is that all right with you?" He was not ready to spill his guts with someone he had only known for a short time.

Rage raced through his body. Dennis was a decent enough guy, but he wasn't his doctor, and he didn't need to know everything about him.

"Okay, Charlie. I'm sorry if you're feeling well. I'll check on you later."

"Thanks. I'll see you later."

When Dennis left, Charlie rolled over and faced the wall. Why had he reacted that way? He felt so angry. Dennis hadn't meant anything by what he said; he was just asking a question. *Get a grip on yourself, Charlie.*

***

It was four in the morning and Charlie woke up in a pool of sweat. His undershirt was soaked through and his hair was damp and heavy. He lay in bed for a moment, trying to remember what had happened in his sleep. The room was quiet except for the occasional snore or two from the other guys. He got up to use the latrine when he heard a loud *boom*!

He staggered back and had fallen on his bunk when another ear numbing boom went off. The other guys jumped up from their bunks, startled, and stumbled after their pants.

Boom! The ship was shaking back and forth violently, and Charlie had to hold onto the side of his bed so he wouldn't be knocked to the ground. The guy above him came crashing down with a thud. Charlie reached for him to see if he was hurt and noticed a gash about an inch wide above his right eye. He had hit his head on the frame of the bunk. The rest of the men were scrambling to finish dressing just as the horn sounded. They were under attack.

"All hands on deck!" the voice over the intercom was shouting. "All hands on deck!"

Charlie ran up with the other guys and met with Dennis as they were going to the upper level. The ship thrashed every time there was a loud *boom*! Steam rose from the engine room as they ran through the narrow hallways. A man was shouting that they were taking on water, another yelling back to seal off the affected area.

Guys were trapped inside one of the decks, which were filling up, and five men were working furiously to set them free. Charlie and Dennis heard this and ran back to see if they could help. The hatch had jammed shut, and all they had to pry it open with was an iron bar. They could hear the men yelling on the other side. The water was coming in waves!

Charlie relieved one of the men, who had run to see if there was something else they could use. At the center of the bar he found his grip and started pulling with all his strength. Dennis placed his hands next to his and joined in the effort. They could hear a slight rubbing sound as the hatch began to budge.

"What if we grease the hatch?" Charlie heard a voice he didn't recognize. He looked to see a lanky man arriving to help. Charlie's arms were tired, and his body sagged from the strain of working the bar with them, but he wasn't giving up.

"Someone ran to get a can just a minute ago."

Just then the man who Charlie had replaced rushed over, his arms extended and his legs pumping. He yanked the lid off the can and slapped on the grease. Now slippery with lubrication, the hatch had the surge of strength that came with men on a desperate mission. They pulled in one smooth, powerful motion.

"Keep going," one of the guys said, "I can hear it moving!"

The shouting from the other side was becoming louder and more frantic, with the water still coming in fast. Charlie wrapped his shirt around his hand to get a firmer grip on the bar and put his whole body weight into it. The hatch began to turn more easily and then *click*, it opened! In one final, giant wave, the water flooded out, knocking all the men down to the ground. Just as quickly, the men from the other side squeezed through the now-open passage and pushed the hatch shut.

"We have to get up to the life boats. She's sinking!"

One of the men motioned for everyone to follow him. Charlie, Dennis, and all the others charged through the hallways and up the steps. The deck was in complete disarray, with half of it on fire and men rushing to board the lifeboats. There were men who were burned or severely injured. Some hadn't made it. Everywhere, the able were helping the injured. And those who were down were placed into the awaiting boats with care and efficiency.

Through the ashy haze, thick smoke filled the air, making it difficult to breathe and equally difficult to see. As Charlie was running for one of the fallen, he heard a loud crash. A huge chunk of twisted metal broke off the prow of the ship and fell into the center of a crowd of men scrambling to safety.

Charlie shouted for Dennis; he knew Dennis had been directly behind him, but Charlie could no longer see him. About five feet away, he could see another wounded soldier screaming for help. Charlie tried to pick him up, but he was too heavy to lift. Reaching under the soldier's arms, Charlie lifted him enough to drag him over to one of the life boats, then ran back to search for Dennis.

He was shouting Dennis's name when he heard a faint call. "Charlie...here. We're here."

He turned a corner and saw that the falling debris had trapped some of the men under its dangerous load. Dennis was one of those men. His leg had been pinned under a piece of the twisted metal and he was struggling to pull it free.

Charlie yelled to the other men for help."Don't worry, buddy, I'll get you out." Charlie grabbed hold and began pulling, but the leg wasn't budging and Dennis continued to scream in pain. He looked around for anything he could use for leverage to lift the twisted metal and spotted, of all things, a golf club. Someone must have been putting earlier that day. When there was little to do to keep the men occupied on board, they became very creative in how to fill their time. Charlie took the club and placed it under one side of the metal object. Then, with all his might, he pushed. Pain ripped through his chest, but he pushed even harder. The metal began to lift, achingly slow, but enough for Dennis to slide himself free. Charlie quickly helped him onto his good leg and they began to head for the boats.

The ship made a deep, horrible rumbling, and it screeched with an ominous sound that could mean only one thing: the ship was going down! Charlie managed to find a boat with space for Dennis and loaded him in.

"Charlie, come on!" Dennis motioned for him to jump in, but the boat was at full capacity and Charlie knew it.

"I'll catch the next one. If I get in it'll be too heavy."

"One more won't matter. Get in!"

Charlie just grinned at his friend and helped lower the boat in the water. Then he ran with the others who remained on board. They headed towards the burning side of the ship, where there was only one boat left. The thick smoke clouded their vision, making it difficult to see if the boat was intact and seaworthy, but it was their only choice for survival. They lowered the boat and got inside.

It hit the water hard, nearly knocking them out of the boat. Once in the water and settled, they could see the boat had indeed sustained some damage and had a slow leak. The water was frigid, and they all took turns lifting it out with their shoes. This did little to keep the level of water safe for passage. As that depressing thought began to overtake any hope, several of the other lifeboats drifted into sight. One by one, men were handed off to whatever boat had space, until the only ones left were Charlie and another fellow named Derrick. Charlie and Derrick maneuvered themselves in the boat so that the leak would be kept on the light end, slowing it to a trickle. They were in the water for what seemed like forever before a rescue ship finally came into view.

It took a few hours to load everyone in the life boats onto the new ship, and a few more hours to treat the injured and bring food, water, and dry clothes to the others. Some of the men were suffering from hypothermia and were being warmed up slowly. Not everyone who had made it into the boats survived. The next day, a full service with a burial at sea was held for those who had passed away. Charlie watched with silent tears as the bodies of his shipmates slipped into the ocean and the icy darkness below.

After the ceremony, he went to the infirmary to check on Dennis, whose leg had been badly injured. Dennis was worried he might lose it. When Charlie reached him, he was resting and Charlie didn't want to wake him, but before he left he gently lifted his blanket to look at his leg. Thankfully it was still there, and Charlie breathed a sigh of relief.

Once again nausea began to plague him, but this time he didn't mind. They had made it through when others hadn't. What was a little nausea compared to the alternative? He survived; he was alive. Surprisingly, he was able to keep down breakfast. It actually made him feel slightly better. After his meal, he decided to go and see what he could do to lend a hand to those in need. He was given the job of helping the cook with meals. Charlie chuckled. He had hardly been able to eat the entire time he had been on board the other ship when his stomach was sensitive, and now he would be working with food. *What irony.*

Beyond working with the cook, Charlie passed his days in the galley, and at night he kept Dennis company.

Sometimes he would read to him and then other times, as Dennis grew stronger, Charlie would take him up on deck for fresh air and more space. Then one night, they were up on deck, where everything was remarkably quiet and peaceful. The sky glowed a deep purple with streaks of indigo. And the stars, millions of stars, shone brightly on the water, transforming it into a sheet of black glass.

"So, are you ever going to tell me why you needed to get out of town?"

Charlie looked at Dennis with a smirk on his face. "Okay, since you're wounded, I'll have pity on you. I'll reveal my secret. But it really isn't that great of a story."

Charlie began to tell his life's journey. It included everyone: his mom, Lillie, Pete, Frankie, John, and Jason. When he reached the present, he emphasized that after his mom died, he had needed to go and do something, something that mattered, something that would give him purpose. But what he hadn't realized until he'd left was that he already had purpose, and it was in Lillie. She was everything to him. How could he not have seen what was right before his eyes? The look in her eyes had shown so much pain, and he'd known then that he had acted foolishly. But there had been no turning back. He had committed to entering the military.

Dennis patted his back. "But you're going home. You'll be with her, and everything will be just fine, you'll see."

"I don't know, Dennis. I've been writing to her every week since I've left, but she hasn't sent me even one letter. I haven't heard a thing from her. I think she's forgotten about me. I'm afraid I've ruined us and we can't be fixed."

"Charlie, you presume an awful lot. You don't know why you didn't receive any letters. You've moved around a lot in the past few weeks. Maybe they're having trouble catching up. Wait until you're home and you finally get to see her. Don't make yourself crazy. If she loves you as much as you know she does, she wouldn't just up and go to the next guy. You need to stop and think. Is Lillie that sort of girl? I don't think so, or else you wouldn't be so crazy about her."

Charlie thought about what Dennis was saying. Although his gut was wrenching, his head told him to slow down and wait until he saw her before writing the ending to something he wasn't sure of.

A week passed and they finally reached Port Chester, a city just outside of Philadelphia. Charlie was packed and ready to go. He needed to get a ride to the train station, and a few of the guys who actually lived in Philadelphia had offered one to anyone who needed it. Charlie accepted without a second thought. Dennis was doing much better, and Charlie was glad they would be traveling the rest of the way together, but despite this, he was anxious, a lit fuse ready to explode. There was this tension in his body that he had never experienced before. He was afraid to see Lillie, but he couldn't wait to get there, either.

When they reached the station, they got to their seats and settled in for the long ride home. The train was filled with other boys going home from the war, and the staff was trying to accommodate all of them. The prevailing feeling of respect and adulation that all the boys received from the staff and civilians on board was overwhelming. Charlie and Dennis hadn't expected such a warm reception from perfect strangers, but everyone felt compelled to tell them how grateful they were for their service to their country. A gentleman who was sitting across from them insisted on buying them dinner, and the food server brought them a free dessert. Afterward they spoke with the people seated around them and enjoyed a nightcap that was sent over from a prosperous businessman several seats over.

It was getting late and Charlie and Dennis were

exhausted. They had propped up their heads on the seat with one of their bags and tried to settle in for the night, but an elderly woman came over to them and with a sweet smile on her face asked why they weren't in a sleeper bunk. Charlie tried to be as polite as he could and explained they couldn't afford a sleeper but that they were fine. They were comfortable, and it was only for one night.

"Nonsense!" she said. "You boys will not be sleeping here like this!" She called over the steward and insisted they be given a sleeper on her account.

Charlie and Dennis stood up. "We couldn't, but thank you, ma'am, for the gesture. We do appreciate it, but we're quite all right here."

"You two boys did not go to war for your country to come home and sleep cramped on a train seat. No, I won't have it!" In fact, she told the steward, "Fill up as many free sleepers that you can possibly find with the boys who are coming home. And I challenge anyone who has a sleeper bunk to give it up for the evening to show them truly how thankful we are."

With that, she handed her ticket for her sleeper to Charlie and Dennis. One by one everyone on the train followed suit. When they were finished, every soldier traveling that evening slept in a bed instead of his seat on the train.

That night, lying in the sleeper bunk of the train, Charlie felt as if he had fulfilled his purpose to his country and to his friends. Now it was time for Lillie.

Chapter Thirty-One

Claire was having breakfast when the maid came in and told her there was someone there to see her. She tightened her robe and went into the parlor to see Jason standing at the window, his face grim.

"What's wrong? Did you get an answer from the doctor in France?"

Jason nodded. "He was there. Charlie had left about five weeks ago. The doc said he was on a ship bound for a port in Philadelphia."

"Oh my god! That's the most wonderful news. We have to tell Lillie! But, wait...Why do you look so... What's wrong?" Claire waited for a response, but Jason couldn't seem to get the words out. "Jason! What the hell is going on?" Claire had never spoken like that before, but she couldn't help it. Her insides turned with each moment of silence. *Why the heck won't he answer me?*

"Claire, the ship Charlie was on...It sank."

"What? How? Wait, how do you know this?" Claire's stomach lurched and tears blurred her vision. This couldn't be possible. *What, he was found and now we have to lose him again?*

"I have a friend in the recruiting office, and when I found out Charlie was alive and on his way home I went there to see if they had any information on when he would arrive. They usually hear about what's going on before the local news. He told me the ship was bound for home and a German vessel attacked them. It hit them hard and the ship went down. There weren't many survivors. They're still sorting through all the information. He's not sure what happened to Charlie; he just knows some guys made it, but they don't know who yet."

Claire sat down and cried. "We can't tell Lillie. This will ruin her. She'll completely fall apart."

"I don't know, Claire. If it were you and Bastian

was the one lost and might possibly be alive, wouldn't you want to know? What if he makes it home and she finds out we knew all along? I don't think she'd ever forgive us."

"Jason, I can't. I can't be the one who tells her this. I just can't look at her face and tell her."

"Think. You're the only one who can. She trusts you more than anyone. If she has to hear this, don't you think she deserves to hear it from you?" Claire put her head in her hands and shook it. She knew he was right, but that didn't make it any easier.

Jason waited while Claire ran upstairs to get dressed. He told her he would go over to the Whitmans' house with her and wait on the porch if she needed him. She rang Bastian and told him everything that was happening. He said he'd meet her at Lillie's and wait with Jason. She thanked him and told him she loved him. She was about to take the longest drive of her life.

***

James was out front speaking with the gardener when Claire and Jason arrived. He was supervising the planting of the new Japanese cherry blossom trees along the pathway of the front lawn. As Claire and Jason approached him, he knew by the look on their faces that this wasn't going to be a pleasant visit. There was a bench under a large oak tree on the side of the property, where they sat down. Jason started the conversation, explaining about the doctor, the telegram, and the letter from Charlie's captain. James scowled at Claire; he wasn't happy she'd gone against his wishes, but it was too late and the deed was done. James sat in silence as he listened to Claire finish the story. When she was done, he couldn't utter a word.

Claire looked into his eyes. "We need to tell her. I need to tell her."

"Absolutely not. Claire, you understand better than anyone. This will kill her. She will not be able to get over this if he doesn't come home. No."

Claire grabbed James's hand and murmured, "I know you want to protect her, so do I. But she needs to know. She needs to have hope. If it were Bastian, I would want to know, and I know if there were a chance that you could have Mrs. Whitman back, you'd take that chance, no matter how slim the odds. All of her life you've taken care of Lillie, and that's wonderful, but James, she's not a little girl anymore. She's a woman. She has the right to know if the man she loves is possibly alive. I have to tell her."

***

Charlie arrived home at ten a.m., and when he pulled up in the taxi, Mr. Russo was sitting on his porch. "Oh my god," he yelled to his wife. "Loretta, come out here. He's home. Charlie boy—he's alive!"

Mrs. Russo nearly exploded out the front door, and when she spotted Charlie, she started screaming in Italian and crying. She ran over to him, kissing him everywhere she could and hugging him with all her might.

"Loretta, let go of the boy. You'll suffocate him." Mr. Russo kissed Charlie on the cheek, giving him a hug as well. "Oh my God, Charlie boy. We thought you were dead. It's a miracle!"

Charlie was confused. "Dead? Why would you think that?"

"Charlie, your captain sent a letter to Lillie. He said you were killed in action on the front. We had a small service, but they never did send the body home. We thought you were buried there."

"Lillie thinks I'm dead? Mr. Russo, I have to get over there now. Can you drive me?"

"Sure thing. Put your bags in the house and I'll get the keys." Charlie threw his bags down in his living room. He barely had time to look around, but what he saw was spotless. Mrs. Russo did an amazing job at keeping up the house, just as she had promised. In his mother's room, he grabbed a small box that he had put in the top drawer of her bureau before he had left. He placed it in his pocket.

Mr. Russo drove at a snail's pace, and Charlie imagined he could have walked faster, but he didn't say anything; he didn't want to hurt Mr. Russo's feelings. When they reached Lillie's house, Charlie was shocked to see Claire, Bastian, Jason, and James sitting on the side lawn. He thanked Mr. Russo for the ride and hurried toward the four of them.

At first glance, Claire looked at him in puzzlement, but then she shrieked and leaped into his arms, giving him a huge hug and then punching him in the shoulder.

"Ouch!" he exclaimed. "What was that for?"

"For scaring the life out of us. Twice!"

By then the others had reached them, and Charlie was excited to see that Jason had recovered. They all hugged him, and then the questions began. Voices overlapping, sighs, and laughter—it all came flying at him. Charlie motioned for them to stop.

"Later. I will tell you everything later. Right now I have to see her. Mr. Whitman, do you know where Lillie is?"

"She's sitting in the garden over by the fire thorns. She sits out there a lot lately. It's almost as if she's waiting for something."

"Do you think she wants to see me?"

James looked astonished. "Of course! Why wouldn't she?"

"Mr. Whitman, I don't know if you know this, but she never wrote to me. I sent her letters every week, but I never received anything from her. I thought maybe she had forgotten about me." Claire punched him again. "Ouch, Claire, cut that out."

"Charlie, you idiot. You didn't get her letters because they were lost, but she wrote you all the time. She became very depressed when she thought you weren't receiving them. It just tore her up. Now go, before I punch you again."

Charlie shot her a smile and ran for the garden.

The gate was closed. He slowly opened the latch and followed the path toward the back of the garden. Finally, he was here in the garden that had filled his loneliest moments and made room in his heart for hope. Sitting in their usual place was Lillie. She had her back to him and didn't seem to hear him come in. What was he going to say? She was there right in front of him. Which words could fit his love? How many times in the wet, dank trenches or the long days confined to a hospital bed had he envisioned this moment?

Too many to count.

As he approached her, she tilted her head ever so slightly, as if she were listening, as if she knew he was there without even seeing him.

In a moment kindly guided by fate's hand, her eyes met Charlie's, and he slid down next her on the bench.

"Is it you? Are you really here?" Tears were flowing down her face. "You're a dream. I'm dreaming?"

"No, my dearest Lillie, I'm here. I'm with you and I'm never leaving you again." He pulled her close to his chest as their arms completed the journey from separation to unity. He gently explained everything that had happened. Then, softly pressing his lips to hers, he felt the very thing that kept him alive all these past months: her kiss. She tasted like everything sweet and delicious in life.

Lillie reached up and caressed his face with her fingers. "Charlie, look at the fire thorns. They're touching. They're together."

He looked deeply into her eyes and their lips met once again. "Yes, together, my darling. Forever we will be together in our garden of two."

And he slipped his hand into his pocket and embraced the little box.

About the Author:

Vicki-Ann Bush currently resides in Las Vegas, Nevada. Originally from Floral Park, New York, she gains most of her inspiration from the beauty of the surrounding desert and the lush landscapes from her childhood memories.

Her other works include, The Dusk Chronicles trilogy and the children books, Winslow Willow the Woodland Fairy and The Queen of It. In addition, Ms. Bush will have the release of her paranormal novella, The Fulfillment, in late fall 2014, published by Solstice Publishing.

Although fictional, The Garden of Two represents the authors experience of young love and the promise of forevermore.

Acknowledgements:

Thank you to Lisa Kovacik and Kathie Lybbert, for helping me with facts and edits on this story. Without your assistance ladies, the garden would have been lacking in both portraiture and definitiveness.

And to Jason Scott, a special thank you. To be cherished, is the sweetest form of love and sometimes, it's deepest dolor.

Social Media Links:

Facebook:
https://www.facebook.com/VickiAnn.Bush.Author

Twitter: https://twitter.com/VickiAnnBush

Blog: http://vickiannbush.blogspot.com/

Website: http://www.vickiannbush.com/

Made in the USA
San Bernardino, CA
08 October 2017